WILD
not
BROKEN

A HEARTHSTONE NOVEL

SARAH KADES

STARK
PUBLISHING

Stark Publishing
Waterloo, ON
www.starkpublishing.ca

Publisher's Note: This is a work of fiction. Names, characters, places, and incidents are a product of the author's imagination. Real locales and names may sometimes be used for atmospheric purposes. Any resemblance to actual people, living or dead, or to businesses, companies, events, institutions, or locales is either completely coincidental or is used in a completely fictional manner.

Wild Not Broken / Sarah Kades – 1st ed.
Trade Paperback ISBN: 978-1-989351-65-9
eBook ISBN: 978-1-989351-66-6

Dedication

To those who are Re-wilding.
Knowing your true, natural nature may
be the grandest adventure of all.
Happy exploring.

Table of Contents

Chapter One

"*On the charge of high treason, the defendant is found to be not guilty.*"

Lillian Kensington, former war correspondent and courier for MI6, stood in the dock in the center of court number one. Tears of relief stung the back of her eyes and her knees threatened to buckle. She fought both. Hers wasn't the first to be tried for high treason in the historic Old Bailey, London's Central Criminal Court. However, there were too many former media colleagues, law enforcement personnel and politicians who had gunned to see her burn for crimes she had not committed.

Lillian would neither cry, nor faint in front of this bloodthirsty crowd.

She was isolated in the raised defendant dock, and apparently safe. The oversized box of oak and glass created a physical, though not bullet-proof, barrier. It also clearly identified her as the focal point of the ungainly space. Oak boxes, desks, tables and benches were everywhere. The bright, arched white ceiling couldn't temper the heaviness of the space.

Standing arrow straight and with her shoulders squared, Lillian looked across the barrister table, past her defense council and the prosecutors, to the judge. During the trial, the woman had been firm but fair. Lillian dipped her head passively. The judge inclined her head a fraction. The movement was small enough Lillian could have imagined it. As far as displays of solidarity, it was a stretch, but the brief action was enough to bolster Lillian.

Someone believed her.

A cautious smile blossomed, while her expensive legal team broke into confident smiles and hearty handshakes. Her not-guilty verdict would cement their already commanding reputations; her trial would be a career-maker. For them.

Noise began to build, and Lillian heard caustic boo's coming from the gallery. Her smile faltered as she raised her gaze and stared in dismay at the jeering gallery. Crude questions and innuendos rained down on her. The judge rapped her gavel for order.

Lillian swallowed hard at the brutal, painful reality that her innocence was irrelevant. What had taken her years to earn—a reputation built on integrity, grit, talent and compassion—had been destroyed in one calculated blow by a terrorist. It had also nearly gotten her killed.

And no one cared.

These people wanted blood because blood sold. Blood soaked in sex sold even more. That she had sex with a double-agent was the only story that mattered to them. The man she thought she was in love with had been selling state secrets. Those she had thought friends, many long-time colleagues, had turned on her. That had been particularly painful, being treated so severely for something she hadn't done and by people she would have trusted with her life. Lillian had naively assumed today she would get her life back. The tabloids and so-called news outlets would stop publishing wild speculations, or outright lies, about her. She could finally put the months of humiliation, shame, and pain she had endured behind her.

Lillian stared at the bright white arch above the judge's raised seat. She blinked, trying to stem the flow of tears that were crowding the corners of her eyes. Someone called her name. Lillian scanned the escalating crowd and caught the eye of a short man. Andrew Burlington. His close-set, black eyes had always reminded her of vermin. He was furiously snapping pictures of her. He called her name again, before shouting a graphic innuendo about her. Laughter erupted around him.

Lillian put a steadying hand on the wooden rail of the box she stood in. Her ears were ringing, and her vision had started to dim around the edges. Panic surged. The last time her ears rang like this a bomb had gone off. Automatically, she moved her weight to the balls of her feet, preparing to flee or fight, while her hand automatically flew to her trouser pocket. Empty. She had to leave her ever-present tactical pen in the car. It wouldn't stop a bomb, but seriously, how was a woman expected to defend herself? She scanned the room again, looking for danger.

An arm wrapped around her shoulder, familiar and comforting. Her *seanmhair*—her Scottish grandmum and family matriarch, had come to support her. Lillian had asked her not to. Lillian had simply fallen too far—she had shamed herself and her family enough.

"Come, child."

"Grandmum, I'm a grown woman." At over forty, female and unmarried, she was knocking on a bit.

But Lillian ducked her head towards the family matriarch a precious moment. Dame Maighread Evans Coille Kensington was a ballsy political force. Even now, the woman had breached protocol by entering the dock.

Lillian could use some of that strength right now.

Her *seanmhair* gave her shoulders a squeeze. "My dear, even strong, grown women need help sometimes. Let's get you out of here." In her grandmother's arms Lillian could almost see herself surviving this.

A commotion off to the side erupted.

"I'll kill you. I swear I'll fucking kill you, you bitch."

Lillian froze. Double-agent Fernando Martinez was screaming at her from the side of the courtroom.

Another arm wrapped around her, buffering her other side. "You're safe. We got you." It was Omran.

She was sandwiched between her grandmother and Agent Omran Forest. She trusted precious few people anymore; she trusted both of them.

Lillian's heart was hammering, and she tried to make herself as small as possible. Reporters shoved cameras and microphones at them, blocking their exit. She could handle the threat of an IED or suicide bomber. That violence was collateral, the aim general. This assault was directed solely at her and oddly more terrifying because of it.

She caught a glimpse of Fernando being hauled away. Four guards were trying to subdue him, and a handful of reporters had swung their cameras in his direction. Fernando didn't fight fair. He was also freakishly quick.

A gun appeared in his hand. Their eyes locked across the courtroom. Lillian's brain tripped as, again, the man she had foolishly fancied herself in love with took aim at her.

Pop. Pop.

The double-tap exploded in the courtroom, followed by a surprised scream. She looked up as Andrew Burlington fell from the gallery. One of the guards had leapt for Fernando, and the shots meant for her had fired high.

Omran yanked Lillian and her grandmother down, his body covering as much of them as he could manage. He only moved when an unconscious Fernando was dragged by guards out of one of the side doors.

Someone was still screaming.

From the floor, Lillian craned her head around. Several reporters in the gallery had been splattered in Burlington's blood.

She scrunched her eyes closed and made herself breathe through her mouth. The smell of blood—that hauntingly metallic, earthy odor—already terrorized her dreams.

"Lillian, we have to go now."

It was Omran. The tone of his voice left no room for hesitation. Lillian accepted his outstretched hand and scrambled to her feet.

No reporters bothered them this time. Omran led Lillian and her grandmum out the courtroom doors. A security detail ushered them into a waiting vehicle on

Old Bailey Road. The darkly tinted windows cocooned them, and as they sped away and out of the Square Mile, Lillian felt a cautious safety. Still, she retrieved her tactical pen from the seat pouch and held it tight in her shaking fist. It was a small, discreet weapon—and working pen— that had become like a talisman.

"Are you okay?" It was Omran. His eyes were worried.

Lillian felt the need to reassure him. "I will be."

Her *seanmhair* turned to her then. Lillian felt raw under her grandmother's attention; the matriarch missed nothing. But her *seanmhair* only squeezed her hand before turning back to look out the darkly tinted window. She had said nothing, yet Lillian knew an uneasy feeling. Her grandmother wielded her power with astute grace, benevolent until she wasn't. The look on her grandmother's face made Lillian nervous—for others. Fernando had started a war, but Lillian didn't want anyone else dying as her *seanmhair* finished it.

"To the estate, Mum?" Omran asked.

The matriarch gave a single nod. Lillian wasn't fooled. The car would drop Lillian at the secure family estate while Omran, her grandmother and the security detail in the front seat would leave together. Lillian didn't have the clearance to know anything more.

As they left the financial district behind, Lillian, still clutching her weaponized pen, closed her eyes. She felt the vehicle gently rock as they merged onto M25, picking up speed. She let her eyelids flutter open and stared at the stark contrast of suburban row housing, and the bright English countryside. A walking path flanked one of the housing developments and she saw a young family with two small children. Envy flickered. Normal people going about their mundane lives. Lillian let out a quiet sigh and squeezed the pen in her hands. Hers was never going to be a normal path.

Much later the car pulled into their long driveway. Several minutes later, it looped around the expansive entrance and pulled to a stop.

Her *seanmhair* gave her a small smile. "Rest dear, you've had an unfortunate incident."

Lillian eyed the additional armed guards she could see, knowing there would be more she couldn't. The estate was always guarded but Fernando's threat was not being taken lightly.

"Are those necessary?" Lillian motioned towards several new guards.

"Yes. As much as I would prefer locking you up safe in the house, that would be rather insensitive of me. The whole estate is as safe as we can make it. Do be careful."

Her *seanmhair* knew her well. "The grounds are secure?"

"As secure as we can make them. I would lock you inside if not."

Lillian couldn't bear to be incarcerated, not again, even if it was at home on their family's ancestral estate.

"Thank you for the additional guards."

Omran simply nodded, his eyes still worried.

Her *seanmhair* patted her knee. "Off you go, then. Agent Forest and I are required elsewhere."

Lillian bristled. One of the guards opened her passenger door. She let herself out of the vehicle. Lillian understood national security, she just didn't like knowing there were decisions being made about her life where she didn't have the security clearance to provide comment.

The guard clicked the door closed. Lillian wanted to slam it.

Without looking back, she ascended the stairs. She waved off the guard who would have opened the door for her and let herself into the large manor home. Once inside, she raced up the left formal staircase and went straight to her wing of the house.

The feeling of being caged-in was overwhelming. She tried pacing. Then breath work. Her shoulder throbbed and her body fought a familiar inner battle. Nearly two years ago, she had been on assignment when Fernando had fired the bullet that had torn a hole through her shoulder, just as severely as he had shredded her career.

Her mind grappled with old fears and scathing memories. Panic surged.

Like a lifeline, Lillian grabbed the remote for her telly. Normal people watched television. She would, too.

The news was on.

Lillian sank down on the settee and stared at the images of women rallying across the country. Her heart flinched with each candle lit. Violent crimes against women were on the rise in the U.K., again, and no one in a position of power seemed to give a fuck. She swiped at her eyes.

Lillian understood fear. Since the *unfortunate incident*, she was afraid of everything and had spent most of the last two years hiding in the family estate home, terrified to leave. Until that fateful day. One of the guards had taken pity on her and asked if she wanted to go with them for one of their training runs. That moment had changed Lillian's life.

Running, pushing herself physically, was the only thing that kept her mind from slipping into the threatening dark abyss. For her, there wasn't a drug on the planet that worked as well as fresh air and the natural endorphins. She knew, her doctors had prescribed the lot of them.

She called the guard station now, requesting a detail.

Lillian clawed off her courtroom clothes in record time. She pulled on running gear—pocketing her tactical pen, she laced up her shoes, before making her way to the side door usually reserved for servants and contractors, where she hesitated. Would she be safe?

Could she afford the mental toll if she didn't?

From down the hall she heard her nineteen-year-old niece, Sophie. "Auntie, is that you? How did it go?"

A pang of guilt washed over Lillian. Pushing it down, she let herself slip out the door, unseen. She couldn't let Sophie see her like this, cowering and afraid. Her niece would only worry more. She needed to run to process the day and be able to put a smile on for dinner.

Lillian shot down the path and darted across the manicured lawn to the adjacent forest. A guard spoke into his radio. She passed two more over the next several meters, both nodded to her and pointed. Her plain-clothed detail fell into sync behind her. They were in running gear.

She gave a grim nod back but kept her pace. Sometimes her detail ran next to her. Today she needed space.

Once in the forest, she picked up a narrow trail and slowed her running to a sustainable pace. Running would bring her relief, for a time. It was a constant fear that one of these days she would break so completely no amount of running would put her back together.

For now, she let the kilometers work their magic as the forest danced past her. The throb in her shoulder finally evened out to a dull ache. Seven kilometers into her run the despair she had been feeling lightened. Twelve kilometers in, the anger started to fade, too. Twenty kilometers in, she started to get hungry.

Lillian took the next trail she knew would beeline her for home.

Crack.

A single rifle shot sounded.

Chapter Two

Colt Tanner winced in the small Texas motel bathroom. The stretched ligaments in his shoulder protested as he twisted himself out of the sleeves of his button- down shirt. In the mirror he saw new gore bruises adorning his scarred body. He half-turned, checking out his shoulder first. Being thrown tonight hadn't done his shoulder, or his pocketbook, any favors. The bull getting a gore in hadn't helped, either.

Colt faced forward again. He prodded the fresh bruises on the left side of his torso. The safety vests bull riders wore offered protection but didn't make them bullet proof, or in this case, horn proof. Pain knifed and he swore, hoping he hadn't broken any ribs.

Wearing only his jeans, he opened the bathroom door. He managed to hold his arm up and motioned towards his ribs. "I can't tell if these are broken or not."

Shayne, one of the guys he traveled with, crossed the small motel room and eyed the bruise pattern on Colt's torso. He gingerly pressed on a few spots.

Colt sucked in a breath and fought the urge to tuck his arm down.

Shayne looked up at him. "Does it hurt to breathe normal?"

"No." Everything hurt, it wasn't isolated to breathing.

Shayne cocked his head, frowning as he continued to prod. "Then I'd say you bruised the shit out of them. Not broken."

"He's not a fucking doctor," Jake called from across the room.

Colt glanced at the bruises in the bathroom mirror. "I promised my sister I'd help her hang beams this week. Her eco-inn opens in a couple months."

"Aren't you moving cattle for the Jameson's this week?"

"I can do both."

"With busted ribs?" Shayne frowned.

"You just said they weren't busted."

He shrugged. "Probably not, but like Jake said, I'm not a fucking doctor."

"I can help your sister," Jake piped in, perking up at the mention of Colt's sister.

"Becca barely accepts help from me, and that's only because I pull the silent investor card," Colt answered. "Besides, weren't you headed to catch the wet t-shirt contest at the Saddle Horn?"

"So?"

"My sister views that as a toxic approach to sexuality, rather than empowering."

Jake grinned. "Until your sister falls madly in love with me, wet t-shirt contests are fair game."

Colt's travel partners were five years younger than him and still reveled in the western hospitality and night life each rodeo town provided. Twelve years on the road and Colt noticed the tarnish of each town and townie before any shimmer or shine.

"Stay away from my sister." Colt said, only half kidding. Becca was a complicated blend of fierce independence and vulnerable sensitivity. He was as protective of her as all the Tanner brothers were.

Colt closed the door behind him. The small bathroom boasted a tub. It wasn't exactly soaker size, but it was clean, and it would help keep the loudest aches and pains at bay another night. Colt closed the plug and turned on the taps.

Riding injured was a reality for a bull rider. A few years ago, Colt had turned to heavy duty pain killers. It had been the darkest year of his life. He didn't fuck around with pills anymore. He kept his pain manageable and minimized inflammation, for the most part, by eating clean, keeping his booze in check, and staying mobile. He also travelled with industrial size bottles of Epsom salts and anti-inflammatory essential oil blends. He added both to the swirling bathwater.

His phone vibrated from the bathroom counter. It was a text from his sister.

Want company? There's a horse in Austin I like.

Colt frowned. That was a hell of a long way to buy a horse. He texted back. *In Arizona tomorrow.*

Shayne knocked on the paper-thin walls. "We'll meet you at the Saddle Horn. And your dad just left another message on my phone wanting to know if you're going to his wedding. You were right. I shouldn't have given him my number when he asked."

Colt swore. His dad had left him a message earlier, but Colt hadn't answered him yet. "Sorry, man. I'll deal with him."

The only reply was the sound of muted voices and the outer hotel room door clicking heavily shut.

His phone vibrated again with Becca's reply. *Next time.*

He gave her message a thumbs-up—she'd only worry if he didn't text back—before finally sliding his battered body into the hot water. His whole body protested.

Without the drugs, everything felt different, including the quiet. It was oddly louder. Scarier. Living on the road was familiar yet had been blissfully distracting. He could go days without tripping *too far* into the crevices of his own mind. Now, Colt was eerily certain he didn't have a full season in him. His body simply wouldn't take the routine abuse.

He stayed in the tub until his fingers pruned and the water turned tepid, facing the silence. Finally, Colt dragged himself painfully out and got dressed.

He sat down in the room's only chair before calling his father.

Bruce answered on the fourth ring. "It's about time you answered my calls."

Colt pinched the bridge of his nose. A pressure headache was building. "Hello to you, too, dad."

"Why do you have to be such a smart ass? You're just like your mother."

Colt stared out the motel window. The small parking lot was filled with trucks. Across the street—which was a small rural highway—the bottom half of a large neon sign blinked erratically. "I'm on the road, dad, what is it?"

"You haven't RSVP'd to my wedding."

"Yes I did."

"When?"

"Two weeks ago."

"I didn't receive anything."

Suspicion flared. "We spoke about it, remember?"

There was a long pause. "I haven't been well. You know that."

"Yes, you mentioned cancer."

"What's that supposed to mean?" Bruce snapped.

Colt hesitated. Bruce Tanner supposedly had a cancer scare a couple months ago. Colt felt guilty for thinking it, but he had his doubts. His father's erratic behavior, memory loss and general unwell appearance seemed more consistent with drug addiction than the generic *cancer* Bruce was touting. Colt hadn't mentioned his concerns to anyone. No one knew of his brush with painkillers, and he wanted to keep it that way.

"Nothing. I'll be there. I'll come to your and Meredith's wedding."

"Do not bring Becca or Tucker."

Colt stilled. "Why not?"

"Those ungrateful spawn of your mother are not invited." Bruce didn't explain further.

"And Gabe?"

"I expect you both there."

Colt felt a muscle start to tick in his cheek. "Right. Please stop calling my friends."

"I'll call whoever I damn well want to."

It was one thing for his dad to be an ass to him, it was another for Bruce to harass Colt's buddies.

"Please, just knock it off, dad."

"Why should I?" Bruce goaded.

"Because I know you don't have cancer."

The instant the words were out, Colt regretted his outburst. He knew better than to show his dad his hand.

There was a long pause before Bruce Tanner hung up.

Shit. Colt had just kicked over a hornet's nest. It wouldn't be long. His dad never waited before he did damage.

Chapter Three

"It was poachers hunting out of season. It's not like Canada will be any safer." Lillian shifted for the third time on the leather chair she was sitting on, opposite her grandmum's desk. She hoped her voice struck the proper balance between conciliatory, yet firm.

Her *seanmhair* was standing, not sitting, behind her desk, a file in her hands. She had looked up when Lillian had interrupted her a few moments ago, but hadn't put down what she was working on, nor taken a seat.

She gave Lillian a look while simultaneously motioning to someone at the door. The small movement made the silver bracelet at her wrist catch a beam of sunlight from the tall windows behind her.

Paranoia crashed through Lillian. She hadn't been aware anyone was there. Such carelessness could get her killed. She braced both hands on the chair arms, ready to spring, and swiveled her head around.

Relief replaced panic. Her grandmum's assistant walked in with her characteristic swift short strides. Ms. Mary Winters was one of those people she couldn't pin down. The woman was efficient, focused, loyal to a fault, and timeless—Lillian had no idea if the woman was a young sixty or an old thirty.

She also moved as silent as a cat, which made Lillian feel only marginally better.

"Mum, here are the documents you requested." She glanced to Lillian. "Good morning, Ms. Kensington."

Lillian smiled, inclining her head. "Ms. Winters, any chance you could help me change my grandmum's mind? She wants me to relocate to Canada."

Ms. Winters eyebrow arched above her glasses. "Not when she has that look in her eye."

Lillian's smile slipped as she glanced at her *seanmhair*. The family matriarch only looked like that when it was imperative her guidance was heeded. Lillian had not heeded her grandmother's last warning. She had lost her career, her reputation, and nearly her life.

Damn. There had to be another way.

Her *seanmhair* set the file she had been holding down and took off her reading glasses. "My dear, you have been through an ordeal. Canada will give you a fresh start. This time it was poachers. I don't want to worry who it will be next time." Her *seanmhair* paused. "And there will be a next time."

"I'm fine here." Lillian knew she wasn't. Fernando wasn't getting more sane, or less possessive, in prison.

Ms. Winters exited as discreetly as she had entered.

Lillian repeated herself. "I'm not moving to Canada."

If she were to relocate, Lillian could think of a half dozen other countries she'd rather move to.

Her *seanmhair* was not listening.

"Bring the North American fur trade journals. They're in the library."

"Beg your pardon?"

"You need a project, and more than your little jogging trips and your meatless recipe nonsense."

Lillian bristled. As a war correspondent and courier for MI6, she thought her grandmum had overlooked what she thought of as Lillian's odd little eccentricities. Now she didn't.

Her *seanmhair* didn't notice, she simply waved her hand. "We have New World fur trade journals in the library, bring them."

"Since when?" Lillian had spent much of her childhood in the family library.

"Oh, I imagine the eighteenth century, possibly earlier. Do grab the personal journals, too, not just the Company ones."

Lillian tried to remember her history lessons. "Company as in the Hudson's Bay Company?"

"Yes, although I think they fancied themselves a company of adventurers, or some sort."

Lillian rolled her eyes. "Guys are weird."

"Of course they are dear. There should be some Northwest Company journals, too, and even a few XY Company."

"What, no American Fur Company represented?"

Her *seanmhair* finally put the files down she had been holding. "Now you're just being sassy. Take the North American content from the library on your trip. Just do be careful with them. Mary can get you a carton."

"How many are there?"

Her *seanmhair* shrugged. "Half a shelf, or so."

"We're hoarding thirty centimeters of Canadiana and Americana in our family library? Shouldn't we send them back?"

"To whom? They're family documents."

"I don't know, to a museum or archive? Over there?"

"They are family heirlooms."

"We have an entire estate filled with family heirlooms. Surely we can part with the documents of historical significance to give others access?"

Her grandmum eyed Lillian shrewdly. It was a look she typically reserved for her political opponents.

"This is important to you. Why?"

There it was. Lillian had wondered if it was only in her head, the undercurrent of friction that had recently surfaced between them. Her grandmum's pointed question and intimidating glare gave her pause.

Lillian held the older woman's stare. "The current global climate on decolonizing for starters. More colloquially, so people can have access to their history and all the tangled roots that affords." Lillian gentled her tone. "Perhaps a better question is why this isn't more important to you?"

"I'll think about it."

"You do that," Lillian retorted before she could stop herself. Her politically savvy grandmum could be shockingly tone-deaf sometimes.

Before, Lillian would have attributed her grandmum's reticence of parting with the heirlooms as family pride. Since the *unfortunate incident,* whispers of doubt had crept in, and her grandmum's actions seemed domineering, even cruel. Controlling access to information simply because she could.

Lillian reminded herself that though her *seanmhair's* life experience and views may be different than her own, that didn't make them wrong. She needed to defuse some of the tension she felt building between them.

"Have you read them?"

Her grandmum smiled then. It was a good start.

"Some. They're fascinating. Those journals were penned at a time when neither the United States nor Canada existed as they are known today. I daresay few understand how entwined those histories are."

"Ignoring history doesn't change it."

With most countries, one simply could not understand history without considering the context.

Her *seanmhair* sat down then. "If you wait long enough, dear, it does. That is why I am so proud of the work you do. We must always read history critically, and with a mind of understanding the wider contexts and agendas at play."

The unexpected praise caught Lillian off guard.

"Careful *seanmhair*, or you will sound as cynical as I am."

Lillian had been a serious child. It had been her response to what she saw as her rather frivolous parents. Her award-winning, yet dangerous career—a path her beloved *seanmhair* had groomed her towards—had turned that seriousness into suspicion. Lillian harbored considerably more cynicism than her four decades on the planet should have accumulated and no one had been more surprised than her to discover she had been duped by a Spanish double-agent.

Worst boyfriend ever.

"My dear, independent thought is not the same as cynicism. And contemplating colonial and Indigenous historic relationships and commercial resource exploitation is just sensible historical context. As is understanding how regular people tried to go about their lives amidst various political and business ambitions."

There was her *seanmhair*. "You really love history."

"I really love having notes to refer back to on how not to make the same mistakes," her *seanmhair* replied.

"I don't think that's how most see it."

"Imagine the world if more did?"

"There's the optimism you're known for." It was a family joke. Her *seanmhair* was better known for holding a grudge.

She gave Lillian a long look. "I do believe that edge you've developed since the *unfortunate incident* is getting sharper."

Lillian tried not to visibly squirm under the matriarch's scrutiny. "I'm fine."

Her *seanmhair* stood then and came around her desk. "Lillian, I need you to listen to me. Your case went to trial because of your connection to me. My enemies went for your throat to get to me, and my allies couldn't be seen as being soft. The trial was for optics only, the evidence was overwhelming and clear." Her grandmum framed

Lillian's face in her hands. "My darling, you didn't do anything wrong."

Lillian whispered, "I fell for the wrong guy."

"You fell for a smooth talker with an incredible backside. What? It's true. Even criminals can have nice asses. That's why we must be ever vigilant." She let her hands drop and softened her tone. "You need to forgive yourself, dear. Besides, our family does tend to fall for foreigners."

"Grandmum!" Deep humiliation swept through Lillian.

"I meant that as a compliment. I was considered foreign to your grandfather's family." Her grandmum made a sound. "And read those journals. The personal ones tend to be quite scandalous. There is one about your several-times great-aunt."

"Why, what did she do?" Lillian couldn't imagine her stoic family ever being scandalous.

"She told her family she was visiting her sister in Cornwall and ran off to the colonial frontier, instead."

"So?"

"With an Irishman."

Lillian gave an exaggerated gasp. "The harlot!"

Her grandmum tsked. "Tease all you want. You know it was considered scandalous to associate with the Irish, can you imagine running away with one?"

Lillian paused as long-faded memories danced through her head. She was no stranger to the allure of an Irishman.

"Good for her, forging a path like that. May women everywhere know the delight in running away with whomever they choose."

Even if they got burned eventually.

Her grandmum's frown was disapproving. "Not everyone is so cavalier. It still matters to some, dear."

Lillian coughed the words, *"Ladies of the United Empire Loyalists."*

Exasperated, her grandmum said, "I understand the group left a lasting and unfortunate impression on you. That's hardly reason to write off an entire country."

"They were awful. With fake accents."

"Yes, well, you'll be in western Canada. It's like a whole different country. Anyway, as I was saying, her father had selected an older gentleman for her."

"Did she love the Irishman?" Most women of the period were forced to marry to secure some semblance of financial stability or familial dynasty ambitions.

"I've always supposed it was a ticket out of town."

"I'm going to pretend it was love, with a rather long courtship."

Her grandmum cackled. "I hear you, darling, loud and clear. One mustn't rush love."

Lillian managed to not roll her eyes. To her *seanmhair* marriage wasn't settling down or securing your future; it was the extraordinary experience of choosing to share your life with your beloved.

Fernando had been Lillian's longest relationship and it certainly had not been the mind-blowing connection her *seanmhair* spoke of.

"Your grandfather came across the fur trade journals—all written in French—as a boy. He desperately wanted to be able to read them. Your great-grandmother swore that was the reason he studied his French lessons at all."

"Wasn't *seanair* the ambassador to France?"

"He was. You could say those journals helped chart a course for his life. We had such an adventure in France." A faraway look briefly crossed the older woman's face. "Anyway, you're going to Canada. Bring the journals and see what you can find. You need a project."

And just like that, the banter between them soured. She was not in need of a project.

Lillian tried another angle. "Sophie's worked so hard. Being invited to train with the National team is a big deal. I'm sure she wouldn't appreciate her old auntie tagging along. She doesn't need or want me."

Story of my life.

"Nonsense, Sophie will appreciate your company."

Escorting the youngest Kensington, a world-ranked biathlete, wasn't why her grandmum insisted Lillian go to Canada and they both knew it.

"I'm not going to Canada."

"Of course you are. Give it three months." Her grandmum walked back around her desk and put her glasses back on. She picked up the file she had been reading before.

Anger flashed. Lillian wanted her old life back and this wobbly version would not magically fix in the Great White North.

Lillian played her last card. "What about Sophie's safety?"

"I'm making arrangements."

Lillian narrowed her eyes. "What kind of arrangements?"

"Over-protective ones. Not to worry, they will not interfere with your day-to-day. They will shadow you and Sophie and only step in if absolutely necessary. You won't even know they are there. And neither does the Canadian government."

"What did you do?"

Her grandmum's political audacity was legendary, though *typically* everything stayed undetected until the files were declassified. The problem was that the potential to ignite international fuses was always just a hairsbreadth away.

"My job," her grandmum answered. "Besides, it's Canada. A Commonwealth country. We're fine."

Lillian folded her arms across her chest. "Did the Canadian government get your memo?"

Her grandmum gave a negligent wave. "They will if they need to."

"*Blimey*, do not start a political pissing match. I can just stay here."

"No."

A knock sounded briefly before Ms. Winters walked back in. "You wanted to make a phone call, mum."

Her grandmum nodded before turning to Lillian. "I'll meet you in the library in thirty minutes. Be a dear and find those journals. You need a project."

"What am I supposed to do with the journals?"

Her grandmum ignored her and picked up the phone.

Lillian briefly considered making a run for it, but she didn't know how to disappear—not like how she would need to, to avoid her *seanmhair's* unofficial security detail, anyway. Or Fernando's crew. She had been a courier for MI6, not an agent.

Her grandmum pointed at the door.

With no reasonable escape routes, Lillian grudgingly headed to the library.

Her new normal sucked balls.

As she was walking to the library, a dark thought surfaced. If Lillian had a target on her back, why did her grandmum want Sophie anywhere near her?

Chapter Four

Dame Maighread Evans Coille Kensington waited for her granddaughter to leave the room. Lillian was cross with her. Maighread couldn't blame her. She would be even more cross if she knew the whole truth.

"Do you require anything further?" Mary, her assistant asked.

"No. I will send for you when I need you."

Mary nodded. "Very well."

When Maighread was alone, she walked over to the plush settee and sat down, thinking. She wanted to kill Fernando Martinez with her bare hands. She still knew how to. What that man did was unconscionable. But she must be wise. These things were delicate, and there were too many moving pieces to jeopardize on that horse's ass.

Maighread leaned over and picked up the receiver of her secure line.

Hating that her pulse leapt, she dialed an old number. She only had to wait one ring.

"Thorsen."

The flutter Maighread felt was short-lived. The voice did not fit the name. *"Who is this?"* she demanded.

"Who is this?" The voice was maddeningly calm.

Maighread sat up straight. "I was looking for a different Thorsen."

"He retired."

"And you are?"

"Not retired."

Agents not on her payroll annoyed her. Agents from independent countries with limited leverage points were unbearable.

"Can I assume we have the same deal?"

"That depends."

"On what?"

"On whether I like you or not."

Maighread was finding it difficult not to sputter. Several years ago, long after her beloved husband had passed, she had a physical relationship with Randolph Thorsen. She had trusted him. It was more than she had allowed with anyone since her husband had died. Randolph was discreet and theirs had not been an overtly romantic relationship. Still, it stung he hadn't told her he had retired. "Mr. Thorsen—"

"Just Thorsen."

Maighread drew in a long breath. "*Thorsen*, are you still keeping tabs on that rancher in western Canada?"

This time there was a long pause. "What do you know about that?"

"I'm fairly certain everything." For the first time, though, she wondered.

The man on the other end's voice changed. "Affirmative. Are you Maighread?"

Maighread dropped the phone. She hastily picked it back up.

"…I'll take that as a yes. I'm being told to help."

"What does that mean?" Her encrypted cell phone buzzed with a new message. She crossed to her desk to retrieve it. It was from Randolph.

He's my son.

Maighread sank into her desk chair. She hadn't known he had a son, either. Not that she blamed him. In their line of work you kept your pressure points quiet.

"Are you still there?" Just Thorsen asked.

"I'm here."

Randolph had a son.

"You got his message."

"Affirmative."

There was a full laugh on the other end of the line. "I like you, Maighread. You'll do. What do you need?"

Randolph was like that, too, suspicious, until he wasn't. He had an unspoken test he put people through. If you passed, you were in. If you didn't, chances are you never would.

Like father, like son.

An unfamiliar longing rose, unbidden and unwanted. She pushed the surprising ember down. A relationship like hers and Randolph's was doomed to remain in the shadows. Watching Lillian and Sophie navigate relationships, Maighread realized she needed more if she were to have one.

Like she had with her husband, or not at all.

Maighread banished the distracting memories and focused on the task at hand — securing her girls the best protection that money and diplomatic backscratching could buy.

Lillian would go to Canada. It would be easier to control the girls if they were in the same place.

Chapter Five

"Sorry again, Becca." Colt walked down the arena tunnel, holding his phone to his ear.

"That dad's blowing another fuse? That's on him. I'm sure he was just blowing off steam and didn't mean anything by it."

"I hope you're right."

The music coming from the arena swelled and Colt pressed the phone tighter to his ear to hear his sister.

"We'll be fine. Sounds like you have to go, we can talk later. Be safe."

"Always." Colt disconnected the call and pocketed his phone, the uneasy feeling still in his gut. Becca tried to believe in the best of people, it left her open to getting her heart broken repeatedly by their parents. Gabe, Tucker and Colt all tended to be more pragmatic. Once Colt had accepted his parents for who they were—in a word, assholes—he stopped getting so bent out of shape.

"*Mr. Tanner, Mr. Tanner.*" Colt stopped in the arena tunnel and turned.

The voice calling his name was quite young. "*May I get your autograph?*"

Colt saw him then. A boy, no more than eight years old, stood in one of the side doorways. The little guy held a pen and scrap of paper in his small hands. A man in a cowboy hat, Colt assumed the boy's father, encouraged him forward. The two were dressed identically in denim, boots, and matching pearl-buttoned western shirts.

Colt smiled and looked at the kid. "Well, hello there. Are you guys having a good time?"

The little guy beamed, proud. "This is my first big rodeo. I watch you on TV all the time."

Colt accepted the pen and scrap of paper from him, signing his name. "I appreciate that. What's your favorite rodeo event?"

"Bull riding!" The little boy pumped his fists down, nearly shouting in his enthusiasm.

"Mine, too." Colt handed the pen and paper to the kiddo.

"We took an airplane to come here. My dad says we're in Arizona. I forgot my hat at home."

The older man smiled before saying to the little guy, "Thank Mr. Tanner, he needs to get going, son."

The little guy stood taller. "Thank you, Mr. Tanner, good luck riding."

Colt smiled. The little guy was so earnest. Colt took his hat off and looked at the boy's father. The man gave a surprised smile before nodding vigorously. Colt held out his hat to the little guy. "Every cowboy needs a hat."

The kiddo stared in awe but didn't reach out to touch it. "Don't you need it?"

"I'm going to put my helmet on in a few minutes and I have another one in my truck."

The little boy accepted the hat and slammed it on his head. He had to tilt his head up to see beyond the brim.

"Thanks!" The little guy spun on his heel and ran back through the doorway.

The father nodded at Colt, before chasing after the exuberant little boy.

Colt smiled as he made his way down the rest of the tunnel. He knew he didn't want kids, yet the sight of that father and son gave him hope for others. Some parent and child relationships weren't fucked up.

Colt was nearly at the end of the tunnel. The arena music picked up tempo and he felt the bass in his chest. It felt good. He heard the buzzer sound. The announcer's voice was muffled but the crowd gave an upbeat roar.

Colt felt the crowd's energy and it juiced him even more. Nothing in the world compared to this feeling.

He made his way to the catwalk behind the bucking chutes.

"There you are, man," Shayne said, handing him his helmet and bull rope. He was standing next to Jake on the catwalk.

"You're next on deck," Jake called. He would be Colt's rope man.

Colt nodded, handing his cell phone to Shayne, who would be spotting him. They wore a similar uniform: jeans, boots, spurs, chaps, and a western button-up shirt with their sponsorship patches. They all wore safety vests. His travel buddies were the classic, wiry cowboys. Colt was built more like a steer wrestler than a bull rider.

Loud music blared and the boisterous audience was on their feet. Colt grinned; the crowd was hot tonight. As he stood behind the bucking chutes, boots shoulder width apart, he rolled his hips in small circles, staying loose. When he shook out his arms, his right shoulder barely offered a protest. The crowd roared again, and Colt felt another rush of adrenaline. Waiting for his turn always built the excitement and energy.

The chute boss signaled to him. "Tanner, you're good. Be ready in the chute, Back Lit sometimes fights a bit."

At the chute boss' words, Colt nodded in his helmet and handed Jake his rope. He stretched left, right, and back left again before tapping the top of his helmet twice and pounding the sides of his thighs once. Colt grabbed the metal bar in front of him. Old scar tissue and the freshly stretched ligament in his right shoulder protested. He let the energy of the crowd drown any lingering pain and reached across the bucking chute. He grabbed the top, far rail and put his left foot on the bull's back. Below him, Back Lit, a Charbray and last year's Bull of the Year, started huffing and snorting.

"Give him a sec," the flankman called.

Colt obliged, moving his left foot off the animal. The flankman motioned for Colt to move again, this time to stand back on the catwalk deck behind the chute.

The Charbray exploded within the chute, bashing back and forth in the tight space. Colt appreciated the stockman knew his animals—getting knocked around before a ride toyed with already revving nerves.

After all these years, the thrill of climbing on the back of a bull had never waned for him. The rush, and not knowing what waited for him at the end of each ride, kept him teetering on an edge. Life on the road was predictable, routine even. Riding bulls kept Colt in the now and reminded him not to take a damn thing for granted.

The adrenaline hit was pretty good, too.

This time the crowd erupted in laughter, entertained by the easy banter between the announcer and the entertainer, sometimes called the barrel man or rodeo clown. He got the crowd hot and kept them that way. Without the entertainer, rodeos would be a bunch of guys playing in the dirt. The entertainer made rodeo a show.

"He should be good now." The flankman called.

The bull's antics had lasted almost four seconds. Colt stopped chewing on his mouth guard and let it slip back into place. Distantly, he heard the music pick up and the crowd's energy swelled again. He replaced his left foot on the bull's back, and a moment later brought his right foot over. In a single fluid motion, Colt lowered himself onto the now-still animal's back, feet forward. Colt had nearly busted an ankle learning the hard way that a bull noticed a misguided spur.

Colt gripped the rope with both hands, jogging it side to side and slightly up, getting the slack out, then nodded. Jake pulled the rope, tightening it, before holding the rope high and taunt. Back Lit stayed docile under him as Colt pumped the rope, making the rosin sticky, before setting the rope handle—simply two sections of braided bull rope—on his knee. Colt rolled the rope over, checking the bell was in place, before rolling the rope back into position, and setting his gloved right hand, palm up, into the handle, lining his pinky just off center. He nodded to Jake. Jake gave a firmer second tug before handing the rope back. Colt pulled it across his open gloved hand, wrapping it behind his hand and pulling it across his palm again. He left a whisper of slack in the loop behind his wrist, before closing his hand around the rope.

Shayne was spotting him, ready to grab Colt by the vest, should Back Lit fire up inside the shoot again. Slipping between static metal gates and a bull was not a place Colt wanted to be.

He draped the tail of the rope in front of him over the bull's shoulders and slid up. Keeping his balance up on the inside of his legs, he tilted forward, anchoring his riding arm against his leg. He dropped his chin to his chest and looked between the bull's shoulders just in front of his riding hand.

Colt nodded like he meant it.

The waiting gateman sprung into action, pulling open the swinging metal gate, at the same time Colt turned his heels in.

The adrenaline that had been building throughout the day hit, and the only thing in Colt's world was Back Lit. The bull leapt out before turning hard, spinning into Colt's hand before sucking back left. The bull bucked and torqued under him. Colt spurred, keeping his center and staying upright.

The buzzer sounded. Eight seconds.

Colt used his free hand to start to release his riding glove. The bull sucked back, spinning right and tight. Colt lost his center. That fraction of a second shifted control. That was all it took.

Chapter Six

The book wasn't supposed to be there. Lillian had walked into the library, and still chafing at her grandmum's overbearing machinations, decided the fur trade documents could wait. Her *seanmhair's* 1778 first edition of Fanny Burney's *Evelina*, also known as *The History of a Young Lady's Entrance into the World*, was another matter entirely. Which was why Lillian stood perched on the library ladder, *Evelina* tucked securely in the crook of her arm, while peering behind a row of shelved books at the small volume that appeared to have fallen behind.

The small nook was hidden behind the upper tier of books and was no more than eighteen inches wide and perhaps forty inches tall. Deep enough for a book to fall and be forgotten. It was all but hidden in shadow, and Lillian could just make out a volume lying flat.

The ladder she was on was well built and sturdy, like most things in the large ancestral home. Still, she was careful to evenly distribute her weight. It had been built before the turn of the last century. If it were in Canada, it would not be still bearing her weight. It would be an artifact, admired behind appropriate museum glass.

Lillian tried to resist her growing dread. She didn't need Canada, she needed friends. Real friends. She could stay with Grace in Jordemorden, or Claire in Cape Town.

The more Lillian thought about it, the more her grand-mum's insistence she accompany Sophie made less and less sense.

But her *seanmhair* always made sense. The woman got to where she was today with unwavering ambitious cunning. Her motivations were direct, if not always popular. Her diplomacy could most accurately be described as a wolf in sheep's clothing.

An odd scratching noise sounded. Lillian clung to the antique ladder with her free hand and squeezed her eyes shut. She pressed her body against the ladder and held herself completely still as her heartbeat thudded in her ears. Her doctors had diagnosed her with Post Traumatic Stress Disorder long before her trial, but Fernando's courtroom blow-up had ratcheted it to unrelenting proportions. Numerous diabolical ways to die flooded her consciousness.

Lillian heard the odd little sound again and had to swallow her shriek. She tightened her stranglehold on the ladder and her legs shook. The force made the ladder shudder, prompting her to rethink her careless quip on Canadian museum choices.

The weird sound was alarmingly close.

Still as a statue and perched on the ladder like a damn bird, Lillian fought for control. The wind outside kicked up. On the other side of the tall library window, several inches away from her nose, a tree branch swayed.

In tandem, the scratchy squeaks resumed.

She closed her eyes and let out a slow breath. No one was here to graphically murder her. At least not at the moment. It had been the wind chasing tree branches. She wouldn't even have heard it had she not been on the ladder.

With renewed grit, Lillian reshelved *Evelina* and dipped her hand behind the row of books. She felt around with her fingers. When she brushed leather, she leaned further, walking her fingers under the volume. With great care, she pulled her arm back and studied her treasure.

The volume was unusual looking. A spider web of cracks across the leather and discoloration on the page edges gave it a particularly utilitarian look. She flipped the book over. A stylized compass drawing with the four cardinal directions was in relief. She held the book up. Sunshine filtered in through tall windows that had been leaded two centuries before. The whisper of another outline was visible, and Lillian tilted the volume in her hand. A figure of a lush female form, like an early goddess statue, was within the compass, fainter than a watermark and infinitely more interesting.

Tingles spread across her skin.

Lillian looped her left arm through the ladder and secured her elbow against a rung. With both hands now free she gently opened the cover. It made a cracking sound as she opened it. Startled, she held her breath.

The old cover held. It was stronger than it had sounded. Lillian felt a rush of energy. The book felt solid in her hands.

Bam.

This time she rounded, ready to launch herself at whatever foe had entered. Breathing hard, she darted her gaze around the room, ready to fire the precious volume she held in her hand to protect herself. From her perch, she could fire subsequent rounds of books as required. As ammunition, they were unorthodox. Thrown with enough surprise and force, though, and she just might give herself a window to escape.

But she was alone.

Across the room, the library door was now shut. The wind blustered and Lillian noticed a set of long curtains billow out. The window behind them was open. The door must have slammed shut in a cross-current.

Feeling a little uneasy, Lillian looked at the book in her hand. Where had the bravado come from?

She gave the room a final scan, assuring herself she was safe. Old houses had personalities. This one was no exception. She had handled her old life of bad food, tight deadlines and random exploding IEDs. All of those she figured out how to deal with. Staring down the barrel of acute paranoia and debilitating PTSD was bollocks.

Annoyed now instead of scared or on the offensive, Lillian turned back to the volume in her hand. She eased a page over, than another. Some pages held descriptive text, while others included vivid plant illustrations that were paired with practical and medicinal information. Other pages contained lists. Sundry items, natural species, and names, locations and dates of what looked like posts and forts were included.

Lillian clung to the ladder, enchanted by the small book. She didn't know how long she stood there, reading page after page of folk knowledge—much would have been considered controversial by the Church—and what appeared to be documentation of sorts.

She sucked in her breath when she turned the next page. She rotated the volume and unfolded the larger page that had been sewn in. It was a hand drawn map. Exquisite in its form and function. She read the inscription, twice. It was an early map of British North America, though pre-Treaty of Paris. It included known waterways that crisscrossed the continent, with some tributaries. Major known lakes and general topographical information was included. Lillian stared at the tidy row of chevrons spanning the drawing as a soft tingling sensation swept through her body.

If she wasn't mistaken, the chevrons represented the Rocky Mountains.

But that didn't make sense. She checked the year again. The map was dated 1751. Lillian didn't think British North America maps of the time included anything as far west as the continent's rocky spine.

Lillian checked the nearby shelves, but none contained the rest of the North American fur trade documents or journals. What was this book doing here, hiding behind these shelves?

The library door opened. This time someone was calling her name.

It was her *seanmhair*. "Honestly, my dear, what ever are you doing? The North American materials are not up there."

Mindful of the delicate book in her her hand, Lillian was careful as she made her way down the ladder. Her grandmum's gaze followed her.

"I went looking for your first edition copy of *Evelina*."

"Very well." Her grandmum seemed to let out a held breath.

Lillian lifted the book in her hand. "I found this. It looks like a fur trade journal of some sorts."

Her grandmum narrowed her eyes. "Where did you get that?" Her tone was more accusing than surprised.

Protective, Lillian vaguely motioned. "Up there. Why, what is it?"

Her grandmum waved her hand dismissively. "It's nothing. You know this library is filled with all manner of random frivolities."

Lillian's journalist instincts were firing. She turned the book over in her hands. "It's lovely. I think—"

"No!"

Lillian raised an eyebrow. "It's a little late to be censoring what I read, isn't it?"

She opened it to a random page and made a sound. "This page talks about how to ease headaches, menstrual cramps . . . holy shite." Lillian looked up. "It lists family planning methods."

Her grandmum's lips thinned.

Lillian pressed. "A woman wrote this, not a man, in the eighteenth century."

"So?" Her grandmum shifted her weight.

"Women didn't write fur trade journals." Lillian held up the small volume. "This is a grimoire, isn't it?"

"Must you be so dramatic?" Her grandmum crossed the room to the sideboard under the tall windows. She poured herself a healthy glass of scotch.

"It is incredible in itself, because it is written by a woman in the middle of the eighteenth century. But it is a grimoire, too, isn't it? What's in here includes typical fur trade records, and feminine knowledge."

Her grandmum sat on one of the settees and took a healthy swallow of her scotch.

Lillian turned a couple more pages. Her hands shook when she found an essay on having visions. "You knew about this book, why didn't you show me this earlier?"

Her grandmum just circled her wrist, swirling the brandy around the glass, remaining stubbornly silent.

The betrayal cut deep.

"It talks about The Sight," Lillian accused. "In high school, when I started having what I could only assume were visions, do you know how this would have helped? I felt like such a freak. Do you know how much that would have meant to me?"

Her grandmum took another long sip and didn't meet her gaze. "I had my reasons."

Lillian looked at the beautiful book in her hand. "What possibly could—"

Then she did the math. "You didn't want to jeopardize your political career."

Her grandmum turned on her. "Do you have any idea how hard it has been to be the only woman clawing my way up in a sea of pompous, entitled men?"

"Of course, I do," Lillian snapped. "I have a vagina and it's only the twenty-first century. It's not like we've left sexism or gender bias in the rear-view mirror."

Her grandmum took another long sip of her drink. She had the grace to look down. "Yes, I suppose you do know. Regardless, I wasn't going to jeopardize my career for a trifle of old wives' tales."

Lillian stared at her grandmum. "I thought I was going crazy, seeing things before they happened. Both you and mum dismissed my questions as frivolous rantings of a silly girl."

"It's not like I was the first one to keep it shelved," her grandmum reasoned. "Your great-grandmum didn't want anything to do with it. Said it was nothing more than an unfortunate family joke."

Lillian's body contracted at the harsh words. Anyone with a pulse should be able to notice the energy vibrating within it. It fairly hummed in Lillian's hands. Finding the grimoire was a sign.

"Yes, we ought to tidy up the library more than once every hundred years," her grandmum retorted.

"I didn't speak out loud."

The older woman had just read her thoughts.

"Yes, well, you fairly shouted your feelings at me."

Realizations started lining up. "Your career, your uncanny ability to know what your opponents are going to do—you live this book."

"As if you don't? Your insights started, what, twenty-five years ago? You should be quite fluent with them now."

Lillian's chest tightened. "Everything stopped in high school."

Her grandmum looked up, stricken. "What?"

"They were so disruptive, and you and mum kept telling me to stop being so silly." Lillian shrugged. "I kept ignoring them and one day they just stopped altogether."

"I didn't know that was possible."

"Tell a girl she's silly and stupid long enough, she'll believe you." Lillian heard the bitterness in her voice. She tried to see her grandmum's point of view, but she couldn't, not for something this important.

"I figured you just quietly went about using your gifts like I do."

"I don't have any gifts. Like I said, that shit was shut down hard."

Her grandmum looked troubled.

Lillian felt exhausted. She stood. "I don't want to fight anymore. I'm not going with Sophie."

"*But you must.*" Her grandmum's voice had turned fierce.

"Why?" This was getting old.

Her grandmum spread her hands wide, imploring Lillian. "It doesn't work like that; I just *know* you must. It's a feeling, an incontrovertible knowing."

"Yeah, we've been over that. I don't get those."

They were at a standoff, and Lillian wasn't sure she wanted to be the one to give first.

Her grandmum stood, too. "I'll have Mary carton the fur trade documents up for you."

"Unless you're donating them, don't bother. They're fragile."

"They're stronger than you think."

Lillian's awareness flickered, like the barest whisper of candlelight in a long, dark night. She *knew* her grandmother wasn't talking about the fur trade documents.

"They're fragile," Lillian insisted.

"You'll keep them safe."

Lillian felt goosebumps rise up her arms.

"I hate it when you do that."

"Do what?" Her grandmum asked, sounding more like her beloved *seanmhair*, than an ambitious political cutthroat.

Lillian eyed her *seanmhair*, understanding more than she had ever had. But that didn't excuse the older woman's behaviour. Whether it was proper security clearance, or North American fur trade documents, her grandmum kept firm control of the flow of knowledge around her. Lillian had built a career helping others give voice to their stories. How would her life have been different if she would have had access to hers sooner?

Lillian looked at the book in her hand and felt a sharp pang of regret. It was pretty clear, if left to her own devices, Lillian made shitty choices that got other people killed. No wonder her grandmum and mum hadn't trusted her with the knowledge in the book she held. She couldn't handle it.

"Stop it."

Lillian asked bitterly, "So you really can read minds?"

"I get impressions. It's different."

"Well, knock it off. My mind is not open for browsing."

Lillian felt a sensation then, like she had just closed a window, but in her mind. She looked up, eyes wide.

Her grandmum said nothing, merely held up both hands in acquiescence.

Lillian blinked. What if she hadn't shut down everything back in high school?

She gave herself a little shake. "Where are the other fur trade documents?"

"You mean you will go, willingly?"

Refusing to go to Canada meant the fur trade journals and letters would continue to collect dust in their private library. Her stubbornness would deny others access to knowledge. Her grandmum certainly wouldn't find a proper archive. She also knew she couldn't go on, jumping at shadows and waiting to be murdered by Fernando.

"I'll go to Canada with Sophie, but I am finding an archive or museum."

She would find a good home for the documents. But first, she would read them. Raw historical data didn't mean as much without knowing their context, and she absolutely wanted to understand the grimoire she had found. That, she could do. She was good at researching.

Maybe Canada would provide a story she could tell. A worthy story. Someone else's.

Chapter Seven

Colt nursed his beer and eyed the crowd of wedding party goers. His father was nowhere to be seen, but Meredith, his new stepmom was making her way around to each table of wedding guests. She was in an elegant, somewhat understated, cream-colored gown and her hair was swept up in a tasteful coif. Her smile was bright, her laughter sincere. Colt didn't have a lot of wiggle room for participating in cheating. Neither he, nor his siblings, had been inclined to give Meredith much of a chance.

Over the last five years, though, she had tried. Colt would give her that. Still, no amount of birthday or Christmas cards would ever change how she had come into their lives. Not for the first time, Colt wondered what she was doing with their father. Bruce Tanner was as arrogant and entitled as Meredith appeared kind and considerate—the whole adultery thing notwithstanding.

The crowd parted and Colt saw his older brother, Gabe on the dance floor. He held Savannah, Meredith's niece. The song was slow, and it was clear the two of them were in their own intimate world. Their joy was painfully obvious. Gabe and Savannah had met at Bruce and Meredith's engagement party. They had ended up working together on an archaeological survey in the Athabasca Oilsands. By the looks of it, their time together had gone rather well.

Colt took another sip of his beer and rubbed his eyes. He was exhausted, sore, and ornery. He should probably just leave. His wreck last night could have been a lot worse. His ribs were bruised, but not broken. They would hurt like hell for a couple weeks, but he'd live. His shoulder was another story. It would need to be taped the rest of the season, and Colt figured his was another ride, maybe two. He doubted his shoulder would hold beyond that. It was sobering, feeling his body breakdown and knowing his career was eight seconds, maybe sixteen from the end. He would ride at Stampede, go out at home.

"Well hello, cowboy." A woman purred in his left ear and Colt fought a cringe.

He turned as a woman dropped into the empty chair next to him, demurely crossing her boney legs and fluttering jewel-clad fingers in front of his face. Her ensemble was expensive and artificial, her body painfully thin. She was close enough for Colt to smell the booze on her breath. Her eyes were glassy enough to suggest it was more than alcohol she was riding.

Colt surreptitiously tried to scoot his chair away. This was not his crowd. He had never felt comfortable in his father's circles, and he certainly was not going to hook up at his father's wedding. Gross.

She followed him, inching her chair over even as he pushed his away.

She stopped suddenly, staring at him. *"Ohmygod, you're Colt Tanner."*

Colt felt oddly cheap and disposable. The woman hadn't actually looked when she had first selected him. Her any-dick-will-do appetite was not a turn on.

"Ma'am, if you'll excuse me."

Colt tried to stand but she snaked out her hand, blocking a quiet retreat. *"The* Colt Tanner."

Colt reluctantly sat back down. "Can I help you?"

"I love cowboys," the woman purred before trying to sit on his lap.

"Christ," Colt muttered. He tried to turn away from her, feigning a phone call.

A clear voice sounded. "Porche dear, Kent was looking for you."

It was Meredith.

The other woman immediately stopped trying to drop her butt on Colt's lap, and looked up, hopeful. "Really?"

Meredith's hands rested on the back of an empty chair. "He's only just arrived. Bruce was just speaking to him in the foyer."

The woman tapped Colt's lips provocatively. "Next time, cowboy," She sashayed off without a second glance.

Colt grabbed a napkin, scrubbing at his lips. "Thanks."

She pointed to the empty chair. "May I?"

Colt eyed his new stepmom and shrugged.

She sat down.

"Who was that?" Colt asked.

Meredith's gaze followed the woman's departure. "Trouble."

Colt didn't like what he was reading in between the lines.

Meredith focused her attention on him. "Have you been on the road?"

"I just got back this afternoon."

In the ensuing silence, Meredith toyed with a discarded confetti wrapper.

"Where were you, dear?"

The term of endearment fell awkwardly between them; Colt did not want to have this conversation, either.

"Texas, but Arizona and New Mexico before that."

"That sounds lovely, and far. Thank you for making such a long journey to celebrate with us."

Another uneasy silence fell.

Colt tried to throw her a bone. "I met Savannah."

Meredith visibly brightened. "Yes, I've never seen my niece so happy. Your brother is quite the young man."

Colt made a non-committal sound. It had been Gabe who had walked in on their dad and Meredith five years ago at the family cottage property. Gabe had accepted a job with Canada's Security Intelligence Service out of grad school to pay off his archaeological student loans rather than accept money from either parent. His last assignment for CSIS had nearly killed him and he had gone to the family vacation property to heal after the near-fatal gunshot wound to his head. He had walked in on Bruce and Meredith instead.

Meredith turned in her seat, scanning the crowd. "I haven't seen Becca or Tucker, have your other siblings arrived yet?"

Colt stared at her. "They weren't invited."

Meredith's face paled. "I beg your pardon?"

"My dad was clear. Gabe and I were the only Tanner siblings allowed to come."

Colt looked across the dance floor. The only reason Colt had shown up was so Gabe wouldn't be there alone. That appeared to be a moot point, as his older brother was currently holding a radiant Savannah in his arms. They both looked a hell of a lot happier than anyone else in the room.

Meredith was frowning in front of him. "I didn't realize."

They were interrupted when two men, clearly inebriated, stumbled into chairs at the table next to them. They reminded Colt of Bruce—entitled and loud. Especially when he'd had too many.

One of them snorted, "I would have married her, too. Do you know how loaded she is? Bruce now has control of her fucking fortune."

The other one peeled into laughter. "What other reason would there be? You can swipe as much ass as you want these days and a hell of a lot younger than that broad's."

Colt eyed Meredith. She sat stone still.

"I'm guessing they are friends of the groom?"

She nodded.

Colt raised an eyebrow. "Want me to break their jaws?"

Meredith wasn't his favorite person on the planet, not by a long shot, but that shit wasn't right.

A slow smile spread across her face. "That is the loveliest wedding present I could ever imagine, but I got this." She leaned sideways in her chair. In her strong, clear voice she called, "Fellas."

The two men looked over. Meredith's smile was icy. When she wiggled her fingers at them, Colt wondered if hexes where real. Meredith no longer appeared the malleable woman. She looked pissed. "Two words, assholes. Pre. Nup."

They sputtered, indignant. Having a woman call them out clearly offended them.

Meredith leaned towards Colt. "Would you think less of me if I did something not nice?"

Colt shook his head, curious.

"Excellent. This will only take a moment." Meredith pulled out her phone from the evening clutch at her wrist. Whatever she was doing, it didn't take long.

Colt couldn't help asking, "What did you do?"

Meredith tucked the phone away. "From the looks of them, I suspect this won't take long. You'll see."

Within moments, both men's phones were ringing. He watched as each left in a hurry, barking into their phones.

Colt looked over at his new stepmom with renewed interest. All of the siblings had figured Meredith was a push-over, Bruce didn't tend to hang out with people who could outwit or outshine him. It appeared Meredith had more steel than they had expected.

Colt felt a brief pang of guilt. His parents' divorce had been messy and neither he, nor his siblings quite knew how to navigate the minefield. Meredith was easier to ignore, than get to know.

Meredith mistook Colt's expression. "Please understand, they work with your father. I've never been comfortable with their ethics. I just pushed over a very expensive domino for them. From their responses, it worked." She looked distressed. "Do you want me to fix it?"

He held up his hands. "Not on my account."

She gave him a small smile and relaxed in her chair.

Colt eyed the elegant older woman. "So, just like that?"

"My dear, I am an old woman with no children of my own. What else am I going to do with my money besides occasionally bully the bullies? And it is my money. My pre-nup is rock solid."

"Remind me never to get on your bad side."

Meredith laughed. It sounded like bells tinkling. "Dear, I've spent five years trying to get on you and your siblings' good side."

"There is that." What else could he say? It was true.

She fiddled with a discarded confetti wrapper. "Thank you for coming today. I apologize that Becca and Tucker are not here, too. Had I known, I would have done something about it. They should be here with you and Gabe."

Colt nodded and took another sip of his beer.

"What's next for you? Will you be heading out on the road again soon?"

"Yeah, the guys and I leave tonight. We'll be in Montana for the next two days, then in Wyoming for a week."

"The guys?"

"My travel buddies. We split driving shifts and can get more sleep."

Teaming up also helped to keep expenses low. When you were in the money, rodeo paid well, when you weren't, you were the one paying to play. Up until last season, there had been four of them that traveled together. Travis, who was two years younger than Colt, had blown his elbow for the final time. There wasn't enough tinker tape in the world that could keep Travis' elbow together again. The joint wouldn't hold, and bull riding required you hang on, tight. Colt pushed thoughts of his impending retirement out of his mind.

"I'm sorry I don't know more about bull riding. It sounds exciting. And maybe dangerous," she added.

"Only if I fall off," Colt added. This was the longest conversation he had ever had with her.

She smiled. "Does bull riding have a shelf life? All you kids seem so young to me, I have to remind myself you are full grown."

"I've got a few more years left in me." He didn't, but she didn't need to know that.

"What will you do after you retire from rodeo?" Meredith asked.

"Now Meredith, the only way to know that is by living, not planning."

"You can always go into modelling."

Colt choked on his beer. It was several moments before he stopped coughing.

Meredith handed him a serviette. "Forgive me, I meant nothing untoward. It's just that I have always thought you have an uncanny resemblance to a popular European cologne model. It's striking, really."

Colt cleared his throat. "Is that right?

A commotion from the foyer sounded.

Meredith hadn't noticed, she was still staring at him.

Colt was almost certain it was his mom who had just crashed the party. Who else could be making such a ruckus?

His older brother, Gabe, had thwarted her previous attempt at Bruce and Meredith's engagement party. Apparently, she wanted a second shot. No woman deserved to be humiliated at her own wedding reception.

Colt stood abruptly. "Meredith, please excuse me, I have to go."

Colt didn't wait for a reply, he sprinted to the foyer.

Chapter Eight

Bruce leaned against one of the open doors of the reception hall foyer. He swirled the martini in his hand, rolling the skewer of olives around and around. The familiar motion soothed his impatient energy. From his vantage point, Bruce could see both of his sons. Gabe was dancing with Meredith's ridiculous granola-eating niece, Savannah. Colt was sitting with his new stepmom, looking amused at something Meredith said.

Ah, Meredith. His lovely, malleable wife. Bruce needed a bank roll and access to powerful people. Meredith had both in spades. That she was hopelessly in love with him made his deception that much funnier. Bruce laughed to himself and took another swallow of his drink.

"Are you supposed to be drinking?" A young server had stopped, hesitant, next to him. "I mean, I can get you a new drink, one without alcohol. Your new wife mentioned we should be mindful of you."

Bruce wanted to backhand her for her insolence, but he noticed Clint Steele step forward.

He fucking hated that guy.

Though he had tried, Bruce had never cracked his children of their embarrassing lack of ambition or predatory drive. Clint Steele had been their neighbor when Bruce's kids were growing up. The man didn't have any children of his own. He had taken one look at Bruce, then taken Bruce's children under his wing. Fucking righteous asshole.

Steele gave Bruce a frosty look before turning to the young server. "Emily, I think I heard Ryan mention he needed help."

The young woman nodded and damn near ran away from them.

"Congratulations, Bruce."

The old cowboy made it sound like a mockery.

"What's that supposed to mean?"

Steele looked Bruce up and down. The set of his jaw made it clear he still found Bruce lacking.

Bruce was not physically intimidated by most men. He knew he could buy them off.

Steele made him uneasy.

"What are you doing here?" Bruce spoke faster to hide his stammering.

Clint took a sip of his drink, something neat. "What do you think I'm doing here?"

They all had believed the cancer bullshit Bruce had fed them, although Meredith had started asking questions. What did the old cowboy know?

"How much do you want?"

The cowboy looked him up and down again, and said, "You're a dick," before walking away.

"Mr. Tanner?" A scratchy voice asked.

Annoyed, Bruce spun around, ready to blast whoever was bothering him. "Do I know you?" But he did.

The man smiled. Bruce hadn't seen anything that cold for five years.

"I believe you have an outstanding debt."

"I don't know what you're talking about." Bruce started swirling his glass around again, confident he would have been apprised if anything had changed.

The man looked at the glass a moment before raising his predatory gaze. "No father would forget he sent his son for slaughter. Even you."

Bruce started to feel lightheaded. No one could know the role he played in Gabe's ambush.

The man smiled his icy smile again. "I see you do remember."

"I gave you everything you asked for."

The man glanced through the open foyer doors to the dance floor beyond. "And yet, he's still alive."

Sweat started to bead at Bruce's temple. How was he going to pay back a blood debt?

"That's not my fault."

The man plucked the cocktail skewer out of Bruce's drink. "Relax, I don't need that one dead anymore."

Bruce stammered before he could help it. "W-what do you need?"

The man lifted the skewer to his mouth, pulling two olives off. He dropped the skewer back in Bruce's drink. "You'll see."

Pop, pop.

A muted double-tap sounded, then people started screaming.

Chapter Nine

Colt came to a halt just inside the stylish foyer. He looked over the heads of the crowd but didn't see or hear his mom anywhere. Becca said their mom had regretted her outburst at the engagement party, but infidelity's sting could be sharp. Shit, was she even here?

Colt made his way through the growing throng of people. Most were standing in a tight circle near the second set of doors. He circled the group. Finding a break in the crowd, he shouldered his way in.

"Excuse me...coming through...excuse me."

Colt stopped at the center of the circle. His father was standing over a man lying on the dark patterned carpet.

"He just collapsed. I don't know what happened, he just collapsed."

Bruce looked shaken, but something in his tone snagged. As Colt was pulling out his phone to call nine-one-one, Gabe materialized next to him.

"No need to hurry. That guy's dead."

The crowd gasped. Several people screamed.

Colt glared at his brother as he dropped to his knees next to the body.

"Well, he is." Gabe pointed. "That's what dead looks like."

Before Colt could chastise his brother for being so macabre, his phone hummed to life.

"Nine-one-one. Police, fire or ambulance?"

Colt held his phone to his ear while he checked the body. "I can't find a pulse."

"Told you—what the fuck?"

Colt turned at Gabe's outburst. His brother had gone sheet white.

"Police, fire or ambulance?"

Colt pulled his hand away from the body. It was full of blood.

"Holy shit."

"Sir, are you there? Do you need the police, fire or ambulance?"

"Yeah, I'm here."

Colt stared at the red streaks of blood on his hand. The red, it was so bright.

"I think this guy is dead. That's police, right?"

The nine-one-one operator started asking him a barrage of questions. Soon, Colt could hear the wail of sirens in the distance. He stood, answering their last questions before hanging up.

"The police and ambulance are on their way." Colt pocketed his phone, trying to avoid getting blood everywhere.

Some of the crowd stepped back then, starting to disperse. Others tucked in tighter.

Gabe didn't respond.

"Gabe?"

His brother was staring at the corpse.

"Dude, what is it?" Colt had never seen that look on Gabe's face. It kinda scared him.

Finally, Gabe looked up. His eyes were oddly empty. "That's the guy who shot me in the head five years ago."

Chapter Ten

Fernando Martinez sat on the lean bed in the grim solitary room. He had woken up in this room several weeks ago and hadn't left since. That was fine. It only simmered the rage within.

He would be out soon. Everyone had a price or a breaking point. His crew was good at finding either, and even now, his network was infiltrating supposedly secure connections and turning government employees into puppets. It was just a matter of time.

Fernando cocked his head, hearing a faint commotion. Several moments later the thick door to his solitary cell swung open. Chad, his second in command, stood in the hallway. "Are you mobile?"

Fernando gave a brief nod. Chad motioned and Fernando followed him. Several turns, a utility corridor, and seven dead bodies later, they emerged through an underground vault to an industrial stormwater drain. It was dark outside. He had wondered. Solitary did not share natural light.

A zodiac bobbed on the choppy water, waiting. Another of his lieutenants was at the wheel. Moments later they bounced across the open bay in the inky darkness.

"Where is she?"

"Canada," Chad answered. "I've made arrangements."

The Kensington bitch had chosen Country over him.

She had chosen wrong.

Chapter Eleven

The private jet banked, and Sophie pulled her attention from the magazine she had been reading to look out the window. Greenland was below. Fjords rose like sentinels from their cloud-shrouded bases in deep shades of green and grey, and she felt her whole body respond in bone-deep awe. Seeing such rugged nature made her feel alive.

Sophie had chosen a sport where she was required to spend much of her time outside. Outside she was free to move; inside was a world of pantyhose and weighty expectations layered with crippling responsibilities.

She pressed her face against the glass. Sophie had seen much of the world, though she wasn't sure it counted. Tagging along on her great-grandmother's diplomatic and political missions wasn't really experiencing the world, not the real one, anyway. Political dinners were orchestrated rituals of compliance. The fjords below them were raw, their power innate, not contrived. What Sophie wouldn't do to feel a fraction of that strength.

"What are you looking at?"

Sophie glanced at her auntie sitting in the posh, oversized seat across from her own. "Fjords."

Lillian glanced out her own window. "I've only ever flown over Greenland. Wonder what it's like."

"I'm guessing cold."

"You know what I mean."

But Sophie didn't. Lately her life had been feeling as shallow and prescribed as those political dinners. If she didn't make a change soon, Sophie was afraid she would slowly bore herself to death in irrelevance.

"Are you and great-grandmum still fighting?"

"We emphatically disagreed on something," her auntie corrected.

"Sounds like fighting. Her jabs at you still not eating meat are getting old."

Lillian shrugged, and Sophie knew a closed door when she saw one. She motioned behind her. "Do you ever get used to them."

Lillian looked beyond Sophie. "Our security detail? Yes. They feel invasive until they block a threat. Then you'll lose your shit if they aren't as close as you think they need to be." Lillian glanced past Sophie's shoulder again. "Those look like Jordemorden guys. You won't see them unless you're in immediate physical danger."

"Sounds efficient."

"They are. They're more hands-off than other systems, but they are eerily effective."

"Wish they had selected more dashing code names for us. We could have been Dragon and Thorn instead of Snapdragon and Primrose. We sound like teetotlers."

Lillian smiled. "*Seanmhair* picked them. And they are supposed to be *code* names."

"Har har." Sophie paused as one of the younger soldiers walked past. "I haven't been to Jordemorden since that global security threats summit with great-grand-mum. How is Grace?"

Princess Grace, granddaughter of the current king, had been the highlight of the trip. She was older than Sophie, sophisticated, and hadn't minded when Sophie tagged along.

Sometimes it felt like Lillian did. The twenty-one years between them at times got in the way.

Lillian eyed Sophie. "Are you doing okay?"

Sophie blustered, "Of course. Why would you ask that?"

"Because your face just fell, and your voice changed."

"I'm fine." Sophie breezed. She would have to do a better job. Her auntie caught too much. "You were saying, about Princess Grace?"

Her auntie smiled. "She's good. Rabidly protective—seriously, are you okay?"

"That's my line," Sophie quipped. "Maybe I am a little nervous."

Her auntie smiled at her. "You'll do great. You have worked so hard. You deserve to be here."

Sophie snorted. "The woman whose spot I took broke her leg in an automobile crash. The next in line just got an ultra-running sponsorship, and the third one in line ahead of me didn't want to move her wedding date."

Lillian was quick to recover her surprise. "So you were the fourth choice. It doesn't take away from all your hard work."

"I'm only on the biathlon team because great-grand-mum made sure we knew how to shoot and have enough cardio to outrun a potential assailant."

Lillian smiled. "She did, didn't she?"

"I'm telling you, if you would have ever tried, you'd be on the team, too."

In their family, you were either an over-achiever or a trust fund brat. You couldn't just *be*. Sophie was on the National biathlon team which gave her credibility and made her a useful accessory to her great-grandmum.

"That's bollocks, and you know it. Don't dismiss yourself so easily."

It wasn't easy, holding her auntie's gaze. "What about you?"

Sophie had watched, over the years, as Lillian's spark had flickered in the turbulent winds of her job. Hers hadn't been an easy career. The last two years had finished crushing her auntie's spirit. "I worry about you."

Lillian shook her head. "Don't. This trip is about you."

Sophie quickly looked down.

Lillian misread her silence. "Sophie, darling, I'm fine."

Sophie snapped her head up. "No, you're not. Fernando is a ridiculous man-child, and your so-called friends are ass-clowns."

Lillian's eyes widened. "Woah, where is this coming from?"

Sophie crossed her arms and stared out the plane window. "It's not fair, is all."

Lillian's face softened. "Life isn't always fair, and we have it better than most."

Sophie looked out the window, avoiding her auntie's gaze. "You're not fine. I hear you crying. I see the ghost you've become. It's not you, and it's not fair. You're two decades older than me, but your social life can't possibly be over because of one bad boyfriend."

"He was selling State secrets. That's pretty bad."

Sophie snapped her head around. "You also said he was really good in the sack. Neither should have any bearing on you moving on."

Her auntie's eyes flashed. "I appreciate your concern, but it's more complicated than that."

"No, it's not. You act like you're broken. You're not broken, you don't need fixing."

"My doctors disagree."

"Your doctors are old-school wankers." She picked her magazine back up and started rolling it in her hands. She could wring those stupid doctors' necks. "You have PTSI, not PTSD. If my doctors would have said my ankle had a disorder instead of an injury, I wouldn't have thought I could heal it, either."

"Sophie, I went to leading specialists in their fields. Brains and ankles are different."

"Not in any way that actually matters. Your doctors are full of shite. Even I can see you are worse now, than when this all started. You can heal, you just need a reason to. We'll start today."

Lillian zeroed in on Sophie's slip. "We? What do you need to heal?"

Sophie smiled a little too bright. "Life, baby."

Her auntie was giving Sophie one of her I-have-a-story-lead looks.

Sophie pressed, "People need a reason to get out of bed in the morning. I know you've got some clinical shit you're dealing with, but while you've been dealing with all this, you lost your faith in your instincts, and fell into a rut. You don't do useless, never have. You need a project."

Lillian splayed her hands on either side of her ears. "Why does everyone keep saying that? Grandmum said the same thing."

"Duh, without your all-encompassing work, you're at loose ends. Running is great and all, but you need more."

Her auntie cracked a grin. "Somehow it's not as offensive when you say it."

That's what Sophie had been hoping for. She rarely agreed with her great-grandmum, but on Lillian, they were in accord.

"So? Am I in a rut or at loose ends?"

Sophie thew her magazine at her auntie. It landed open to a cologne ad and Lillian dropped her gaze. "Bet he could get me out of either."

Sophie cackled at the bemused look on her auntie's face and looked down. The man staring up from the glossy magazine page was undeniably sexy, his raw masculinity fuel for the hottest fantasies.

Sophie fanned herself. *"Ohmygod, yes."*

"What?"

She pointed. "You and the *Archambeau* cologne guy. With great-grandmum's connections, I'm sure we can track him down."

"And do what exactly?" Lillian asked dryly.

Sophie waggled her eyebrows. "That's up to you and the hot cologne model."

It was nice to hear her auntie's laugh again.

"Let's not make plans to molest an unsuspecting cologne model."

Sophie ceded. "Fine. But it's not molesting if he's into it."

"Your commentary on the *Archambeau* guy aside, let's revisit your earlier assessment. You think I'm in a funk?"

"And you don't trust your instincts anymore," Sophie added.

"I guess I haven't been myself lately."

"Auntie, I miss the old you." Inspiration struck. "We can do anything with a plan. Let's call it *Project: Re-Wilding.*"

Lillian furrowed her brow, looking utterly unconvinced. It was one of her auntie's looks that would normally have Sophie diving for cover and feeling like an idiot.

Not today. Her auntie needed her.

"ReWilding as in returning to the core of who you are, the real you, where your identity is *you*, not your career, or what others think you should be. Careers are supposed to support a person, not define them, and other people are way too good at telling us who we are, or who we are supposed to be." Sophie leaned forward. *"Who are you?"*

"Shit, you're intense."

"I know. I kinda like it." Sophie warmed to her new-found courage. "Okay, no espionage, no human trafficking, no bombed schools, no contact with any former loser colleagues or *friends*," Sophie emphasized with air-quotes, "no war anything. But you do need to get back to work."

"You've just axed everything I write about."

"There are literally millions of things to write about that aren't how shitty human beings can be to each other. Great-grandmum's right, you need a project."

"She gave me one. She sent me with family fur trade documents. They look interesting enough—"

Sophie yawned loudly. "Sorry, did you say something? I just fell asleep I was so bored."

"Ha-ha." Lillian opened her satchel on the empty seat next to her and pulled out the book she had found in the alcove in the library. "I do have something."

The hair on the back of Sophie's neck stood on end.

"What's that?"

Lillian's face held fascination, and maybe a bit of trepidation.

"Grandmum freaked when I found it."

"Good. I like it already." She held out her hands. "May I?"

Lillian passed her the book and Sophie felt her body tingle, like a brief surge of energy had flowed through her.

"What the fuck is that?"

Lillian nodded. "I know, right? It like hums."

"Jesus, what it that? Does that happen to you often?"

Her aunt shrugged. "I've felt similar a few times before. Mainly with books."

"Nerd. I haven't." A memory tickled. "Actually, there was one textbook. A political science one."

Sophie hadn't thought about that class in a long time. Her teacher had taught her concepts and views she had never considered before, ones her great-grandmum would have undoubtedly considered political blasphemy. The notion that the economic and political engines of the world could run on anything other than the threat of retaliation, fear, greed and deception had been eye-opening. Sophie had been fascinated ever since, not that she had done anything with it.

She gently turned several pages. "Some of the plants listed don't grow in the U.K. Holy shit—this section is from North America. This page covers menstrual cramps." Sophie looked up. "What is this? It's like a natural history atlas and women's studies book rolled into one."

She gently flipped a few more pages. "If ever there was a ReWilding manual, this would at least make it into the appendix."

Lillian smiled. "Now who is the nerd? I've never seen anything like it. I'm certain it was penned by a woman, but it has fur trade recordings, plus rather shocking feminine wisdom. It's kind of weird, truth be told. I mean, what exactly is it?"

Sophie turned another page. "It's a New World grimoire, that's what. How did we miss having a witch in
our family tree?"

"That's a bit of a leap, but I like it. Grandmum's not
talking and I'm certainly not asking my mum."

Sophie snorted. "Can you imagine? It would intrude
on her socialite activities."

She came across a larger page that had been mindfully
folded and sewn in. "This is stunning."

Lillian's eyes sparkled when she said, "That's a map
of North America from 1751. There might be a reasonable
explanation, but conventional history has assigned an
Anthony Henday, who had been working for the Hudson's Bay Company at the time, as the first white guy as
far west as the Canadian Rocky Mountains in 1754."

"So?"

"So, fur trade documents are penned by men. The one
in your hand seems to be written by a white woman three
years *before* Henday made his way that far west."

Her auntie was nearly vibrating in the plush oversized
seat. Sophie looked back down at the book in her hands.
She liked when the improbable happened, and when her
auntie was happy.

Lillian continued. "Do you know how important a
find this is? Back then, few women were taught to read
and write, and men didn't take their white womenfolk to
the hinterlands in the mid-eighteenth century. It simply
wasn't done."

"I feel a *but* coming."

"Many took what was called a *country wife*. They married local Indigenous women whilst they were away."

Sophie's snapped her head up. "They were bigamists?"

"You know the rules. If a union wasn't blessed by the church, it wasn't considered a 'real marriage' so legally, it wouldn't have been considered bigamy."

"Fuck, the church pisses me off."

"I know." Her auntie sounded world-weary.

"The kids would have been considered bastards in the eyes of the church and British society. By-blows, as it were. How could the men knowingly do that to their kids?"

"None of this is news," Lillian said gently.

"Doesn't make it right."

"I know. Marrying for love is a relatively recent development. They were financial transactions long before love came into the picture."

"Why did the women 'marry' the white traders anyway?" Sophie asked, stubborn.

"How do I say this delicately? We don't have a monopoly on marrying off our daughters and sisters in the name of political alliances or business acumen. Country wives were extremely valuable. They knew how to survive in unknown, hostile landscapes, and had valuable social connections. Business was like it is today, it matters who you know."

"Fuck, I hate history."

Sophie knew she was sounding like a broken record, there was just so much *shite* out there.

"It's relatively recent that women have had a choice. Many still don't. The financial disparity, and in some cases, need for physical security, is simply too great."

"It's bullshit."

"That's easy for us to say. We have the financial means to never have to get married, and a crew of special forces protecting us."

"How do you know all of this stuff?"

"I started researching as soon as I found that book in your hands. I think the woman who wrote it was named Obedience Beatrice Evans."

"*Obedience?*" Sophie forced herself to lower her voice. "That is an awful name."

Lillian agreed. "If she wrote that volume, she didn't take it to heart. She supposedly ran away to the New World with an Irishman. I haven't come across him beyond his name, Seamus O'Malley. I did find a single letter from her sister in Cornwall. Her sister called her *BeeBee*, by the way, not Obedience."

"Good." Sophie crossed her arms, mad on behalf of her long-dead great-aunt.

The plane engines sounded overly loud in the ensuing silence.

Sophie glanced at the men hired to protect them. "Ever just want to punch them? Just let all your angst fly? They look like they can take it."

"No."

"Yeah, me neither."

A small smile played on Lillian's lips.

Sophie could no longer see the fjords below them, just a heavy blanket of clouds far below. She couldn't help *BeeBee,* but she could help her aunt still living.

"Auntie, I was thinking, falling for the wrong guy does not mean the rest of your life is fucked."

Her auntie's eyebrows went up again. "I'm not following."

"Hear me out. If I went through what you did, there is no way in hell you'd let me give up on me."

Lillian's eyes were stark. "Sophie, I have nothing left in my tank. I'm tired. All my fight is gone."

The private flight attendant arrived with their meals.

"Then it's a good thing our food is here. Fuel up, auntie. You are going to *ReWild.* You're going to get your self back."

She handed the grimoire back to Lillian. "Here. I would feel awful if I spilled anything on this. I don't want to be another person that let you down."

Lillian safely tucked the volume back in her satchel. "You could never let me down."

Sophie knew she would.

When she finally got up the nerve to admit she didn't want to compete anymore.

Chapter Twelve

L illian ran like someone was chasing her. Her chest heaved, her legs hurt, and still she ran harder as she clutched her tactical pen in one hand and bear spray in the other. Even with an elite security detail shadowing her, she was never without either on the trail. Or the public library. She had gone into the city every day this week to pour through the records collection, trying to find a whisper of her ancestor.

There had been a time when Lillian had been fearless, when worry was nothing more than a verb to practice conjugating in other languages. Those days were long gone. Now she sought control and avoided the untamable. She ran to give her mind something to grapple with and exhaust her body enough to sleep. It was a stifling way to live, but at least she was alive.

The kilometers flew past as she kept up a good pace. She was on an unpaved road that wound high through crown land in the Alberta foothills. Thick green grasses undulated in waves around her, interrupted by the occasional copse of poplar. There were splashes of color, too. Wildflowers, many the likes of which Lillian had never seen, dotted the landscape. Rolling hills, some topped with what looked like spruce forests, played peekaboo with the distant Rocky Mountain peaks.

Sunlight and a deceptively cool breeze were her only consistent trail mates.

Besides her security detail.

They would be discreetly surrounding her. A normal person wouldn't even notice them. She had blown past normal a long time ago. Sometimes one of them would run next to her, other times she knew they were somewhere nearby. Like today. Never staying predictable was the name of the game.

The air was cooler and drier than she was used to. These mountains were also obviously higher above sea level than England. Her lungs and blood were having a hell of a time adjusting to the difference. Still, she pushed her body harder.

The sun had warmed the surrounding vegetation and Lillian tried to savor the exquisite earthy perfume. But Sophie's words chased her.

People need a reason to get out of bed in the morning.

Lillian ran harder. She had no job, no deadlines, nothing worthy to accomplish or strive for. It was the middle of the day, and no one would notice or care if she researched family history or binge-watched crappy TV.

You're in a funk.

She attacked the next incline, a steeply graded curve. Lillian missed her old life, her old job and the unrealistic deadlines. She missed Omran's annoying orders, take-out curry chips from Jocks, running *without* bear spray.

You're not broken.

Four hundred meters up the steep ascent her ill-adjusted body faltered. Heaving, she stopped and bent over, still clutching her tactical pen and bear spray. Lillian held her body bent as she emptied what little remained in her stomach.

Her earpiece sounded. *"You okay?"*

Embarrassed, Lillian cautiously stood upright. She holstered the bear spray and slid the weaponized pen into the side pocket of her running tights. "You heard that?"

"*Affirmative.*"

Lillian pulled out the small water bottle at the small of her back. "Sorry. That must have sounded awful." She rinsed out her mouth and popped a piece of mastic gum.

"*We've heard worse.*"

She smiled at her detail's dry humor. "I bet."

Lillian tilted her head up, letting the sunlight warm her face. A hawk circled high overhead, it's cry a piercing lament that Lillian felt in her core. She watched as it angled down, suddenly dropping out of the sky. In a moment it pulled up, something small clutched in its talons. The bird of prey flew off, leaving Lillian alone, such as she was, and feeling too much like a small creature caught in powerful talons.

She tried to shake the odd feeling off and broke into an easy jog. A feeling, not quite like déjà vu, arose. Along with it came the certainty she needed to check the carton of fur trade documents. Her *seanmhair's* assistant had crated the items from the estate library, but Lillian had yet to crack the carton open.

This time when Lillian surveyed her surroundings, she considered Obedience Beatrice Evans. Had her ancestor, centuries ago, crested this very hill? Would she discover that another ancestor had?

Doubtful. Lillian was being fanciful now. But as the stubborn spark lingered, she realized something was very wrong. Lillian stopped walking, and the dust from the gravel road swirled about her running shoes. Scanning the horizon, she looked for what had tweaked her attention, and cover. This stretch of gravel didn't have a ditch to speak of, nothing deep enough to use as cover anyway. The road she was on disappeared over one of the larger rises of the rolling hills of silvery green scrub brush, and now it worried her she couldn't see what was on the other side. Cover was a copse of poplar trees at least two hundred meters away on the other side of a barbed wire fence. The grid road that had been her private little haven only moments ago now felt like an exposed gauntlet of unseen dangers.

Her doctors in the U.K. had assured her that paranoia was a routine symptom of PTSD. Too bad they didn't have a textbook or graph to tell her if she was actually being targeted. Moments ago, she had been humbled by the stark beauty of the land. She had let herself forget, even momentarily, that Fernando was in prison but his mercenaries were not. Now she saw vegetation too stingy to take cover in and hills too big to see past. A red-winged black bird called from the top of a cattail at the edge of a pond. Slough. Distantly she recalled they called them sloughs here. Great, now she could add delirious to her list of things to worry about.

Her stomach tightened again, warning her of an impending danger.

"Something's up, guys," she said into her earpiece.

Indecision could get a person killed. Lillian was ready to run, she just didn't know in which direction to flee. Her car was at least sixteen kilometers away. She had just decided to make a bolt for the trees when her earpiece sounded.

"Copy that. There's a large herd of cattle in the next valley over."

She swung her gaze back to where the road crested, and a brown furry body flashed. Another brown body came into view. Soft lowing followed and a small herd of dusty brown cows ambled a few steps before stopping and staring at her. She exhaled and let her stance relax. She had been scared by a few cows. Not arms traders, drug lords, renegade soldiers, or Fernando's crew.

Chagrined, Lillian took a step forward and the cows turned, heading back where they had come from.

"We can share the road," Lillian called after them, but the cows disappeared over the rise.

Lillian smiled; the cows were kinda cute. She'd check out the view from the top of the hill and then turn back.

Sprinting up the last few meters to the crest of the hill, Lillian shrieked as a gigantic horse shied in front of her. The large animal reared, sharp hooves windmilled precariously close to her face. Instinctively she threw herself back. Stumbling, she hit the dirt hard. She let momentum carry her and rolled into a back shoulder roll before springing to her feet in a fight-ready position.

The horse was now stamping instead of rearing, and she noticed he had a rider.

The cowboy had kept his seat, although how was beyond Lillian. He was built like his horse, taller than most with corded strength to match. He spoke in low, soothing tones to his mount, his body moving in concert with the animal he had quieted with remarkable speed.

Lillian stared and let her hands drop from their battle-ready position to her sides. She was no longer in danger from the horse, the rider was competent. Her earpiece had gone off as soon as Lillian had shrieked, but she wasn't listening. What was going on in front of her? The horse pawed again, once, before blowing out a big gust of air. It stood still, at ease and waiting for its rider's next direction. Lillian wasn't often awed—she had seen too much—but the pair before her were magnificent.

"What the hell are you doing?"

"I beg your pardon?"

The cowboy gave a fast glance behind him and cursed. "You. Here. Why?"

His speech was positively barbaric. Lillian held her hand over her brow to block the glare of sunlight and followed his gaze down the other side of the rise to see what all the fuss was about.

Lillian didn't know cows particularly well, but a sea of bobbing heads, like a wave of motley-colored browns flowing in the sunshine, were headed straight for them. There must have been hundreds of them.

She watched as the handful that had previously crested the rise and turned back around, met the oncoming herd. Those at the front of the herd, started to turn when met with the now-oncoming traffic. Lillian watched in awe as the handful that had turned around became a dozen. Then twenty. The tidal wave of beasts was literally going back out. And gaining momentum.

The cowboy cursed again. "Get on." He kicked his boot out of his stir-up and offered his left hand. *"Now."*

Lillian did not trust strange men. She barely trusted known men anymore.

"Are there more of you?" he asked, his hand still out for her to take but he wasn't looking at her. His gaze was locked behind them again.

She didn't understand his distress, and her attention had snagged on his profile. Did she know him?

He turned back to her. "Look lady, I need to know you're not going to get trampled. Is there anyone else who could be in danger?"

The brief moment of recognition passed. Lillian could see four riders in the distance urging the gigantic herd to stay on course—straight for them.

Holy fuck, was she in the middle of a cattle drive?

Her earpiece buzzed. *"Roger that. This guy's clean. Exit now. I repeat, you're clear to exit now."*

The cowboy in front of her wasn't carrying a firearm and his face didn't ping any immediate threats from the intel her detail could access from the field. The easiest way for Lillian to get to safety was via the outstretched hand. If needed, at least one of her detail would be a sharpshooter. Her security detail still did not have official permission to be here. The paperwork alone was enough for her to grab the stranger's offered hand. "It's just me."

Lillian planted her boot into the empty stirrup and, with the cowboy's gritted help, hauled herself up and behind him. From the way he moved and the pinched expression on his face, he was riding injured.

The horse shied and she pressed as close behind him as she dared and wrapped both of her arms as gently as she could around him. Her right arm brushed sturdy nylon. He was in a brace of some kind.

With his left hand, he held her arm firm against him, the other held the reins.

"Don't squeeze your legs more than you need to stay on."

She didn't understand that cryptic remark until she felt him tighten his own legs around the horse and the animal immediately shot forward. In reflex, her arms cinched around him.

"*Oof.*" The cowboy half-turned his head to look back at her, their bodies bobbing as the horse cantered. "I'm going to need to breathe, ma'am."

Lillian loosened her grip as much as she dared and felt his intake of breath. She was pretty sure he was sporting injured ribs, too.

Yet he had offered her protection.

She let her body match his, and his horse's, fluidly. The physical contact was startling. She hadn't touched anyone—person or animal—in a long time.

Lillian held on only tight enough to stay upright. The cowboy looped them wide and out of danger.

He turned his head again. "Still okay?"

Lillian nodded against his back. He smelled like sunshine and dust.

"Good."

He angled his horse again, this time bringing them into position at the back of the herd. The other riders were also fanned around the back of the herd, like an invisible net bringing the herd in. It worked.

Lillian stared in wonder as the tide stopped turning. Her awe turned to alarm as the ocean of ambling bodies became choppy waves of running hooves. The herd was breaking away, though this time moving away from them.

"Hold on." In a flash the cowboy turned right and headed straight for an opening in the fence line. Within moments they were at the copse of trees she had spotted.

He held out his left arm for her. "Get down and get in those trees. You'll be safe there."

Panting from fear, and maybe even exhilaration, Lillian took his left arm for balance and slid off the horse. He waited until she had slipped into the grove before spinning his horse around and charging away after the herd.

He was out of sight in seconds.

Lillian's earpiece hummed to life. *"We have a visual. Confirming secure."*

"I'm good, I'm good," Lillian said, breathless. "You could have said there were *a few hundred* cattle."

"Roger that," came the dry reply.

She wound her way through the aspen, following the wee forest higher and higher. Branches clawed at her face and shoulders and caught in her hair.

The ground gave a weird rumble. She pressed on as fast as she could, not wanting to miss a second of the unfolding drama.

Finally at the front edge of the cluster of trees, she wrapped her arm around a trunk and looked down, watching. The herd still looked like an out-of-control wave.

Her knight, if she still believed in such a term, was in the thick of it, his mount and the other riders funneled the stampeding herd into tighter and tighter formation, slowing their pace but not turning their direction. The land before her stretched out in rolling glory, handling the cattle, horses, cowboys, an unofficial security detail, and one disgraced English war correspondent.

The choppy sea of cattle settled. Some even stopped to munch on the succulent grasses on the edge of the gravel road.

Lillian sank down and sat on the grass, still cradling the tree trunk. In that unlikely moment, she wondered if she had just witnessed why people would actually choose to live here.

Chapter Thirteen

"For the hundredth time, I wasn't shot. Neither was Gabe or Savannah. They're safe. I'm safe. Everyone is fine except the dead guy." Colt winced at his lack of finesse. He sounded like Gabe.

Colt had just arrived at his sister Becca's eco-inn ranch, and they were still standing in the foyer area. He figured he had about four seconds to calm her down before she red-lined and kicked into full-blown momma bear mode. She was protective of her siblings. Her maternal instincts were significantly more primed than their mom Samantha's were.

"How can you be so calm? You were the one who found him?"

Colt used the boot jack to slide out of his boots. He placed them neatly on the large mat Becca had placed in front of the main door.

"When I checked him for a pulse, I didn't know he was dead. If I dwell on it, yeah, it'll get weird."

Colt didn't mention that Becca and Tucker not being invited to the wedding had inadvertently kept them out of harm's way. He had been thinking about it a lot. Few things genuinely terrified him. Since Gabe was shot in the line of duty five years ago, Colt had a new-found fear of losing one of his siblings.

He walked quickly through his sister's large living room and headed down the back hallway.

Becca trailed after him. "This is Canada. Who the hell has shoot-outs at their wedding?"

"Good question. Meredith is flipping out."

"I would, too!" It was a rare display of solidarity for the woman their father had left their mother for.

They walked into Becca's oversized kitchen. Chalk marks lined the ceiling and several long, distressed eight-by-eights were piled in front of a row of cabinets.

"Those the beams you need me to put up?" Becca's eco-inn was scheduled to open in a few short months and Colt tried to help her out when he could, and when she'd let him.

"Yeah. I need coffee first, though. You?" Becca filled the kettle with water before putting it on the stove.

"Your coffee? Hard, yes." Becca had come back from Germany making wicked good coffee.

"Do Gabe or Tucker know anything?" She started grinding coffee beans.

Colt placed both hands face-down on the counter. "There is something you should know."

Becca pulled the French press off her drying rack and poured the ground coffee into it. "That sounds ominous."

There really was no delicate way to say this. "Gabe recognized the dead guy. He is certain it's the guy who shot him five years ago."

Becca hooked the back of one of the stools at her large kitchen island. She pulled it out and sat down, looking stunned.

"Not in a thousand guesses." She rubbed her temples. "He's *sure*?"

"He is. It was five years ago, though, and a pretty traumatic experience. Memories can be fluid."

"What the fuck is dad into?"

"What about Meredith?"

"Oh please, that woman's only flaw is she fell for dad and acted on it."

Again, his sister surprised him with her non-viperish comments about Meredith.

Becca ran both hands through her hair. "Don't get me wrong, I *really* don't like her. But if I were to bet anything important on who's connected to the dead asshole, it'd be dad, not her."

When had his little sister grown up so much?

Colt leaned against the island counter. "She seemed genuinely distressed. Dad seemed put-out. Someone getting murdered at a family wedding is bad enough. It would be a hell of a lot better if the dead guy wasn't the one who shot Gabe five years ago. If anyone knows who he is or why he was there, they're not saying."

Becca dropped her head down onto the counter. "Why is our family so dysfunctional?"

Colt slung his arms around his sister's shoulders. "We're interesting."

"I want boring," she mumbled, but leaned into him.

"If there can be such a thing as fluke gunfire and really sketchy coincidences, I'm chalking it all up to that until someone with a badge tells me differently." Colt had to.

It was the only way he was going to keep himself sane from worry.

The kettle whistled. Becca dragged herself up and crossed to the stove. She finished making the coffee and left it to steep. "Do Tucker or Gabe know anything else?"

"Not that I know of."

"I hate this."

"I know." She looked so sad. Colt walked over and gave her a real hug.

She wrapped her arms around him and held on tight. He tried not to wince as his ribs protested.

"Thanks. I know you're not a hugger."

He wasn't. "You worry too much."

"You don't worry enough." Her voice was muffled in his shirt.

"Until we know different, I'm letting it be wrong place, wrong time. You should, too."

"Fine." She pulled back. "Why are you wearing the brace?"

"My shoulder popped a few nights ago."

Her eyes widened. "Popped as in dislocated? Colt, you shouldn't be moving cattle, let alone hanging beams."

"I didn't dislocate it, I just annoyed it." He didn't mention his bruised ribs. The dead body at their dad's wedding had everyone jumpy, and his sister was stressed enough getting everything ready for her opening weekend in the fall. Colt didn't need to give her anything more to worry about.

Becca eyed his arm brace. "We can do this next month."

As a rule, Becca didn't ask people for help. Colt pulled the silent investor card so she would at least accept his. If she kept up her solo, grueling pace, she was going to run herself ragged before her business even opened.

"Gabe and Savannah would help you if you asked them to."

Becca laughed so hard tears started running from the corner of her eyes. "Have you ever done a home improvement project with our oldest brother?"

"No."

"Take my word for it—don't. Just don't."

"Noted." Gabe could be a bit intense. "What about Tucker?"

"That man is a culinary genius. Those skills do not translate to anything with a hammer. And I wasn't kidding, we can do this next month when you're healthy."

Next month Colt could be in worse shape.

"Nah, let's do it now. It'll be one more thing you can cross off your list. I promise I'll use the driver left-handed."

"You're sure?" Becca had that look on her face; Colt knew she needed help but didn't want to press.

He waved off her concern. "Where do you want the beams?"

The eight-by-eights were strictly ornamental. The large house had plenty of exposed structural beams. Becca had wanted *pretty* ones in the kitchen to match. Becca walked Colt through where the long, rough-hewn wooden beams would be positioned, pointing at the ceiling as much as she motioned to the precise drawings she had sketched to scale.

"Sounds straight-forward. I have quick-snap scaffolding in my truck."

Becca helped him unload and they set up the scaffolding in her kitchen with relative ease. He poured them coffee as she double-checked her math and where she had marked off on the ceiling where the beams would go.

They were able to easily raise the decorative lumber into place using a rigged lever. She already had the oversized ladder in the kitchen, and he maneuvered it into place.

Becca grasped a rung of the ladder. "With it set up like this, I can screw the beams into place."

Without thinking of the repercussions, he blurted, "Nope."

His sister gave him a withering look. Colt gave her an exasperated one right back.

"Sometimes a man needs to feel, you know, manly."

"And standing idle while your little sister climbs a big, tall ladder and uses power tools makes you feel less of a man?"

"Well, yeah. Kinda."

Becca rolled her eyes. "Men and their machismo."

Colt shrugged. "It's not that you can't do it. You are freakishly the most self-reliant person I know. Actually, I think you and Clint are tied. Anyway, it's not that you can't do it, it's that if I don't, then I'm the loser putz who didn't step up."

Becca had her hands on her hips. "And what, be a man?"

"Is there any way you would see this as respecting the feminine instead of toxic masculinity?"

Becca tousled his hair like an auntie would a little kid. "Aww, the bull rider has a sensitive side."

"Why do I hang out with you?"

"Because I'm the only woman in your life who is not a groupie or your mother."

"Right. I need to expand my circle. Have any single friends?"

"Not a chance, bro. And I'm just messing with you. To you it's manners, not undermining my feminine might." She motioned to the ladder. "Alright, get your ass up there and be all manly like a good boy."

"Thank you." Colt pocketed a handful of screws as long as spikes. "I swear, it's like pulling teeth trying to help you."

"Quit whining."

Colt climbed the oversized ladder, smiling. Becca handed him the cordless driver, before holding the ladder steady. They fell into an easy work rhythm.

Becca admired the first beam. "Nice work. I had my doubts on your ambidextrous aspirations."

"Ye of little faith." The beam did look good. Colt was impressed with the level of detail Becca was incorporating. The inn had a warmth and character that few accommodations he had ever stayed in had managed to achieve.

"Want to hear something weird?" Becca said from the base of the ladder.

Colt lined up another screw. "Sure."

"Dad bought me the old Chasseur place."

Colt's hand slipped and the cordless driver he was using skidded, plunging the screw at an odd angle. It would have been a mess if the rough-hewn wooden beam he was anchoring hadn't already been sporting knots and abrasions.

Colt looked down at his little sister. "Why'd he do that? I thought he wasn't speaking to you."

Becca shrugged, both hands still gripping the metal ladder. "Tucker figures Meredith put him up to it. Meredith gave dad the money to buy it for me."

"Why would she do that?" Colt backed the screw out of the wood and tried again. This time it bit in clean and straight.

"Pretty sure she feels bad for how her and dad's relationship started. You know, that whole adultery thing. Do you think I should have gone to their wedding, even not invited? I mean, he is our dad."

Becca's usually cheerful face had become tight and drawn.

Colt felt compelled to remind her, "Dad's being a dick to you and Tucker, that's on him. I only went so Gabe wasn't flying solo. I didn't know if it would get weird, Savannah being Meredith's niece and all."

He sunk in another screw, careful as the long, slender metal chewed a straight trajectory through the knotty pine.

"I know. Still—"

"Dad has stopped and started talking to you and Tucker so many times I've lost count. He got sick and didn't tell anyone until Gabe pried it out of him. Then he married the woman he cheated on mom with. None of that is on any of us, including you."

"Then why do I feel so shitty?"

Colt used her old nickname. "Kiddo, mom and dad are really good at pulling those strings. You've got to stop letting them."

Becca made a face, but Colt saw that her eyes were wet with unshed tears. "That land is perfect. It has water for the livestock, perfect terrain for all levels of riders, stunning views that will look picture-perfect on marketing material. Not to mention haying fields and existing oil lease royalties that will help keep everything afloat."

"It does sound good," Colt retrieved another screw and loaded it on the end of the driver. The electric whir of the power tool temporarily muted Becca's answer.

An uneasy feeling sparked.

Rumor had it, Officer Jason Chasseur had finally pulled together enough money to buy back the family ranch his father had sold years ago. There was bad blood between his sister and Officer Chasseur. Colt didn't know the reason, and it was none of his business, but if his little sister had anything to do with scooping the officer on that particular stretch of land, it was not going to end well.

"Everything I need is on that land. I'm just afraid of dad's strings. I've poured everything I have into this inn. So have you. I want, no, I *need* this to work."

"Don't go there, either. I was happy to invest in this place, and in you."

Metal bit through a wood knot, making a harsh whirring sound. Colt repositioned the driver before giving it steady pressure and power. The long screw sunk in, secure.

Becca waited until it was quiet again before she asked, "What if he takes it away? What if dad gets mad, like he does, especially lately, and goes all weird? I can totally see him suing me or something. This is my livelihood, but he could throw a tantrum and take it all away."

"Is it in your name?"

"It's in both of ours. Apparently for five years, then it reverts to me. I didn't even know that was a thing."

Colt sunk in four more screws.

"You can run your business without the new land. I know, I ran the numbers with you. Don't build or invest in anything on the new stuff until it is totally in your name. Until then, use it for trail rides and marketing photos."

"I suppose. It just feels like a shoe is going to drop."

"With mom and dad, there is always that distinct possibility." Colt didn't ask her about Officer Chasseur's offer on the land. That fire was already too hot.

"Speaking of marketing, you don't by chance have any European contacts, right?"

Colt froze on the ladder. "What do you mean?" Did Becca know about his modelling?

"I want to target a European demographic, I'm just hesitant to pick a marketing company cold. I don't have money to burn on ineffective ad campaigns."

Colt exhaled. "Right. Um, not really. I can ask around if you want?"

"Thanks. I know I need to wrap my head around the marketing stuff, it's just that horses and hammers are so much more interesting."

"I get it." There was something else bothering Colt. He fitted another screw before he asked, "Why did you want to meet in Texas?"

"I told you, I wanted to check out a horse."

The whir of the driver was the only sound for several moments.

"Yeah, but in Texas? There was nothing closer?"

"We've both done the drive a million times. It's not that far."

"It's across the continent. Weren't you just in Montana buying horses?" Colt sunk another two screws in.

"So? I got a lead on a mare. She must have been good, too, because she was snatched up before I had a chance to drive down."

Colt switched tactics. "Jake thinks you're sweet on him." It wasn't true, Colt was just fishing.

Becca snorted. "Remind me to ignore him harder."

"Becca, seriously, what's going on?"

She looked up the ladder at him. "When I was in Germany, I loved it so much."

"Then why did you come back?" He had always wondered. She had a solid career as a regenerative specialist, an incredibly rapid-growing field.

"Every day I had my hands in soil—healthy, vibrant soil."

"That is the point of carbon drawdown . . . wait, did I get that right?" Colt hadn't even known what regenerative agriculture was until Becca got her degree in it.

She smiled at him. "Yes, that's right. This is going to sound crazy, but as chatty as that soil was, it's like I didn't *know* the conversation. Not there."

She was right, Colt had no idea what she was talking about. He made a non-comital sound.

"What I mean is, I had no *connection-connection* to the land there. It was beautiful and lovely, but it made me miss the land here, that much more. I can hear the land here. It's like I know the language."

"I don't hear the land like that, but if it's anything like working with livestock, I get it." Sort of.

Becca gave him a watery smile. "And you guys are a total pain in the ass, but I missed you all, too. Now I'm back and it's nothing like what I expected."

Colt hadn't realized his little sister had missed him. He had visited her in Germany, but he had been on the road when she had returned nearly two years ago. And apparently too self-absorbed to notice anything amiss.

"What isn't what you expected?"

Becca shrugged. "I don't know. Maybe it's just dad being so weird lately, and him and mom still being at each other's throats. Gabe up and moved to Toronto. I'm happy for him and Savannah, but that was really fast. And Tucker talks nonstop about making detective. He's crazy happy, but did he forget how Gabe got shot in the head? Did he forget what that was like?"

Colt climbed down the ladder and gently wrapped his arms around his sister.

"What are you doing?" Becca asked. "This is like three hugs in one visit. Am I really that needy?"

"I missed you, too." And Colt certainly hadn't forgotten what it was like when Gabe had gotten shot.

Becca swallowed. "Thanks. No one ever told me."

Regret whispered up. "You have three brothers; we don't talk like that." He tweaked her nose. "It'll be okay."

She slapped his hand away. "How do you know?" She sounded mulish, like when they were kids.

"I don't. I just know we'll figure out whatever comes up."

She swiped at her eyes. "How very adult of you."

"I can be the adult sometimes."

"You climb on bulls for your job, you're an idiot."

"Ouch. Tough crowd."

"All I want to do is pull my family around me and keep you guys safe." She gave him a pointed look. "But I can't do that because you guys keep playing with bad guys and bulls."

At least she wasn't snarling. Her safety mechanism had always been to snap back when she was hurting.

Colt purposely teased, "What about mom?" He repositioned the ladder.

Becca's eyes widened. "The last time mom was here she brought a date."

"So?"

"For me! I was training horses and the guy just stood there, making suggestions."

"Is that really so bad?" Colt said, lighting the fuse and waiting for the fireworks.

Becca sputtered. "He works on a rig. He's never ridden a horse in his life, let alone trained one."

Colt burst out laughing and pain fired across his ribs. He tucked his arm in.

Becca nodded at his injury. "Like I said, *idiot.*" She paused. "I worry about you. I worry about all of you."

"Don't."

Colt knew his little sister had always been sensitive, he just hadn't realized how that played out on a day-to-day basis. Another realization hit him. "Sorry dad didn't invite you and Tucker to the wedding. That was pretty shitty."

It likely stung more than he had realized, too.

Becca turned away. "Me too."

Now Colt really was feeling like an idiot. His sister was hurting a lot more than she had let on and he was an oaf who hadn't noticed.

She cleared her throat. "Shall we stop rehashing our dysfunctional family and finish up? I can make you a sandwich before you head out."

"Sure." Colt climbed back up the ladder. He grabbed the last three screws from his pocket. He slid two between his lips, before loading the third on the driver.

Becca had resumed her hold on the ladder. "I want to hear all about the woman you met yesterday."

"What woman?" Metal chewed through wood with swift precision.

"The one you rode double with."

"Ahh, that one," he said out of the side of his mouth.

Brief though their encounter was, the woman was proving to be a beautiful distraction. Her eyes had been lit with careful intelligence, and whatever she did to keep fit was working. The bright memory of her had lifted the heavy melancholy of his impending career end.

"You never ride double." Becca's voice was decidedly chipper.

"Not really, no." He sunk in another screw.

"But you did yesterday."

It wasn't a question, so he didn't bother answering. Instead, he counted screw holes. The beams needed to be well-anchored, not only for Becca's safety but for her paying guests that would start arriving before the end of the year. He drove in the last screw, before looking down. Becca was looking a little dreamy when she said, "You two meeting like that, it's like fate or something."

Colt wondered how she could be so naive. Their parents had taught them more than Colt ever wanted to know about how relationships worked. Namely, they didn't. Sometimes abysmally so.

"I am out of screws. If your math is right, we should be all good." Colt climbed down the ladder. "And it's nothing like that. I was working, she was walking. No fate was involved. And how did you know?"

Becca rolled her eyes. "Duh."

"Right. I swear, you are more connected than any of Gabe or Tuck's surveillance people." Becca knew things at a freakishly fast turnaround, which is why if Officer Chasseur had put a bid on the old Chasseur place, Becca should have known about it.

She shrugged. "I don't gossip, but I listen. I like knowing things. Like when my brother is meeting fascinating women and making room for her on his horse."

"It wasn't a big deal. She was in the way. I moved her."

Becca cocked her head. "Would you have moved a guy that way?"

"Of course."

"Liar." Becca started packing up tools. "You've met plenty of hunters coming out of the bush when you're moving cattle. Never saddled up with them."

Colt was losing traction, fast. "Who said she was fascinating?"

"You did. Like I said, I listen, to what you don't say, as much as to what you do. You like her."

"I liked getting her out of my way. Besides, it's not like I'm going to ever see her again. I have no idea who she is."

"Then you really are an idiot."

Colt folded the ladder. "Where do you want this thing?"

Becca motioned with her hand. "There is fine. I'll do more work tonight. Want to come over for dinner? Gabe and Savannah will be back. They took a day trip to Yoho."

Colt leaned the ladder against the counter. "Nah, I need to wash up and pick up the guys. We're supposed to leave in an hour."

Becca frowned. "I thought you were home through Stampede."

"Just a quick trip down to the four corners."

"That's a thirty-hour drive. I hate when you travel all night."

"It's part of the job. That's why Shayne, Jake and I travel together."

Becca rolled her eyes. "Jake is an overgrown child."

Colt laughed. "I know, why do you think he's so fun to travel with?"

"Your idea of fun is seriously different than mine. How many rodeos are you hitting?"

Colt shrugged. "Six this trip. We'll be back up for Stampede." He was not telling her he had scratched all of his entries except Stampede.

"You could stay here permanently, not just for the summer."

Colt's hand shot up, as if he could put a physical barrier between them. "This is your gig, not mine. I invest, I help you build. I'll help train your horses and help get you ready in any way I can and that you'll let me. But I am not settling down. Even if I was, it wouldn't be here."

"What's so bad about here?"

It was an old argument. "I have my reasons."

"Your recovery takes longer after each wreck. Another bad concussion—" she broke off. "You're too old for bull-riding and too young to get any more broken. How many times have you blown your shoulder? And ribs, do you even have any left? And don't get me started on your second elbow surgery."

Maybe he should tell her—

The door interrupted them.

"Hello? Becca dear? I have a date for you." The sing-song voice of their mom filtered in from the front door.

Colt grinned. "That's my cue, gotta run."

Becca lunged for him. "Don't you dare leave me with her."

Colt ducked out of reach and grabbed the handle of the back door. "See you in a week."

"Colt Tanner, do not abandon me. Why doesn't she parade blind dates in front of you?"

"Start riding bulls. Believe me, no one wants to marry a bull rider," Colt said before slipping out the backdoor.

Chapter Fourteen

The sun had finally dropped behind the mountains, taking the heat of the day with it. Lillian was back to sitting cross-legged on her living room floor. She had taken a break to run on her treadmill, but that was an hour and a half ago.

Most of the contents of the carton her *seanmhair's* assistant, Mary, had packed lay in tidy piles around her, as was Obedience Beatrice Evans'—*BeeBee's*—journal grimoire. So far, Lillian had found various correspondence, reports, and a few personal journals of traders. The time frames either overlapped, or gave valuable context, to her several times great-aunt's rather daring life.

Obedience Beatrice Evans was not fitting into a tidy box. She was a force, one not easily reckoned with. From what Lillian could ascertain—and to be fair, some of it was reading in-between the lines, *BeeBee* had fled an arranged marriage, running away to the New World with an unlikely ally, the Irishman her grandmum had mentioned. Seamus O'Malley was returning to resume his work as an unlicensed fur trader. It wasn't legal, but it was lucrative. *BeeBee* had begged to travel with him. She risked the perils of a brutal frontier with a near stranger to avoid an unwanted union. Lillian didn't want to imagine what *BeeBee's* betrothed must have been like to warrant such a dangerous escape.

From the maps and context, it looked like *BeeBee* and Seamus travelled deep along the upper Missouri River and its tributaries in the mid-eighteenth century. The territory was well past the routine operations of the French and British authorities warring for colonial control. It was dangerous work with shifting alliances. As far as Lillian could tell, European women in the mid-eighteenth century, wives or not, did not venture beyond established colonial towns. It simply wasn't done. Yet it appeared *BeeBee* had done exactly that, making it as far as the eastern slopes of the Rocky Mountains. Reading the historic documents, the North American fur trade seemed more akin to guerrilla commerce than the watered-down fluff history books had been touting.

Lillian looked up briefly as shadows, the first in hours, flickered across the room. She stood, rubbing her eyes, and stretched. She was stiff from sitting so long. Lillian bent over at her hips into a forward fold and let the tension drain from her stiff limbs. She blew out a breath, sinking deeper into the stretch.

Her mobile beeped and she pressed a button on her earpiece.

"Lillian?" It was a welcome, familiar voice.

Still upside-down, she answered, "Omran! Ohmygod, I miss you."

"You sound weird. Are you running?"

Her awareness flickered. The moment was brief yet snagged her attention.

Lillian flipped upright.

"No, and no one is chasing me."

She glanced around the condo, but nothing seemed amiss. Sophie wasn't home—again.

"How's Canada?"

"Awful."

"Really?"

"No, it's just me. Sophie is having a great time. She's even been on a couple dates. Nothing serious. Couple guys from the Canadian team."

"What about you?"

"You've got to be kidding?" Lillian's heart had frozen solid during the *unfortunate incident*. It would take an impossible heat to thaw.

"It's been two years—"

"Ask me after a million."

"Roger that."

It was so good to hear his voice. His familiar, crisp voice shot past her usual reserve. Perhaps that was why she whispered, "I'm still a wreck."

"Understandable."

Angst jumped within her. "Yes, but it's not livable. It's not sustainable. I'm so scared I'm running on a fucking treadmill. This isn't a life."

She closed her eyes. *Fuck.* She hadn't wanted to admit that. He'd only worry more.

"What? Don't you have your detail?"

Lillian closed her eyes. "I'll be fine. This is just something I'm still figuring out how to work through."

"Do you need me to come?" There was a catch in his voice.

Lillian clutched her mobile. "I adore you for asking. But you can't fix what I have."

No one could, it was up to her.

There was a short pause on the other end. "I can be there in ten hours."

"Don't be silly, I have arguably the world's best talent protecting Sophie and I. That was just the last two years talking." She cleared her throat. "How are you doing?"

"Besides worrying about you?"

She smiled and walked over to the fridge. "Besides that." She pulled out the jug of cold water and poured herself a glass.

"You know me. Same."

Omran's *same* was anyone else's extreme.

"Have you found anything you want to work on?"

Lillian hedged. "I'm doing some freelance reporting. I'm almost a regular at one of the local news outlets."

"That's good." Omran's voice rose, clearly happy for her.

"My next assignment is a rodeo."

"Oh."

The single word fell hard. To be covering sports and entertainment after wars and genocide was a hefty drop.

"Yeah. *Oh.*" Lillian took a lusty swig of water.

"What do you want to do?"

"There's a documentary crew doing an anti-oilsands film that's been bugging me to join their team."

"You're not interested?"

"Not really. The world has moved on to renewables, hydrogen energy and molten salt reactors. If I work on something, I want it to be how to move forward."

"So do that."

"What?"

"Find something you believe in and write that."

Lillian hesitated. She believed in *BeeBee*. But Lillian was still wrapping her head and heart around why the woman's story so compelled her. It felt acutely personal, and Lillian wasn't sure she wanted to share.

Omran mistook her silence. "You need to start somewhere. Get your spark back."

"My spark is fine."

It was flickering brighter each day, in fact, thanks to *BeeBee*.

"Pull my other leg."

"That's not a leg," she answered.

"That only works if you're a dude."

She laughed at their old joke. Both of their lives would have been easier if they had been attracted to each other. They were not, not like that. Omran was bi, so technically it was possible. He was also the closest thing she had to a best friend, and she didn't want to fuck it up with sex.

She heard a ping on the line. "You have to go?"

"Yeah. I'll let you know if I hear more about Fernando. Keep your head up, and get your spark back."

Omran hung up.

Lillian smiled, feeling better. She brought her glass of water back to living room, setting it safely out of the way.

She was enjoying her research; it was like a historic treasure hunt. Lillian's Canadian experience was proving to be exploring *BeeBee's* story and daydreaming about the cowboy from the cattle drive. Both kept her busy while she grappled with the inexplicable fear that had ballooned the day after the cowboy had whisked her off to safety. Her doctors had assured her it was the nervous excitement of narrowly escaping a cattle stampede that had triggered her renewed inner turmoil.

Lillian fought hard to believe them but was losing the battle. Her burgeoning fear was too real. She could barely bring herself to venture outside the condo, even with an elite security detail, and Omran didn't know the half of it. Picking up the bare necessities now felt like a high-stakes gauntlet, and running outside was no longer an option, her fear was simply too great. She ran on her treadmill, in hiding, and researched a remarkably brave woman who had been born three centuries before. Thank God for digital archives. She couldn't bring herself to venture back to the library.

Lillian looked across the room to the sliding door of the condo balcony. Hiding was no way to live. *BeeBee* would never cower in her flat waiting for a man to kill her.

She considered the evidence. There was zero intel her and Sophie's location had been compromised. Her security detail would let her know if something was amiss and they hadn't.

Needing to believe that her doctors knew best, Lillian forced herself to take a step forward, then another. When she stood at the shrouded balcony door, Lillian forced herself to lift her hand and brush the curtain aside. If she was going to get better, she had to face her fears. With unsteady fingers, she unlocked each safety mechanism on the sliding glass door.

It's a feeling, an incontrovertible knowing.

Lillian fought against her *seanmhair's* words. The paranoia was her PTSD, her doctors had said so. It wasn't real. They were experts, she was the broken one.

When no one rushed the room, Lillian slid open the door an inch. Then two. She fought the hysterics that were erupting in her mind. The fear of being taken out by a sniper was too great, and she merged into the shadows of the fading day. She forced herself to go through breathing exercises, to face her demons, from the shadows.

It's a feeling, an incontrovertible knowing.

Heart pounding, she gave herself ten seconds; eight . . . nine . . . ten.

Pop, pop.

Lillian hit the floor and slammed the sliding door shut. She reached as far as she dared to slide each lock home.

Through the closed door, she could hear an altercation in the parking lot. Terrified and flat on her stomach, Lillian nearly shrieked when her mobile rang.

She rolled away from the windows before springing into a low crouch. She darted across the room and scooped up her device. It was a text.

Threat identified and neutralized.

Lillian dove for her earpiece and popped it into place. "What? What just happened?"

"Threat identified and neutralized."

It was like pulling teeth with these guys. "Yeah, I got that. Explain."

"Two unfriendlies are currently being processed, you —."

Lillian sank down to the floor, leaning against the sofa.

"Got it. Copy that." She held her head in her hand. "Actually, I don't want to know the rest. Not right now. Sophie's safe?"

"Affirmative."

"I'm safe?"

There was a brief pause. *"Affirmative."*

"Snapdragon out."

Lillian pulled out her earpiece. The fear she had felt had been real. What if she wasn't losing her mind?

What if she was finally healing?

Chapter Fifteen

Lillian stared in dismay at the shelves under the of-interest banner in the quaint mountain town bookstore. There were celebrity book club picks, the latest in juice cleanses, as well as classic vegan recipes. Several volumes on the outdoors, and a handful of new releases on World War II were also included. Books on contemporary war apparently didn't make the cut here. Arms trading, human trafficking, child soldiers and drug runners were also suspiciously absent.

What could be more of-interest to a reader than the shocking dangers faced around the globe?

"Auntie, this one looks good." Sophie held out a book. The cover was a majestic picture of yet another photogenic mountain top. It proudly announced fifty-two hikes for the serious weekend warrior.

"Have a go at it. It looks fun."

Lillian had no intention of reading a book as frivolous as how to conquer mountain peaks on your weekends. And pretending that hiking a mountain was even re-motely the same as being a soldier made her stomach turn.

"You're ranked twenty-second in the world; I'll leave the mountain peaks to you."

Sophie rolled her eyes and put the book back. "I train, I don't bag peaks."

"Right. I'm going to go find the current events section."

Reading made her feel connected to something that mattered, even if she was only a spectator this time.

"*Auntie no.*" Sophie put a staying hand on her arm. "What if you know someone in one of those books, again? That set you back weeks last time. You promised."

"Darling, I'm fine. We're in Canada in the middle of nowhere. Hardly the backdrop for another *unfortunate incident.*"

A loud crash sounded.

With lightning-fast reflexes, Lillian grabbed Sophie, pressing both of them into a row of bookshelves that had an emergency exit. Sophie stood calmly in Lillian's protective grip, her voice patient as she said, "Auntie, we're safe. A stack of books just tipped over by the cash. I saw it. We're okay. We're both safe."

Lillian tilted her head. She could hear store clerks talking as they tidied up the fallen pile of books.

She dropped Sophie's arm, trying to hide the action by smoothing out her summer skirt. "I knew that."

Sophie glanced at their security detail above the rows of books and Lillian felt her face flush. Their detail hadn't overreacted to the crash, either. They were still pretending to browse shelves in the aisles on either side of Lillian and Sophie.

"Auntie, I'm nervous, too. But our detail is fucking solid, you know that. They neutralized the crew Fernando sent. And if he sends another one, they'll do it again."

Lillian couldn't bear the thought of Fernando going after Sophie. She blew out a breath. "You're right. And Grandmum or Omran will let us know if Fernando escapes from prison."

"We're safe." Sophie paused. "Auntie, you know Fernando methodically undermined you, right? He targeted your trust in yourself, he tried to hijack your instincts."

It was hard not to flinch at the damning words. Lillian knew she had been manipulated. She felt like a fool.

"Seriously, you understand that, right?" Sophie held her gaze, daring her to hear the truth.

Something inside Lillian shimmered, like a whisper of possibility. What if Sophie was right?

"Let that percolate. Now—" Sophie turned Lillian around to look out the store windows. "We're not in the middle of nowhere, the TransCanada is right there."

Outside, cheery hanging baskets with cascading flowers decorated each lamppost, while aspen trees, decked out in their bright green summer leaves, fluttered in the breeze. Spruce and pine also dotted the trendy urban landscape, and a handful of blocks away, the cross-country highway flowed. Mountain peaks loomed over everything, their stark greys, blacks and browns provided a stunning contrast to the brighter shades of summer foliage.

It was also quite lovely.

Sophie pointed to the bustling sidewalk. "You need to get out more. There is so much to do here, so many really great people to meet. You'll see."

Lillian couldn't help but smile. Her niece made a compelling case. The people outside all looked normal. Happy.

"I'll think about it."

Lillian slipped away before Sophie could press further.

Sophie called after her, "Nice evasion technique."

Lillian grinned as she turned the corner.

She stopped suddenly. There, on an end cap, was a cover with a grizzled cowboy on horseback in a sea of cattle. The title announced, *Still Driving*. Images of *her* cowboy flooded her mind, the one who had whisked her away to safety. But it was the book beside it that she picked up. The cover was a historic photo of an Indigenous woman standing next to a horse with a travois, a wooden palisade in the background. The title, *We Have Names*, did not pull any punches. From a contemporary viewpoint, history was dominated by astonishing biases, and women's voices painfully irrelevant to the documented historic record. If women were mentioned at all, they were typically without an identity, a generic *female*, *wife* or *daughter*.

Lillian opened the book as she turned down the next aisle.

And ran headlong into a wiry body in a checked shirt.

"Begging your pardon, miss." The older man nodded his head. Lillian suspected had he been wearing one, he would have tipped his hat.

She was immediately charmed by the senior.

"That's my line, sir. I ran straight into you." Lillian tucked the history book into the crook of her arm.

"My dear, old men still appreciate a chance be a gentleman, makes us feel useful, you see."

His eyes crinkled at the corners in a series of deep, weathered lines, his disposition clearly prone to smiling. He was clad in what Lillian had come to learn was one of two uniforms for this mountain town, either ready to jump on a horse or scale a mountain. The man's denim trousers, checked shirt, and cowboy boots aligned him with the rancher crowd. He was old enough to be her father, but probably too young to be her grandfather.

"Do you know where the current events books are, by chance?"

"Just past that big potted plant, miss." The man hesitated a moment. He glanced straight at her security detail before asking, "Will they mind if I ask you for your autograph?"

Lillian blinked. Only those connected to—or evading—law enforcement ever noticed her detail.

He held up the book in his hand. It was one of hers.

Lillian's stomach lurched. She hadn't dreamed she would be recognized here. Anywhere in England, sure, but not backwoods Canada. The older man holding one of her books seemed nice enough, like one of the good guys, actually. And his attention to her work made her feel worthy again.

She gave a half smile. "That photo shoot was dreadful."

The man looked down at the picture. "Looks like it was taken in action."

"It was taken after the action. I wanted to get back to the hotel, they thought a candid photo would resonate more with readers."

The man held out his hand. "I'm Clint Steele."

She shook his hand. "Lillian Kensington."

"It is an honor to meet you. I've read all of your books." He lifted the book in his hand. "I lent this one out and haven't gotten it back. Had to pick up another copy."

His earnestness wrapped around her like a cocoon.

"Thank you, that means a lot." Quieter, she added, "especially now."

Clint tugged on his ear. "I heard you ran into a bit of trouble."

"You're kind, and I appreciate you putting it so mildly."

"What are you working on now?"

"Nothing like that. I'm afraid I'm still too radioactive."

"I thought you were cleared of all the charges?"

"I was."

"So what's the problem? You're one hell of a re-porter—begging your pardon for my language."

Lillian felt like hugging the man.

"What I wouldn't have given to have met you two years ago. No, for now, I'm just freelancing local-interest pieces."

They paid lousy, but Lillian had never touched her trust fund, and she didn't want to start now. Being black-listed was making it rather difficult. Her grandmum was paying for the security detail and had made certain Lillian and Sophie had more than enough money to live on. Lillian just didn't want to accept the help.

"Would you mind signing my book? It's not every day you meet a famous author."

Lillian smiled, endeared. "I think infamous is more accurate, but it would be my pleasure."

She retrieved a pen from her satchel and accepted the book from Mr. Steele.

"Who should I make it out to?"

"Me, please, *Clint*."

With quick strokes she penned a salutation and signed it. She handed the book back to him.

He held it in both hands and remained.

"Yes?"

"Are you just visiting then?"

It was there, on the tip of her tongue to avoid whatever he was asking. But his eyes were kind, and it felt good to meet someone who still believed her. "I've relocated here for a few months."

His eyes brightened. "I could use someone like you."

Panic flared. "Oh, uh. That's very kind of you, but I'm not– that is, I don't think . . ."

The older man shook his head, his eyes twinkling. "Ma'am, you misunderstand me. I mean to hire you. A family friend is opening an eco-inn and dude ranch. She says her target demographic is mostly Europeans, and a higher-end clientele than I'm used to. She needs help with her marketing material. Write-ups about the terrain, the different packages, photos, that sort of thing. Is there any chance you would consider that sort of work?"

Lillian's brain shifted gears. "An eco-inn?"

"Yes, Becca's degree is in regenerative agricultural practices. That's what she was doing overseas until she moved back a couple years ago."

Lillian was intrigued. "That's a rapidly growing essential field, why did she switch?"

"Great question. Let me know if you find out."

Lillian would have been blind to miss the older man's concern.

"She is lucky to have you looking out for her. And I owe you an apology for jumping to conclusions earlier."

"Are you kidding? You made my year. I'd love to set you up with one of her brothers, but you young kids are too sophisticated for anything as ordinary as old-fashioned matchmaking."

The man had an easy grace that kept disarming her.

"I'm sure they're wonderful, but I'll just stick with writing, for now. An eco-inn sounds like an interesting marketing project."

Already her brain was pinging with possibilities, and Becca sounded like an interesting woman to meet—regenerative agriculture was one of Lillian's soft spots, and she desperately missed friends.

Clint shrugged again. "Becca's vision for how the land can be experienced is special. So is your writing. I think you two might work. Fair warning, she's hopelessly stubborn accepting help, but she's swamped with getting everything else up and running." He hedged. "I doubt my budget could come close to what you're worth."

If he only knew how far she had fallen.

And she liked him. She could use a friendly face on this continent besides Sophie.

Lillian handed him her business card. "How about you email me the details and we go from there?"

Clint was quick to accept the card. "That would be great. Thank you, Ms. Kensington." He held up the book. "And thank you for signing this. You made my week."

He had made her year with his kindness. "My pleasure."

Sophie walked up as Clint headed to the cash register. "Are you making friends with the locals?"

"I think I just got a job."

"Cool. What's that?" Sophie pulled on the book still tucked under Lillian's arm.

Her face fell, though, when she saw the covers. Sophie handed them back. "That looks boring."

Lillian tucked it possessively back into the crook of her arm. "Women's history is not boring."

Sophie eyed it again. "Is that for research on *BeeBee*?"

Lillian brightened at her niece's question. "No, at least I don't think so." She looked at the cover. "Well, maybe."

Sophie pulled a romance novel off a display and flipped it over. "What's the job?"

"An eco-inn's marketing material to attract European clients. The owner was a regenerative agriculturalist."

"Of course she is. Only you could run into a total stranger and come out with a cause to work on." Sophie re-shelved the book and pulled another. She held the paperback up. The cover was adorned with a chisel-chested warrior-type. "Does he know anyone that looks like this?"

The cover was rather delicious looking, and oddly reminded her of *her* cowboy. Lillian only raised an eyebrow. "Are you quite done?"

"Never. I can't believe you won't let me ask grandmum to track down the *Archambeau* cologne guy. Omran totally would."

Lillian hadn't told anyone, but for the last two years, the *Archambeau* cologne model had been her therapeutic crush. Every time she saw one of the ridiculously hot pictures of him, her day got brighter. She knew it was silly, the guy wasn't real. But one day she might meet a man—a kind, decent man. If he happened to be as hot as the *Archambeau* model, that was okay, too.

The model had helped her through a really shitty time, and he'd never know it.

She ignored Sophie's audacious suggestion. "It's a paid gig. It might not be covering a war but it's more meaningful than the fluff pieces I've been doing here so far."

Sophie rolled her eyes. "You don't need paid gigs; you need the feeling of self-sufficiency they provide."

"That's not—"

"Bullshit. You have a classic guilt complex. We have what ninety-nine-point-nine percent of the world doesn't. I get it, it's not fair. But punishing yourself doesn't make other's lives any easier or better."

Lillian stared at her niece. No one in her family had ever suspected what drove her to take such chances, to go to such areas of decay and deprivation.

Sophie stopped. "What? I said I get it. And it makes sense, in a warped sort of way."

Lillian's mouth was suddenly dry.

Her niece's eyes widened, and she wrapped an arm around Lillian in a quick hug. "Don't freak, I just mean it doesn't all have to be child soldiers, mass rape, or the latest biological weapon released. Someone needs to write about bliss, unicorns and chocolate. Why can't you take a turn writing that?" Sophie waggled her eyebrows. "For instance, that cowboy you're interviewing for Stampede is supposed to be crazy hot."

"*Sophie.*"

"You could use hot."

"I tried hot, I got burned, bad." Lillian's devastation went deeper than anyone knew.

Sophie stopped abruptly. "No. Do not let him ruin the rest of your life. It's not fair."

"I told you, fair's got nothing to do with life. The last twenty years has hammered that point home. Why do you think these idiot fluff pieces are driving me crazy?"

Sophie's sad smile held a wisdom beyond her nineteen years. "Oh auntie, did you not just hear me? They're not what's driving you crazy."

Lillian suddenly felt bare, exposed. But her niece was looking at the back of another book.

"Readers need feel-good stories. It's okay if you do, too."

The gentle support slipped past Lillian's armor. She pulled her niece in for another hug.

"What would I do without you."

Sophie hugged her back. "Never set foot on Canadian soil and spiral into the tedious boredom of the superfluous life of our parents?"

Lillian cleared her throat. "Right. Did I thank you for that?"

"Canada wasn't your first choice, not by a long shot. But I'm glad you're here."

Lillian wasn't sure she wanted to find what was left under the rubble of her life. Maybe Canada would help her stay lost.

Sophie suddenly feigned shock. "Look at us, where's our stiff upper lip? This is positively disgraceful."

She linked her arm through Lillian's and leaned in. "Now that I've got you in good spirits again, might I remind you, you've met royalty and spies, but never a bull rider." In a saucy voice she murmured, "Consider the possibilities."

"I'm quite certain I could go my entire life without meeting a man whose job it is to strap himself to large angry animals."

Sophie dropped her voice into a scandalous whisper. "*Auntie,* the animals are not angry. And he doesn't strap himself, he hangs on."

"There's a difference?"

"A huge one." Sophie flicked her long hair back over her shoulder. "In fact, I challenge you to find out the difference."

"Quoi?"

Sophie's smile held feminine certainty. "Auntie, we're surrounded by intelligent, well-muscled men with stamina, who like to frolic in the great outdoors. Go find someone worth riding."

Lillian's mouth dropped open.

"Don't look at me all shocked, you need to feel something besides hurt and sad. An orgasm is a good start. I'm serious, a healthy sex life is whole body maintenance. And at least one of us should be getting some. I'm training all the time." She held up the books in her hand. "I need to go pay for these. I'm getting you the one with the hot cover."

As they made their way to the cash, Lillian spotted a copy of the *New York Times*. Sophie slapped it out of her hand with impressive speed. "Absolutely not."

"You are positively militant."

"And you are going to be too busy with your homework. Find someone rideable. I hear Stampede is a good place to start—*Oh*." The books Sophie had been carrying slipped out of her hands and fell to the floor.

There was a young man in front of her. He automatically bent down, retrieving the fallen books.

"Here you go—" He stopped midway up. The look on his face as he stared at Sophie could only be described as smitten.

Straightening, he said, "Hi."

"Hi," Sophie answered back, a little breathless.

Lillian gently took the books out of his hand. He barely noticed.

"I'll be outside," Lillian murmured.

Chapter Sixteen

"*B*ombings continue as militants groups clash. Civilian casualties now number in the tens of thousands—*" Colt punched the search button on the truck's stereo. Static accompanied the ticking green digital numbers that gave a muted glow to the dark truck cabin. The digits finally stopped on the same station. "*...targeting aid organizations. Four more have been added to the growing list, making this the bloodiest month since—*"

Colt turned the radio off. He supposed it was a luxury to simply stop listening; no one was bombing or shooting at him. He thought of his brothers; Gabe was former CSIS, and Tucker was a homicide detective. Colt was the odd man out. Bulls were not bullets.

The flashing white lines of the interstate paced on. They had since Sheridan, Wyoming. Shane and Jake were both snoring softly in the crew cab. Pre-dawn light whispered on the undulating Montana sage plains. Colt knew the sight would only get more striking as the sun rose.

His phone discreetly beeped. Colt put in an ear bud and answered just as quietly, "Colt here."

"Good, I caught you awake." It was Clint Steele.

"It's four in the morning."

"It's light out, ain't it?"

The eastern horizon was just starting to flush with barely-there light, the west still cloaked in total darkness.

"Not really."

"Well, it will be light enough when I finish my coffee. I got a job for you."

The older man was more honorary uncle than neighbor. Clint had been a part of Colt and his siblings lives for as long as Colt could remember.

"I'm not touching that back fence."

"Widow McCormick, god bless her, will find another suitor and only then will we move on fence negotiations. No, I need a guide. I ran into a freelance writer in town. She's from the U.K. and I think she could help Becca with her international marketing campaign. Do you mind taking her out on the land, show her the trails, stuff like that? Take my camera. Becca's been working so hard, I thought we could help out."

"Yeah, of course. How'd you get Becca to agree?"

"I'm as surprised as you are. That kid is going to run herself ragged. Where are you now?"

"Just south of Sweetgrass." They would be across the border soon and make it through Calgary before the morning rush.

"How'd the trip go?"

"Shayne and Jake were in the money last night. Shayne is in fourth, and Jake moved up to eleventh."

The top ten money-makers of the season earned a spot in the Canadian Finals. Colt had gone five times and won it twice.

"You didn't ride all week."

It wasn't a question.

"Nope." He might as well tell the older cowboy. "I rode Back Lit in Texas. I fell in the well after the buzzer."

Clint had been a bull rider back in the day. He knew what falling in the well meant.

"Oh."

"Thought I'd go out in front of a home crowd."

It was a long moment before Clint answered, "I can understand a man wanting that."

Colt knew he would.

The older man cleared his throat. "Back Lit is feisty. You always could ride the rank ones."

"The only ride that matters—" Colt recited.

"Is the one you're on."

Silence fell, both lost in their own thoughts.

Clint spoke first. "About that freelance writer."

"Yeah?"

"She's really pretty."

"So's my new saddle."

"You're always so quick to dismiss settling down."

"You never did."

There was a pause. "I would have."

Clint's voice had taken on an odd quality. It made Colt wonder what regrets the old cowboy had.

Chapter Seventeen

L illian wound her way through the crowded outdoor exhibition grounds. The Stampede had a particular charm, and it was hard not to get swept up in the excitement and overall revelry. Rambunctious—and often sunburned—festivalgoers crowded the spacious grounds, and every now and then she caught glimpses of her security detail. She trusted them.

It was a heady sensation, trusting again.

Lillian had not understood the email her managing editor had sent about the Stampede dress code. She did now. Every other person was wearing a cowboy hat and cowboy boots. It didn't take an anthropologist to pick out the real deal from the ones having fun playing dress-up. What surprised her was the sheer volume of those participating. She didn't know if it spoke to community spirit, an innate desire to fit in, or romanticizing an ideal of a simpler way of life. Lillian had seen the numbers. There was nothing simple about the world of professional rodeo or chuckwagon racing. Neither were for the dabbler, not at this level.

There were enough food vendors to fill a town and enough beer gardens to rival any British event. The midway looked large, and she had never seen so many barns in one spot, not that she had ever looked particularly hard. She passed several large buildings with signs inviting revelers in to watch any number of show and showcase. Everything from dog and light shows, to sheep herding and heavy horses, to cowboy obstacle courses.

It wasn't the largest fair grounds Lillian had ever been to, but the likes of which she had never seen. A small spark flickered within her. She was actually enjoying herself.

Until the wind shifted.

A blast of barbecue smoke hit her. She covered her nose and quickened her pace, trying not to breathe in the smell of charred animal flesh. Her stomach turned and her eyes started watering. The wind shifted again, and she could breathe.

"Auntie!"

Lillian froze. Sophie was walking as fast as the huge crowd would allow and was holding the hand of a young man. The pair stopped in front of her.

Sophie stared at Lillian's ensemble.

"What are you wearing?"

Reflexively, Lillian smoothed out her new denim skirt. "I heard there was a bit of a dress code here. Is it too much?"

"No, you look great." Sophie gave her a considering look. "Country suits you."

Lillian's mouth dropped open.

Sophie just smiled. "This is Craig. From the bookstore."

Lillian found herself sizing up the young man. He needed a haircut. But his clothes were clean, if a bit worn.

Judging by what she could only guess was an auto parts logo on his t-shirt, and the staining on his fingers and nail beds, she guessed him likely a grease monkey. His eyes were kind, though hesitant, and he had the build of budding manhood from his broad shoulders to firm jawline. If he was older than Sophie, it wouldn't be by much.

Lillian held out her hand and smiled. "Nice to meet you, I'm Lillian."

The Handshake could reveal a lot, namely what the other person wanted you to feel.

Craig visibly relaxed before accepting her outstretched hand. It was firm enough to be attentive, yet a respectful pressure. This man was not a pushover, nor a bully. Lillian decided she liked him.

The young man ducked his head a bit. "Nice to meet you."

Sophie asked, "What are you doing here? Your speed is not an agricultural fair."

Lillian dipped her chin. "I took the rodeo assignment."

Sophie clapped her hands together and bounced up and down. "You're interviewing Colt Tanner!"

Lillian checked the details on her phone. The subject heading was in fact *Colt Tanner, bull rider.*

"How did you know that?"

"How do you not? He's a local celebrity. And he teaches inner city kids how to ride horses, how cool is that? Craig kinda knows him."

Craig had stardust in his eyes. "That guy is awesome. He punched a grizzly once who was mauling him. That guy has bal—I mean, he's pretty cool." The young man's esteem for the bull rider tipped into hero-worship.

"We were just heading out." Sophie eyed their security details circling nearby. "Craig's going to show me the foothills."

Lillian wanted to be happy for her niece, but what she really wanted to do was bubble wrap Sophie and keep her safe, including her heart. But all she said was, "Are you guys home for dinner?"

"We'll grab something."

"You have an early training practice tomorrow, don't you?"

"We won't be late. Doesn't the rodeo start soon?" Sophie asked.

Lillian checked the time and blanched. It had taken her longer than she had expected to make it through downtown and across the grounds.

Craig pointed. "If you hug that perimeter, you'll avoid the bulk of the crowd. It'll lead you to one of the arena side entrances that usually doesn't have as long a line-up as the central ones do."

Lillian gave him a grateful smile. "Thank you."

Sophie grinned. "Have fun interviewing Colt Tanner."

Lillian had interviewed hundreds of people more relevant than a bull rider. Her fall from grace had been steep.

"You, too. Be safe."

Don't do anything stupid like I did.

Sophie waved over her shoulder. "Always."

Lillian watched her niece and Craig walk away holding hands. Lillian made her way to the stadium as Craig suggested. The line moved quickly, as he had guessed. The venue wasn't soccer-stadium big, but there had to be nearly twenty thousand spectators for the afternoon rodeo.

Lillian had just found her seat and sat down when the back of her neck tingled in awareness. She casually turned around, as if absorbed in the merriment around her. Spectators of every age imaginable made up the crowd, from happy families in matching western wear, to inebriated executives. Good grief, they were in matching western shirts, too, with company logos trailing down their sleeves or bannered across the front pockets.

She spoke into her ever-present earpiece. "Guys, something isn't right."

"Copy that."

The feeling of being watched grew stronger. Lillian discreetly gathered her satchel and casually re-slung it over her head and across her torso. The crowd was still swelling. She felt her own anticipation rising as her now near-unbearable flight response was triggering.

"We have identified a potential bogey. Exit when—"

She couldn't hear her radio as an announcer's voice boomed over the loudspeaker. Blaring music cued, and pyrotechnics exploded on the infield in front of the crowd. As diversions went, it was more than she could have hoped for. Lillian bolted.

The crowd had all gotten on their feet, giving her a protected exit. She wasn't listening to the announcer's voice until he said *Colt Tanner*. Then the crowd erupted in boisterous cheers for the local favorite, giving her more cover. Lillian didn't risk sneaking a look, she would see the poster boy soon enough.

If someone didn't kill her first.

She wove through the throngs of people still making their way to their seats, dodging a shocking number of empty beer cups. She kept scanning for anyone who didn't fit in, anything or anyone that looked suspicious. She changed directions, made U-turns, changed up her speed, and took opportunities to glide along with packs of rodeo-goers through numerous flights of stairs and the main concourse. If her detail had followed, she didn't notice.

Like a whisper, she slipped out an unmarked exit as the national anthem started playing.

Chapter Eighteen

The buzzer sounded. Eight seconds. Colt dropped his left hand, loosening his rope and freeing his right hand. The bull under him stopped spinning, planting his front legs. The back half of the bull's body torqued, sending its rear legs off the ground. Colt was ready for it. The motion shot him off the bull's back, and Colt landed on his feet, upright and out of the way.

"Ninety-one! That ride was good for ninety-one! If he can hold it, he's got a spot in the finals on Sunday."

The crowd cheered. Colt pumped his left fist in the air and trotted to the chutes. The crowd didn't know he couldn't lift his right arm above his head. He climbed back onto the catwalk, letting the roar of the crowd dull the screaming pain in his shoulder.

Shayne nodded. "Nice ride."

Jake clapped him on the back. "You're buying tonight."

Colt pulled off his helmet and waited. There was one more cowboy left to ride. The cowboy left was an Australian, and damn good. The speakers crackled as an eight-count country song rang through the arena and the edginess of the crowd swelled.

A gate swung open and the bull, Rocket Fuel, sprang out. The cowboy on him was in the zone. With an undeniable agility, the Australian rode. Colt smiled to himself;

it was pure poetry. Damn, he loved this sport. He would miss this. Being a spectator wasn't nearly the same as riding.

The bull shifted and the cowboy stalled, his balance dissolving in a split second. Rocket Fuel tossed his head up, slamming into the front of the cowboy's face.

The Aussie wasn't wearing a helmet.

On contact, blood spurted wide, but the real concern was how the cowboy had gone limp. He was knocked out cold. Rocket Fuel gave a final toss, throwing the unconscious cowboy, hard. He landed against the chutes, before slumping to the ground like a rag doll. He laid there, unmoving.

Rocket Fuel docilely trotted out of the arena.

Colt closed his eyes, sending silent words to whatever deity that watched over cowboys, that the guy would be okay.

Medics rushed to the downed cowboy. Of those behind the chutes, a few murmured to each other, but most were deadly quiet as they watched, arms crossed with boots braced shoulder width apart.

The announcer's voice rang through the arena. Colt didn't pay attention, he was watching, trying to will the fallen guy to be okay.

The medics shifted their field assessment. Still bracing the fallen cowboy's neck, they moved him to the spine board. Minutes later, they had him lifted and were carrying him out of the arena. The grandstand crowd, somber now, left en masse.

Jake turned to Shayne. "You ready?"

Shayne nodded before clapping Colt on his left shoulder. "Have a good interview."

The guys knew Colt tolerated interviews only because his sponsors required he smile pretty. Colt felt like a fancy pants every time a camera was on him. "Thanks."

Jake added, "See you on Sunday."

Colt nodded.

His buddies left. Colt looped his bull rope and slowly headed out, too. He answered greetings from those he recognized around him, though everyone had a somber air about them now. He heard one of the stockmen talking to a saddle bronc rider about the wreck.

Colt headed towards the tunnel to get cleaned up. He had an interview to smile through.

Chapter Nineteen

From his vantage point, Fernando Martinez saw six agents closing in on gate *K43*, flight one-one-seventy to Berlin. His decoy had worked. He slipped into the stream of travelers heading towards the baggage claim. It was unlikely, but possible, they would lock down the terminal.

He would be long gone.

Once upon a time he had followed orders and the rules. Caught bullets meant for lesser men. That ladder was not worth clawing up. Five years ago, he had found a more lucrative path. Now, he was the one giving orders. His crews were soulless mercenaries without the red tape of governments. Fernando was like their king — oh yes, he liked the sound of that.

His phone pinged. It was his second in command, Chad — it wasn't good news.

The second attempt to grab the Kensington bitch had failed. Fernando knew Lillian would have security support, he just hadn't expected them to be better than his crews, or that they would go on the offensive.

The failures had created an unfortunate personnel gap. So had firing Chad's original selection.

Fernando hesitated.

The single time he had met Chad's connection, the mercenary's cold eyes had communicated brutal competence. Fernando had immediately wanted such a violent man under his control. But expertise came at a high cost.

The mercenary picked up on the third ring.

"I thought you fired us." The man's voice was as menacing as Fernando remembered.

"How did you know it was me?"

"Did you forget what I do with people who ask stupid questions?"

Fernando swallowed. Few people scared him.

"That was all just a misunderstanding. I have a job for you."

"You know we don't work on credit."

"You'll get your money." He forced bravado into his voice. "I need you on a job now."

"When?"

"I need you to start today. She's—"

The voice interrupted, *"Are you paying today?"*

"I'm telling you, that was a misunderstanding. I'll pay half today and the other half in a week."

"No, you'll pay all now."

"But—"

"That's two strikes."

The man hung up.

Fernando let out a string of expletives, startling several travelers. Mercenaries were so fucking *mercenary*. He was the one in charge. Why did Chad even work with this guy?

Fernando could be in Canada by sunrise or fix his cash flow problem.

He made a call.

"Get the blueprints, then pay the Canadian crew. Yes, the original one." He paused. "Ax Chad."

Chapter Twenty

The summer sun beat down on Lillian as she wound through the throng of partygoers. She had taken a maze of hallways, a courtyard, two barns and finally had skirted the edge of the midway. She now stood in front of a large building, the crowd still swelling behind her.

Her earpiece buzzed back to life. *"Threat has been identified and neutralized."*

Relief washed over Lillian. Her instincts had been right, again.

She cleared her throat. "Thanks guys."

"Debrief forthcoming."

Her earpiece went silent. They weren't exactly chatty types.

Lillian ducked inside the building. She crossed a throughway and into an oversized arena where row after row of vendors were set up, several jockeying loudly for customer attention. Lillian joined the steady stream of shoppers, looking for a corner to tuck into.

She walked past numerous rows before stumbling upon a large, gaping opening. She walked through the decorated doorway. The new room was as big as a warehouse and serenely lit. It sported artfully grouped trees and shrubs, small indoor ponds, fine art vendors, and what looked like a well-stocked wine and cheese bar.

And it had Wi-Fi.

Lillian made a single circuit of the large space. There were tourists, as well as artists and workers squiring about, but nowhere near the crowds elsewhere on the grounds. She ducked behind a small forest of potted trees and a pond, making herself as comfortable as she could perched on a garden boulder, before pulling her laptop out of her satchel.

It might be a fluff piece, but Lillian had been counting on watching Colt ride. Without that context, she felt unprepared for the interview. She typed *Colt Tanner bull riding videos* in her browser window.

The search returned thousands of hits.

Lillian clicked on a video. It was surreal watching someone ride a domesticated, yet far from tame, animal—on purpose. The cowboy rode with one hand raised up above his head, the wings of his chaps flapping as he rode. She studied the scene, but it was hard to know what details were important. The video took a dark turn, then. Lillian watched in horror as the cowboy lost his balance and dropped off the side of the bull. Two men, dressed in an odd combination of shorts and safety gear, sprang into the shot. Their antics lured the bull towards one of them, as the other darted in and helped the cowboy safely back up the rails.

The video ended.

Lillian had no words. How was she supposed to describe *that* to readers?

Her earpiece buzzed. Omran. "We got a hit. An image of Fernando Martinez was recorded at Charles de Gaulle. It looks like Fernando boarded a flight to Berlin under an assumed name, but we haven't confirmed that yet."

Lillian closed her laptop. "When?"

"Forty-five minutes ago."

"Then it wasn't him who just followed me." She explained what had happened.

Lillian heard the clicking of Omran's keyboard. "None of the digital trap doors have been triggered. On paper, your location is still secure."

"Tell that to the Jordemorden guys. They neutralized another crew."

"You okay?"

"Yeah, I was fine as soon as I got out of the stadium."

"I haven't seen an update yet, what did your detail say?"

"*Debrief forthcoming.*"

"Chatty, aren't they? You know the drill. Pay attention, stay alive." Omran said quieter, "We need you to stay alive."

"No shit."

Omran made a sound.

"What?" Lillian asked.

"Your vocabulary, it's...different."

"Less stuffy?"

"Less something." Omran pivoted. "Any movement on your history project?"

"How did you know I was doing a history project?"

"I monitor all incoming requests—"

Lillian finished for him, "And I requested Ms. Winters send any letters from the family library that pertain to an Obedience Beatrice *BeeBee* Evans, or a Piety Frances Davies, nee Evans."

"You did. They should arrive by morning."

Lillian felt a jolt of anticipation. "Thanks."

"Anytime." Omran paused. "I miss you."

"I miss you, too. Tell my *seanmhair* I miss her, as well."

"You should tell her yourself."

"I will."

"When?" Omran must have found out about Lillian and Maighread's cross words.

"Later."

"Whatever you say. Stay safe." Omran hung up.

Lillian was surprised to realize she wasn't homesick. Somewhere between researching *BeeBee*, her security detail routinely extinguishing threats, and one fantasy-inducing cowboy encounter, Lillian felt oddly expansive.

It was disorienting.

She opened her laptop back up and watched several videos of Colt Tanner. Each one was as bizarre as the last. The videos didn't reveal much detail of his face; his hat was either pulled low or he had his safety helmet on.

The wrecks were another story.

She winced every time his body took a beating.

Having enough, she pulled up archival databases instead. She tried several before getting a hit at a western research center. She reread the entry, twice. They had a journal of one Seamus O'Malley, though date was included. It might not be *BeeBee's* Seamus. She really hoped it was.

Buzzing with excitement, Lillian followed the online instructions and booked an appointment to view the journal.

Her timer discreetly chimed.

It was time to meet the rodeo star.

Chapter Twenty-One

L illian flicked her tactical pen around her thumb, catching it between her index finger and thumb. She was seated at a picnic table in one of the numerous pop-up outdoor barbecue restaurants. The picnic table's umbrella, decked out with the logo of a local brewery, took the sting out of the blazing sun, but just barely. It wasn't the first time she noticed how intense the sun was here.

So was the ever-shifting wind. The restaurant's oversized barbecues billowed the spicy smoke of grilling meat, mixing with the smell of spilled beer from the adjacent outdoor beer garden.

Lillian tried to discreetly cover her nose. Her managing editor had picked the place. At least her back was to a solid wall, one of the few on the whole grounds. There were also multiple exit points. Perhaps it's biggest selling point, though, was absolutely no one with intel on her would look for her here.

"Are you Lillian?"

Lillian's gaze slid across the table, stopping as a belt buckle the circumference of her fist glinted in the sunlight. She stared at the perplexing sight, dropping her pen.

She snatched the pen from the table and looked up.

The cowboy standing in front of her was tall. His shoulders were wider than most, and his Stetson hat sat so low on his forehead she couldn't see his eyes. She had the ridiculous thought he wanted to avoid as much of the interview, or maybe her, as possible.

How did he know?

The wind shifted again, sending the barbecue-drenched air elsewhere. She drank in the clear air. "I'm Lillian. You must be Colt Tanner." She started to stand and held out her hand.

"Ma'am, please don't get up. Clint would have my hide."

His eyes were still hidden by his hat.

"Who is Clint and why would he have your hide?"

"Never mind—just old school manners." He accepted Lillian's handshake.

She sized him up like she had Sophie's friend, Craig.

Colt Tanner's hand cradled hers, his size and strength obvious but not oppressive. She had met men who used a handshake to show dominance. Or overt seduction, like Fernando. Colt's handshake was neither. She was surprised in the speed in which he took his hand back. Lillian tried not to stare as he folded his tall frame into the bench seat across from her.

Colt lifted his head a fraction. From below the brim of his hat she saw eyes the color of a North Sea storm, a whole lot of grey and just as moody. Intelligence sparked in them, as did caution.

He was as wary of her as she was of him.

Before she could explore the thought, recognition

slammed into her.

"It's you."

It was her cowboy. The one she had been daydreaming about since he had whisked her away to safety before riding off into the sunset. Alone.

Damn. There went that fantasy.

Lillian tightened her grip on her tactical pen. She looked past him, scanning the diners and crowds for an accomplice. "Are you following me?"

He paused a beat. "Beg your pardon?"

"I asked if you were following me? Why are you here?"

Coincidences meant set-up and she was not being anyone's patsy again.

He looked around, scanning the crowd behind them, like her. "What are we looking at?"

Lillian didn't answer, she was too busy trying to find the setup.

The cowboy tapped the table twice. "You are the one interviewing me, right?"

Was he signaling to someone? She slid her hands into her lap and opened the tactical pen. She flicked glances between him and the crowd. Possible threats were everywhere.

He turned to look behind him again. "Seriously, what are we looking at?"

Suddenly a man she didn't recognize appeared behind Colt and slapped him on the back. "Nice ride today, Tanner."

Colt smiled at the newcomer. "Thanks. That spinner

helped me out."

Lillian hesitated, watching the exchange. She was sure she noticed Colt Tanner hide a wince as the other man clapped him on the back.

"Good enough for a ticket to Sunday." The man's phone pinged. "Congrats again, see you at the finals." The man nodded to Lillian. "Ma'am." He took his call and walked away.

Lillian tried to decode their conversation. "You're Colt Tanner. The bull rider."

On the edges of her awareness, recognition fluttered. She was sure she had seen him before, and not just at the cattle drive.

"I'm sorry, were you meaning to interview someone else?" He crooked his thumb and motioned over his shoulder. "It's okay, I can totally go–"

He stood, looking way too happy to leave.

Lillian put a hand on his arm. "Please, I apologize. If you're Colt Tanner the bull rider who has also allegedly punched a grizzly bear, then yes, I would very much like to interview you. Please."

Colt looked at her hand still on his arm, hesitating. Slowly, he slid back onto the bench seat.

"Don't put the bear thing in."

"Okay."

"I'm serious. Grizzlies have enough people problems."

"I promise." She eyed the cowboy in front of her. "You don't like being interviewed, do you?"

Colt grabbed two menus from the center of the table

and handed Lillian one.

"Mind if we order first? I'm starving."

She accepted the menu. Her story instincts were in full drive, and a hundred questions swirling through her head.

She scanned the menu instead. Two neat rows of carnivorous options stared back at her. She flipped it over, hoping for a second page of options.

Those storm-colored eyes looked back at her. "Something wrong?"

Lillian was unsure how to proceed.

He guessed, "You're a vegetarian? Vegan?"

The cowboy was quicker on the uptake than she expected. Still, she had zero expectation he would understand and braced herself for the verbal assault. In her experience people were quick to point out another's failings.

A breeze kicked up, drenching them both in barbecue-laced smoke. Colt frowned then, creasing his weather-teased face, so serious. He looked down at the all-meat menu he was holding.

Others at a nearby tables snickered. Her back stiffened until she realized the group wasn't paying attention to her. This continent had the definite perk of the near absence of British tabloids. She bit the inside of her lip, willing her raw emotions to quiet the fuck down.

Colt looked up from the menu. "You're covering the rodeo and you don't eat meat?"

"Yes, but it doesn't impede my ability to think or write," she snapped.

His expression frosted. "Never said it did."

Lillian exhaled. "No, you did not. I apologize, Mr. Tanner. I'm being a bit of a blighter today. It won't happen again."

"You can call me Colt." He glanced at her phone. "Are you recording this?"

"Not yet. I haven't asked your permission."

He made a noise that could mean anything. Panic bloomed within her. Losing an assignment as frivolous as this one, would be a new low, even for her.

"I apologized," she reminded him.

"This interview is for the paper, that's it, right?"

Lillian was confused. "Yes, the digital and print versions. The special edition feature piece. I assure you I am not here under false pretenses."

He seemed to weigh her words. "This your first rodeo?"

"I've been reporting longer than you have been climbing on the backs of bulls." She didn't mention she was used to covering real news, nothing as ridiculous as a rodeo.

"I meant it must be troubling covering the rodeo and being a vegetarian. It's hard when your personal values and professional responsibilities don't overlap."

"Oh."

The cowboy in front of her was not fitting into the tidy little box she had assigned him.

"That's rather astute."

"Kind of hard to miss that polarity."

"You'd be surprised," she muttered before admitting,

"Mr. Tanner, you're not what I expected."

"I asked you to call me Colt."

She studied the man in front of her. Supposedly he was large for a bull rider. He was proving to be a hell of a lot smarter than she had given him credit for—the whole bull riding thing, notwithstanding.

"You did." Lillian inclined her head. "*Colt.*"

She heard a series of high-pitched squeals and turned to see three young women in the shortest jean shorts she had ever seen, rush their table. They each wore variations of a checked shirt, but with ample cleavage and belly rings showing.

Lillian glanced down at her own outfit. There was no denying the exquisite softness of the flannel shirt she wore or the sensible durability of her denim skirt. In her previous life there had been desert khaki or couture. She felt like a fraud, but at least she was a comfortable one.

The young women advanced on Colt. It was like watching a car wreck. Lillian was horrified yet found she couldn't pull her gaze away. The women could have been in their teens, or a decade younger than her—it was hard to tell these days. After throwing her a single irritated look, they swarmed Colt, talking at once and batting their eyes at him, with their come-ons and rabid attention.

Lillian had never felt so invisible.

She didn't want to be the center of attention—far from it—but when she had had a career, she had never been so dismissed by the likes of such illiterate fluff . . . and here she was doing the same thing to three women. Ashamed, she heard her mentor's voice. *Judgement is easy, understanding takes effort.* She didn't know these women, their stories, or their motivation. So they were ruining a perfectly screwed interview, what did she care?

But she did. Lillian felt rather possessive of the attentive cowboy. He was *her* attentive cowboy for the length of the damn interview.

She heard Colt sigh. Shocked, Lillian stared. His expression was polite, but vacant, and his absolute lack of interest was tangible. Lillian watched with unexpected delight. The girls flaunted, posed and pouted to get him to give an inch, but he disarmed their advances with what could only be called smooth practice. He wasn't rude or mocking, just firm in his lack of interest.

Lillian had grossly misjudged this man. He might be a rodeo star, but he wasn't blinded by his own dazzle. She picked up her pen, and twirled it around her fingers, now watching the spectacle like an anthropologist. Another blast of barbecue smoke assaulted her, and she tried to discreetly cover her nose. She took shallow breaths through her mouth and waited for the breeze to stop or switch directions.

When the girls finally trotted off in a huff, Colt visibly relaxed.

"Are you going to ram that thing in my larynx, or were you ready to defend my honor?"

Lillian dropped her hand from her nose and looked down at the pen she was still wielding. She would have gladly run off the—what were they called? Oh yes, *buckle bunnies,* for him.

She clicked her pen closed and laid it precisely along her notebook before answering.

"Consider it professional courtesy."

Damn, he noticed her hesitation.

Gone was the phony politeness he had used with the groupies. Those grey eyes were assessing her, not missing a beat. Uncomfortable awareness tingled. Colt Tanner listened to the silences.

"All three of them were beautiful and willing. Why did you say no?"

Those handsome eyes flashed dark as any storm. "I make my living in rodeo so clearly I have to screw anything that wags in front of me, is that what you mean? I have tack older than them. Besides, since when is beauty synonymous with percentage of skin showing? You strike me as more of a 'brains' woman."

"Are you calling me ugly?" Lillian blurted.

His eyes flicked down for a fraction of a second. "That's what you got from me calling you a 'brains' woman?"

Lillian stared hard at one of the pearl buttons on his western shirt as humiliation swamped her. His job might be in the entertainment industry, but that didn't mean he was for sale. Or irrelevant because he wasn't living through a war. She hadn't realized she had become so cruelly jaded.

She made herself lift her gaze and locked eyes with his stormy ones.

"I'm broken. And I mean broken-broken."

His eyes softened a fraction. "Aren't we all, in some

way or another?"

"Some more than others."

"Is it a competition?"

Lillian felt a small smile crack. "No." She couldn't blame him if he left, but was surprised how much she wanted him to stay. "Now what?"

Colt tugged off his cowboy hat and swiped his hand across his hair. It looked soft and their conversation had turned so prickly.

"This interview started off on the wrong foot for both of us. I've been on the road way too long to have any patience, and you look like you're three carrot sticks away from snapping."

Lillian gasped.

He smiled. Two dimples flanked the sides of his mouth.

"Sorry, too soon for plant jokes?" He held a hand up. "Don't answer that."

He put his hat back on and filed the menus back in the table caddy. "Truce? And for the record, I don't care what you eat."

The cowboy was giving her a re-do. Relief swept through her.

Lillian nodded and held her hand across the table. "Truce."

He took her hand in his. A confetti gun went off somewhere nearby and she held on.

Colt eyed their hands, still entwined. "You okay?"

Lillian snatched her hand back. "Yes, of course."

"Good. Let's get out of here. There are a few food

trucks set up that will serve more than ketchup as a plant-based option. We can find one and do the interview there." Colt's voice shifted to curious when he asked, "Why did you pick this place?"

"My boss recommended it. Said you'd love it."

"I've never met the man."

Lillian shrugged. "That's what he said."

Colt had walked to her side of the table and held out his hand. She looked at it. He waited a half-beat before starting to drop it. Understanding finally dawned, and Lillian shot out her hand, accepting his.

The dimples reappeared.

With her hand in his, she unfolded herself from the picnic table bench, releasing him promptly. Lillian scooped up her phone and deposited it and her notebook in her satchel.

"Do you always carry your pen in your hand?"

She shouldered her satchel, keeping the discreet weapon gripped tight.

"Yes."

He eyed the pen in her hand briefly, but didn't press further. Colt's long-legged strides beat hers to the till and he paid for their drinks.

As they headed to the restaurant exit, she pointed behind them in dismay. "I was supposed to pay for those, this is an interview not a date."

"Got it, you're buying dinner."

"It's not *dinner*." She insisted.

Colt raised an eyebrow.

"I mean we will eat food, but it's not *dinner*-dinner."

"Right. If it was a date, you'd want me to pay for dinner?" He nodded, the dimples back. "Works for me, U.K."

Lillian tried not to sputter.

Colt could have his pick of women. There was no way he would choose a prickly British outcast, and one nearly a decade older than him. Even now, his tall frame and broad shoulders were drawing appreciate stares as they walked through the crowd. Colt was built like the security details she had gotten so used to. Well, except he wasn't armed. She had learned to tell who was carrying and who wasn't.

"Want to talk about whatever has you frowning like that?" Colt asked.

"This is your interview," Lillian countered.

"It was worth a shot."

"Why don't you like to be interviewed?"

"Ooh, Gretzky is denied. The article won't be covering that topic."

"Who's Gretzky? Is he a bull rider, too?"

Colt stopped. "Seriously?"

Lillian felt like she had just failed an unwritten test.

"So, not a bull rider, then?"

Colt shook his head as if in pity. He started walking again but paused long enough to grab two ketchup sachets from the to-go counter and handed them to her. "Just in case your blood-sugar is low."

Lillian took the small, squishy white packets. "Is this a clue about Gretzky?"

"I'm embarrassed on your behalf. Come on, we need

to get some food into you before you ask if we can drive to Toronto this afternoon."

That joke she got.

"Ooh, could we?"

"Don't even—"

"Relax cowboy, I've looked at a map."

Lillian discreetly slid the ketchup sachets into her shoulder bag, a precious souvenir from the unexpected and lighthearted moment. She looked up at the cowboy next to her, appreciating his dazzle.

Boom!

An explosion rocked through the crowd. Lillian felt Colt's arms wrap around her, tucking her into his larger body as he moved them around an oversized wooden planter.

Her earpiece buzzed. *"Funhouse, your three o'clock, go! We're covering you."*

Lillian grabbed Colt's hand and led him through the scrambling crowd. She was surprised he followed her lead without question. Shouts filled the air—but no screams.

She found the funhouse and pulled Colt through the exit doorway. They took the mismatched stairs and she crouched low, hiding behind plastic gargoyles, and pulled him down, too.

They had a clear view of the restaurant. Lillian peeked her head around the oversized gargoyle, assessing the threat. She had a better chance of evading danger if she knew what the hell was coming.

"Are you okay?" Colt asked.

Lillian ignored him. There were some people still running away, more were looking around in confusion. From her vantage point she could see the planter Colt had first tucked them behind after the immediate blast. He had found the only nearby relative safety in a disturbingly short amount of time.

Unless he had known the blast was coming.

She rubbed her arms, suspicion chilling her. Several security personnel raced up to the restaurant. Her detail had swarmed the funhouse.

"Lillian, are you okay?" Colt repeated.

She turned on him. "How did my boss know you liked this place?"

"No idea. I told you, I've never met the man."

The city police were now on scene and focused on the outdoor kitchen area of the adjacent beer garden. A fire crew appeared. Lillian noticed the emergency crews were focused on a propane tank and what looked like a gas hose. None of them looked overly worried. They would either be in for a nasty surprise . . . or the explosion really was an accident.

Lillian played a card. "That's the second time you got me out of danger."

Colt eyed the tactical pen clutched in her fingers before meeting her gaze. "Maybe you should explain what you meant by *broken-broken*."

Chapter Twenty-Two

"I forgot my own rule, let the locals pick the food places." Lillian licked a drip of tzatziki sauce off the corner of her pita and Colt felt his body tighten in response. He wanted to thump his forehead down on the table, repeatedly. A woman couldn't give more No Trespassing signs. Her disdain for him was palpable, his attraction to her a million kinds of stupid.

She hadn't said much after her impressive crowd-evasion display. When he had sat down, Colt had given Lillian as much space as possible. If she was afraid of men—which likely explained her behavior—he was larger than most and certainly didn't want to upset her.

They were seated at an out-of-the-way picnic table next to a caravan of food trucks. The noise of the midway rose and fell, a symphony of squeaky metal and rock music, carnies and fair goers.

Reporters usually annoyed him. This one was an ornery, fascinating puzzle. Like a bull. But prettier.

"Your boss isn't a local?"

"He's from somewhere called Saskatoon."

"A Saskatchewan boy."

"If you say so."

"It's the next province over." Her accent certainly wasn't local. "Do you travel often?"

"I used to," Lillian said, her voice frosting.

This was by far the weirdest interview he had ever done.

Colt watched as Lillian put down her pen long enough to devour the rest of her meatless Mediterranean wrap. He got the feeling pleasure, culinary or otherwise, wasn't typically tolerated by the uptight Brit. It was oddly gratifying she seemed to be enjoying something—anything— with him.

Colt ate his own wrap. He would have preferred beef on a bun, but the rabbit food was pretty good. Colt was no stranger to plant-based dishes, but he didn't have to tell U.K. that. His brother Tucker had just made police detective, but was also a closet gourmet chef.

Once finished, Colt crushed the paper wrapping and wiped his hands on a serviette. Lillian tidied herself with significantly more daintiness, and Colt felt like an ogre.

She didn't seem to notice. Lillian retrieved a small pad of paper from her satchel and picked up her ever-present pen. "The research I did suggests bull riders have other employment."

"Is there a question in there U.K.?"

"What do you do for money when you are not hanging on the back of a bull?"

Colt steepled his fingers on the table in front of him. "I start horses for mounted units—"

Lillian interrupted, "Sorry, I don't know what that means."

"'Start' instead of 'break.' It means to train a horse to accept a rider."

"That used to be called breaking a horse?" Lillian

sounded appalled. "That sounds medieval."

No shit.

"It's not my approach, but yes, some still use that method. I also fill in as a ranch hand."

"Is that what you were doing when we first met? I didn't thank you properly for your help the other day."

He shrugged. "You're welcome."

"What were you doing?"

"Moving cattle."

She gave him an inscrutable look. "I had wondered how the rest of that day went. There had to have been hundreds of cattle."

"You were worried about me?" A sense of masculine satisfaction rolled through Colt.

She cleared her throat. "Do you do anything else?"

U.K. was flustered—nice. "I have my guiding licenses and lead pack and sometimes fishing trips into the mountains on both sides of the border. Model." *Why the hell did he mention that?* "I give a hand to search and rescue folks when I'm in town. Teach kids to ride horses." Colt shrugged. "There's always work to do."

Lillian's eyes had widened. "Did you say model?"

Colt lowered his voice and looked at the table. "Nothing local. It was all overseas."

"Ohmygod, you're the *Archambeau* guy! That's why you looked familiar."

Colt glanced over each shoulder. "Quiet down, will you?"

Lillian glanced left, then right. A table of middle-aged women were talking excitedly and glancing their way, but the rest of the diners weren't paying them any attention. "Why are we being quiet?"

"Because it's embarrassing."

Lillian actually laughed. "Being the poster child for the number one selling men's cologne in Europe is embarrassing?"

"It's not like I cured cancer, I took my shirt off and made pouty faces for the camera. It was all rather ridiculous."

"Then why'd you do it?"

"I needed a new horse trailer and it paid well."

"You do realize you could likely walk into any modelling job in Europe, right?"

"That's what my agent keeps telling me."

Lillian's eyes bugged. "Then what are you doing here?"

Colt stared at her. "Living."

He didn't add that when he did that work he had been high as a fucking kite on prescription and non-prescription pain killers.

"Can I tell you something?" she asked.

"Sure."

Lillian tapped her pen against the table a couple times. "I've had a really shitty couple years. What I'm going to tell you will sound stupid, and please don't read anything into this, but those photos of you helped me. So, thanks."

No one had ever told him anything like that. Colt was unsure what to say.

"Um . . . you're welcome?"

She cleared her throat. "Moving on. You work in America, as well?"

Colt crossed his arms. "I have dual citizenship."

His parents' divorce five years ago had been messy, and Colt had been happy to be anywhere but home. His mom had been born in America, making his citizenship a matter of paperwork.

"I'm still surprised you're not modelling anymore. I know guys who would kill for that opportunity."

Colt frowned as he imaged the men in her life: tailored, well-groomed, impeccably mannered, probably called Winston or Rupert.

His tone was sharper than it should have been when he said, "I work hard and live simply. My life suits me just fine."

Lillian sat up straighter and scribbled something in her notebook. "Can I quote you on that?"

He leaned back. "Sure."

Colt watched her jot down notes. Whatever gig she had before this one, he doubted it was covering local fairs and festivals. Lillian Kensington had an intensity he had never seen in a reporter before.

"What about family? My research said you are a bachelor, what happens when you want to settle down?"

The interview had just skated onto thin ice. Time to tap the ice in warning.

"Are you throwing your hand into the ring?"

Her neck flushed a lovely pink. "Of course not, I'm asking for professional reasons."

"And here I thought you were turning sweet on me."

Lillian scanned her notes, cool as a cucumber. "It would take a hell of a lot more than being a model."

Ouch. This one-way turn-on sucked.

Lillian looked up from her notes. "Why do you do it? Why do you ride bulls?"

Colt smile turned brittle. Years ago, he had learned what people wanted to hear and it wasn't the truth. It had been a humiliating experience.

For half a second, he considered breaking his rule. This uptight Brit, though not interested in him, might actually get him. And Sunday would be his last ride. No one was going to ask again.

"Colt?"

Sanity returned. He opened his mouth, ready to deliver his rehearsed, perfect pop answer.

Lillian's cell phone discreetly pinged.

She ignored it. "You were saying?"

Colt gestured. "Please, go ahead."

He let his gaze wander over the midway.

She silenced it. "It can wait. Why are you a bull rider?"

Her phone immediately pinged again.

Lillian frowned, flicking a look at the call display before pushing the phone away. "Please continue, I've mucked up enough of this interview."

The phone started pinging a third time.

"I get it, you're polite." Colt pointed. "That sounds important."

Lillian hesitated a moment. "Sorry, thanks." She turned sideways on the picnic table bench and leaned forward at the waist, resting her elbows on her knees.

"Sophie? What is it?"

Noise from the midway swelled and she lifted her hand to cover her ear.

She was wearing an earpiece.

It was impossible not to hear her conversation.

"What? . . . Slow down . . . Where's Coyote Creek?"

A long pause followed.

"The RCMP's cruiser got stuck chasing you? Where's your detail?"

Lillian darted a brief look at Colt before hunching over more.

"You would be in jail already?"

That caught Colt's attention.

"You'll have to wait until Monday morning?" Lillian's voice had turned to a soft shriek.

Colt gently tapped her arm. When she looked up, he dangled his truck keys in front of her. She stared at them a second, then shook her head. "I can't ask you to do that—*no, not you, Sophie, I was talking to Colt.*"

Lillian pinched the bridge of her nose. *"Yes, that Colt Tanner."*

Colt smiled.

Lillian sat bolt upright. *"Sophie, do not speak to a copper like that."*

Colt waved his hand. "I can give you a ride. I'm going near Coyote Creek anyway."

Lillian tucked her phone against her chest. "Oh, no, thank you. I couldn't possibly—"

"Just say yes. It will make life easier. And really, I'm heading that way, anyway."

She hesitated. "I insist on paying you for petrol."

"Whatever, sure."

He'd give her a ride; it was the decent thing to do. Then they would part ways. Her immunity to his profession had at first been a breath of fresh air. But he was too old to chase crushes, and Lillian Kensington was proving to be too complicated to be anything more.

Chapter Twenty-Three

Lillian clutched her satchel and tried not to freak out sitting in the front seat of Colt's half ton pickup truck. He hadn't said a word in miles, but his right hand was slung casually across the top of the steering wheel. His relaxed vibe was in stark contrast to the terror she was feeling.

She didn't have many weak spots left anymore. Sophie was one of them.

She knew physically, her niece was fine. It sounded like the kids had simply gone for an off-road country drive and had gotten stuck in mud. Sophie's detail had her in sight. Still, Lillian fretted. The police were involved, though she wasn't exactly sure why.

Her mobile rang, shattering the silence.

After a quick glance, she silenced the phone and shoved it into her satchel. Her Canadian doctor was spouting the same crap her British one had been chastising her about for the last several months. She was not up for their expert opinions right now.

Colt slid her a look. "You okay?"

"Fine."

Her voicemail pinged and she ignored that, too.

"It got a lot chillier in here when your phone rang."

Lillian fought a smile. "Do you read bulls as well as you read people?"

He laughed. "Bulls are way easier than people."

"I believe you."

Quiet filled the truck cabin again and Lillian stared out the window. Lush valleys punctuated the otherwise grassy hills and scrubby brush. The wind toyed with the tall grasses, looking like waves rippling across a green sea. Further back, patches of spruce and pine crowned some of the crests. Above it all, the mountains stood, their stark grey bodies brooding as dark clouds thickened around their peaks. The sun, still shining, didn't stand a chance in that gathering storm.

"One could run away for days here."

"Sorry?" Colt asked.

"In England, if the traffic isn't shite, we'd have hit a border or an ocean by now." She stared out the window. There was just so much land.

"It'll be okay, we'll figure it out. We're almost there," he repeated.

She was learning 'almost there' was relative here.

"Sorry the interview was so, weird."

The corners of his mouth lifted. "It happens."

"I've never met anyone as understanding as you are."

"You say that like it's a bad thing."

"In my experience it is."

Colt shrugged. "I used to get bent out of shape. Then I decided it wasn't worth the hassle. Now I just cut my losses and walk away."

"Just like that?"

"Yup. Just like that."

Lillian felt pulled to his clean logic. "I didn't want to come here."

"So why did you?"

"It's complicated."

When he didn't ask her to elaborate, she wondered if

he had assigned her to the walk-away category.

"We're almost there." Colt's voice gave nothing away.

He turned off the highway and the truck thudded over a series of large parallel bars. The large truck bounced and swayed over the terrain. Lillian grabbed the convenient handle on the cab's ceiling adjacent to the truck door.

Colt laughed at her fierce grip on the ceiling handle.

"That was a Texas gate, it's supposed to be driven over."

"Aren't we in Canada?"

"Last time I checked."

"Then why is it called a Texas gate?"

"Why are French fries called French fries?"

"They're not, they're chips." Lillian fired back.

"Wherever they're from, they pair nicely with a steak sandwich." He paused. "In Texas they're called cattle guards."

"I'll take your word for it."

Lillian looked behind her, watching the paved road disappear. She might have travelled around the world, but most of her assignments had been in urban areas.

An uneasiness surfaced. "There's no road, how can we be almost there?"

Colt ignored her question. "You going to hang on to the *oh-shit* handle the whole way?"

Lillian kept her grip on the handle and scanned the rolling field in front of them. Seriously, where was the road? She slipped her free hand in her satchel, reaching for her tactical pen.

And came up empty.

Adrenaline exploded in her system. Had he stolen it? She dared a quick glance at Colt. He didn't look crazy, or mean. But she knew monsters didn't always look the part.

She discreetly eyed the truck cab for a weapon. The space was tidy. Only a cluster of paperwork and a cell phone charger were within sight or reach.

Panic surged. What was she going to do, attack him into submission with paper cuts? It would be useless to try and use the charger cord on him, he would be way too strong in hand-to-hand combat. His shoulders were massive.

Her fingers found a ball point pen. With the element of surprise and enough force, that could work. It better work. When would she stop trusting the wrong people?

Sweat beaded at her temple and Lillian hoped the astute cowboy wouldn't notice.

"What are you doing?"

If not for her seatbelt, Lillian would have shot off the bench seat.

He was darting looks at her. "Seriously, are you okay? We'll have cell reception again when we hit the top of the hill. We're almost there."

A new level of fear spiked. It had never crossed her mind there would be no cell coverage. She searched for her phone. No bars.

"Sophie called, though." Her voice came out a croak.

Colt had lied to her.

His arm shot out and she instinctively ducked. Lillian jammed her hand back in her satchel, wrapping her fingers around the ball point pen. Her hostile situational training flooded her mind. *Do not wait until you are in custody.*

Well, she blew that one. It was now or never.

Colt had reached behind her in the backseat. Lillian was ready for him. She waited for the right moment, her hand curled over the civilian pen.

A rainbow darted across the cab as sunlight glinted off contained liquid.

She blinked.

He was handing her a bottle of water.

"You look tense. Here, have some water. I figure they're over this rise and in the shallow gully beyond. Usually it's dry by now, but we had a wet spring. It's an easy place to get a whole lot of stuck."

Lillian slowly exhaled. She had almost stabbed a man in the throat over a bottle of water.

He still held the water out to her, his eyes on the road. "Here. It'll be okay. High speed car chases don't really work in mud. Your niece should be fine."

She accepted the bottle of water and kept the pen in her hand. Automatically she started rhythmically clicking it.

"Thinking about going for my larynx again?" Colt eyed the pen in her hand.

"Maybe. You know how to show a woman the middle of nowhere."

He shot her an incredulous look. "We're four-hundred meters from the highway."

Lillian looked in the side mirror. The highway was a dark ribbon, clearly visible, and indeed right behind them.

Lillian crossed her arms. "Showoff."

"Spatially challenged."

Lillian opened her mouth to retort, but no quip came out. She took a sip of the water instead.

They crested the hill, and the scene below was so ridiculous she sputtered on her water, inhaling some. Colt slammed the truck into park. She held up a hand when he looked ready to pounce to the rescue, to slay any foe. Even a drink of water.

The image was ridiculous and only made her cough harder. Finally, she got out, "I'm fine, I'm fine."

Colt glared at her. "It's not funny."

Lillian coughed again before asking, "Do you always rush to rescue damsels in distress?"

"Lady, you're the furthest thing from a damsel in distress, with the possible exception of my sister. You two are the most fiercely independent woman I've ever met."

"Fernando didn't think so."

When concern was in those clear, grey eyes, not recognition, relief flooded Lillian. Colt was not Fernando's hired muscle.

Breathing easier, she pointed out the windscreen. "That *is* funny."

An assortment of pickup trucks, tractors and three RCMP cruisers convened at the bottom of the hill. Even at a distance, Lillian could see all of the vehicles, save for a single police cruiser, were stuck in the largest stretch of mud Lillian had ever seen. It was as big as a small parking lot.

Colt gave her another long look. Finally, he turned, too. A small smile teased the corner of his mouth. "That's Alberta mud."

Lillian gave him a questioning look.

"The soil, it has a high clay content. If you ask my sister, she'd recite something about glacial lakes . . . never mind. Is that your niece?"

Lillian nodded. Sophie was the only woman in the small circle below.

"The kid next to her is Craig Cameron. He's a good kid. Got the short end of the stick on stepdads, but he's solid."

"I met him earlier today. He seemed pleasant enough." Though a run in with the police had her concerned.

Of course, she had been wrongfully accused of treason. She had to at least hear the kid out.

"I'd be surprised if this turned out to be anything. Craig's not like that."

Three Mounties were talking to Sophie and Craig.

Colt leaned forward, and the hand slung across the top of the steering wheel tighten.

Lillian followed his gaze. In the distance, two riders were approaching on horseback.

He looked back at her, his eyes stormy. "What happens here is off the record, is that understood?"

His vehemence was unexpected, but she agreed; if the British tabloids caught word, they wouldn't hesitate to crucify Sophie if they could.

"Absolutely."

"I'm serious."

"So am I."

He nodded. "Good. That's my brother and sister on horseback."

Suspicion flared anew. "Your family just so happen to be out riding, here, now?"

"That's not a joyride, they're working. See the gear strapped to their mounts?"

Lillian wasn't sure how to respond.

"Never mind." Colt slammed the truck into drive.

Lillian grabbed the dashboard as they careened down the steep hill. "Is this speed necessary?"

Colt dodged a small boulder and accelerated out of the swerve.

"I'm creating a buffer. You won't believe it, but I'm the sane one in my family."

"The sane one is a bull rider, of course."

They were closing in on the scene. A fourth officer walked around a vehicle, talking on a mobile and looking angry. He had mud clear up to the knees of his trousers.

She pointed through the windscreen. "Who is that and why is he so angry?"

Colt brought the truck to a jarring stop. "Prepare yourself for way more fireworks than any grandstand show. My family is a bad soap opera. Consider yourself warned."

"What does that even mean?"

He didn't hear her. Colt had already launched himself from the truck.

Chapter Twenty-Four

"What the hell are you doing here?" Officer Jason Chasseur glared at him. Colt walked past Officer Chasseur a few paces, wanting to pull the Mountie's gaze away from the approaching riders. Lillian had hightailed it to Sophie and Craig.

"Jason, always good to see you."

"Is it?"

Colt tucked his hands in the front pockets of his jeans and glanced at the other man's soiled work pants. "Knee-high mud—it's a bit bold, but nice look."

"Shut up. Not now Colt, not fucking now." Jason crammed his cell phone into his front shirt pocket. He stomped his boots and mud flew in several directions. "What are you doing here? Aren't you riding today?"

"Already did."

"I'd ask how you did, but I really don't care right now."

Colt grinned at the officer's candor. "I have twelve years on four of the guys in the top ten. That's a lot of years of bust-ups when they're coming in fresh and hungry."

Jason eyed him. "You're not hungry anymore?"

"I'm tired." The words were out before Colt could censor them.

Jason recovered first from the unexpected share. "This

is a goddamn mess."

A burst of static sounded, and Jason answered his radio. Another call had come in and the Mounties had three vehicles stuck here.

"How can I help?" Colt asked.

"Won't your sister disown you for that?"

"Naw, our dad's the only one prone to that. Besides, what are neighbors for?"

"In my experience, being a pain in the ass," Jason retorted, stomping more mud off his boots and pant legs. "Hey what's up with the dead arms and drug dealer at your dad's wedding?"

Colt held up his hands. "Not a fucking clue. I ride bulls. I don't run in his circles. Never have."

Jason seemed to weigh his answer. "You've got a point."

Colt had always thought the RCMP officer to be a decent guy. The kind of neighbor you wanted to know, not piss off like his sister had. People needed each other, especially living out here.

"Your cruiser is the only one not up to its axles in mud. Do you need to head out? I can stay and help."

But Jason had just noticed Becca and Tucker riding up.

"*Aw hell,* what is *she* doing here?"

Colt closed his eyes. Shit.

Everyone started talking at once. Voices were rising, horses were sidestepping, and normally docile people were acting like idiots.

Colt met Lillian halfway back to the truck.

"After I assured myself the kids were fine, I thought it

prudent to wait up here."

"Good call."

They stood a distance away, watching the drama.

"What's with the boiling tempers between those two?"

"It's my sister's land."

"You make that sound like a bad thing."

Colt nodded towards Jason. "Only for that Mountie."

"Will she take it out on Sophie and Craig?"

Colt shook his head. "It would be out of character if she did."

"Will the Mountie?"

"He's fair, but anything involving my sister, especially this particular stretch of land, is a wild card."

Colt wished he was still at Stampede, having a beer and listening to live country music.

Lillian blanched then. "My niece is yelling at that copper."

The young woman was giving a young officer hell. She motioned towards Craig, then the old pickup truck, before shaking her finger at the young uniformed man.

Angry voices below carried on the breeze. Even the mud seemed to be getting thicker.

Colt turned to head back to his truck.

"Where are you going?"

The catch in her voice stopped him. Colt spun around and stomped back into the medley. Tucker was holding both horse leads and looking resigned. Becca was bellowing at Jason.

"*I* will decide if charges are pressed or not. In case you

have forgotten, this is *my* land."

"You've been watching too many American TV shows. That's not how the law works up here. And like I'd forget the spoiled princess who ran to her rich daddy to buy this land out from under me."

Becca stopped. "What are you talking about?"

Jason voice was laced with scorn. "Nice touch, waiting until I had finally scraped enough together to put an offer on my family's land. But you knew I couldn't compete with Bruce Tanner's deep pockets. That's a new low, even for you."

Colt and his brother Tucker both took a protective step forward.

Tucker said, "Easy there Jason."

"Truth hurts, doesn't it boys?"

Confusion had replaced Becca's glare. "That's not how it went."

"You can honestly tell me you didn't have anything to do with your daddy's obscenely high offer?"

Becca's face had paled. "I didn't know you had put an offer in to buy it."

"Yeah right, save it for the next dip-shit who dares want something you have in your crosshairs."

"I didn't know."

The underlying tension that had always existed between Becca and Jason had exploded since the land deal. Even from the road, Colt had heard Jason had finally pooled together enough money to put an offer on the land that had been in his family for generations. It was hard to imagine Becca wouldn't have known.

Colt walked forward, physically putting himself between them.

"How about you guys hash this out without an audience. Right now we have bigger problems than hurt feelings. The McTavish's are moving cattle through here. No one wants six hundred head of cattle added to this shit show."

The low growl of a diesel engine sounded. A large, commercial-grade tow truck crested the hill before rumbling towards them, interrupting the tension.

Jason gave Becca a hard look, before turning to the crowd. "You heard the man."

Becca was watching Officer Chasseur walk away. Tucker handed her her horse's rein's. They both swung into their saddles and rode off. The others were making their way towards the powerful truck.

Except Colt.

With a little luck, he'd soon be on his back porch, beer in hand, a medium-rare grilled steak in front of him as he watched the sun dip behind the mountains, taking the screwed-up day with it.

Lillian came up beside him. "You okay?"

Colt crossed his arms. "This is why I ride bulls."

"They don't get stuck in the mud?" Lillian said, deadpan.

Colt fought a smile. "Something like that?"

"Was that the fringe fireworks show?"

"Now your sense of humor comes out?"

Colt wondered if he had any vegetarian options at his house other than ketchup. He'd start a garden tonight if it meant she'd keep looking at him the way she was now, and the sense of humor was a noticeable improvement from the earlier, crankier Lillian.

"Shall we see if we can all go home?" Lillian asked.

"First rules for dinner, and now a plan for sleeping arrangements. You are organized."

"Have a care, it's been a long day." She elbowed him in the ribs. "Jesus, you're built like a steel pole."

Colt sucked in a breath, trying to breathe through the pain.

"That's not a compliment any man would turn down."

She reached out to him. "Are you okay?"

"Yup." Her elbow had felt like a two-by-four to his ribs.

She placed her hand on his arm. "Colt, what is it?"

"I banged up a rib or two riding a few days ago. It's still a little tender, is all."

Lillian pulled her hand back. "You rode with broken ribs?"

She was looking at him like he was an idiot.

"*Cowboy-up* is not some trite expression for too-tight t-shirts or cheap beer koozies."

"Of course, not."

Colt's patience frayed. "Rodeo is not a bunch of backwater assholes jacking off. It is a legitimate professional sport. We don't have a contract protecting us, so if we don't ride, we don't earn. So yes, I ride broken."

A tense silence descended.

Lillian ceded first. "Seems I have more to learn here beyond finding out who Gretzky is."

Colt gave her a long look, sorry for his outburst but feeling too raw to do anything about it. "We should go join them."

"Okay."

They started making their way back towards the group.

"Can I get a spreadsheet, maybe a ledger of the dynamics?" Lillian asked.

"What?"

She looked up. "A spreadsheet, you know, so I can keep track of everyone."

He cracked a smile. "You're sharp, you'll pick it up."

As they walked up, Sophie's hand was firmly in Craig's. They looked like a young, united front. The teens nodded to them, but didn't say anything.

Jason hung up his phone and looked as crumpled as his mud-soaked uniform. "The pickup truck is still reported stolen, I have to book you kids for grand theft." He glanced at the beat-up old truck. "Make that just theft."

"Officer Chasseur, my mom said I could use it. It's my stepdad's old work truck, he doesn't even drive it anymore. She would have let him know I have it."

"Your stepdad reported it stolen. He's the one that told us where to find you."

"He did what?" Craig's voice cracked. "Why would he do that to me?"

"Do you have another number I can try your mom at?" Jason asked.

Craig shook his head. "That's the only one. She's not

at work today."

"I'll keep trying to get ahold of your mom and clear this mess up, but we need to take you two in now." Jason called over to another officer. "Cooper, take my cruiser and get these kids to the detachment."

The younger officer trotted over.

Colt was surprised Lillian's niece looked as calm as she did. In fact, Sophie was reassuring Craig. He heard her say, "we'll get it sorted," as Officer Cooper placed them in the cruiser. They drove off without incident. If Colt was in another country and got mixed up with the police, he'd be sweating buckets.

Jason swung his fore fingers together. "Are you two... I mean, who am I calling to pick the kids up? They're technically adults, but I'd prefer if Craig had a place to stay tonight that wasn't his stepdad's."

Colt knew what Jason wasn't saying.

"Yeah, of course. Craig can stay with me."

Jason let out a breath and held out his hand. "Thanks, Colt. I appreciate it."

Colt accepted the handshake. In another lifetime, they could have been friends.

After the officer walked away, Lillian pressed, "You'll give Sophie a ride, too?"

She looked so worried.

"I said I would."

Lillian visibly relaxed.

Colt still felt shitty for losing his patience with her. "Sorry I blew up back there, about rodeo."

"I'm sorry I judged you rather harshly."

He opened his mouth to protest, but she stopped him. "No, I did judge you harshly. And not just to your face. I'm not proud of myself, and I'm sorry, too."

Colt had never had anyone apologize to him like that. He wasn't sure what to do with it.

He invited her to dinner. "Want to wait at Becca's? It'll be easier than driving into town only to turn around again. And Tucker's cooking tonight. The food will be worth spending time with my family." He eyed her. "That said, they're a bit rambunctious."

Lillian raised an eyebrow. "Your sister—"

"Is completely sane when Officer Chasseur isn't around. I promise there won't be any more fireworks."

Unless his parents showed up.

Chapter Twenty-Five

Lillian stared, transfixed. She stood with Colt in his sister's foyer. He had taken off his cowboy hat and turned to hang it on a hook behind him, his western shirt pulled tight across his wide shoulders. She smiled to herself; it was no wonder his image sold high-end cologne. The man had an undeniable—almost elemental—sex appeal.

"Did you say something?"

Lillian flushed. "Nope."

She hung her satchel on the wrought iron hook next to his hat and smoothed out her plaid shirt. "You're sure your sister is okay with me coming?" Lillian had spent so long being shunned by those she had thought were friends, she was having a hard time being accepted within minutes.

"We're good. She loves entertaining, especially if Tucker's cooking."

Lillian looked around. Soft, late-day light was illuminating the foyer. A gentle breeze flared long, hand-embroidered curtains that flanked tall vertical windows. Faceted prisms suspended from branch curtain rods swayed and rainbow-colored light danced across the log benches and walls. Stunning black and white photography of mountain lakes and horse close-ups adorned the walls.

Long hallways led off either side, and to the front, a large room with no less than seven doorways opened up beyond. A robust, hand-stretched glass sculpture sat tastefully atop a wide sideboard. Peeking behind the windowed cabinets below were stacks of folded jackets and baskets of what looked like hats, gloves, and scarves. Form and function.

"This place is incredible," Lillian whispered, reverently, looking around.

"Becca's done a great job with it. I'm really proud of her."

Warm touches and mindful details were everywhere. Lillian's flat in England had been professionally decorated and was nowhere near as welcoming as Becca's inn felt. Lillian had travelled so much with work she hadn't bothered changing anything the decorators did. After the *unfortunate incident*, she had moved back to the family estate.

She took a step closer to Colt and almost ran into him.

"Seriously, it's just dinner," he said.

"You mentioned that."

"And there's cell coverage here, you'll hear the call about Sophie and Craig."

Lillian nodded. The officer with the muddy pants, Officer Chasseur, had confirmed Craig's story with his mother and now was just finishing the paperwork. The kids were fine.

She wasn't. Lillian tried to delicately toe out of her new, unfamiliar boots. She lost what little balance she had. And took a header into Colt's waist.

He gave a grunt on contact.

Colt had caught her shoulders and pulled her up, but not before she had face-planted—if only for a second—just below his belt.

"Oh my god, I'm sorry!" Mortified, her cheeks flamed, and she snapped her eyes shut.

He cleared his throat, twice, before he shook a jean-clad leg.

"Good thing I didn't have one of my big belt buckles on."

"That's not considered big?" It looked as big as a dessert plate.

"Not even close."

Bewildered she asked, "But why?"

Without missing a beat, he answered, "PPE for beautiful women falling into our laps."

He thought she was beautiful. "What's PPE?"

Tucker called from somewhere towards the back of the large house, *"We're back here. Are you guys coming?"*

"Be right there." Colt called back, before asking her, "I know I'm sounding like a broken record, but you're good?"

She was mortified. Turned on. Still precariously close to the abyss' edge of crazy. But standing this close to him had her feeling better than she had in months.

"I'm good. Thank you." She did need to make a call, though. "Where's the loo?"

Colt nodded down a hall. "Second door on right," and used his thumb to indicate behind him, "kitchen is through here. Go all the way to the back of the house. Do you want me to wait?"

She eyed the multiple doorways and hallways. "My phone has a GPS. Are all ranch houses this big?"

"Becca's opening it as an eco-inn."

"Right. You said that." This time she held the wall as she unceremoniously kicked out of her boots. "I'll be there in a sec."

Lillian ducked into the loo. When she heard Colt's retreating footsteps, she slid the lock closed.

She flipped on the light and gasped aloud, barely containing a shriek as she saw herself in the mirror.

Her earpiece hummed to life. *"We have the house surrounded. Do you need assistance?"*

She had forgotten about her security detail.

Lillian dropped her head back, staring at the ceiling. "Negative."

"Copy that."

Her earpiece went silent. Her security detail's level of competence, and utter detachment, was like a superpower.

In the large mirror, Lillian could see the speckles of mud dotting her face and clothing. Her hair was a riot of tangles. The wind had pulled most of her plait loose. As quickly as she could, Lillian brushed off what dirt she could and washed her hands and face. She finger-combed her hair before wrapping it into a loose bun.

Lillian looked at her reflection in the mirror. She was rumpled, smudged with dirt, and her eyes had a twinkle she hadn't seen in ages. With nervous energy, she pulled out her phone and made a call.

Chapter Twenty-Six

Dame Maighread Evans Coille Kensington hit the play button again on her laptop. Hard rain beat against the massive windows flanking her study walls. A warm fire blazed cheerily in the fireplace. A soft knock sounded, and Mary entered, carrying a serving tray with a fresh pot of tea and a small plate of biscuits.

"Thank you, Mary."

The woman nodded. "What are you watching?"

Maighread smiled at the shenanigans on the screen. Her granddaughters were in a mess alright. There was mud everywhere. "The girls."

"Is Lillian taking your calls, yet?"

Maighread shook her head. Lillian had been quite upset, and rightly so. Maighread had been unforgivably selfish keeping the special journal secret all those years ago. It wasn't an easy thing, realizing how her personal ambitions had highjacked her better judgement. She had hurt her granddaughter to get ahead, to fit in.

The cost of conforming always had been too high.

Mary looked at the screen. "What on earth? Is that Sophia scolding a man in uniform?"

"Indeed. And she's doing a superb job of it, too, if I do say so." Maighread couldn't hide the pride in her voice.

Mary straightened and *tsked*. "Looks troublesome, if you ask me."

Maighread watched the screen. "Looks like good fun to me."

Mary snorted. "You would. You have them all fooled, you know."

"Nonsense."

She hoped Mary was right. That she was still the same woman who could have fun like that, like her granddaughters. What she wouldn't give to go back, to dare enough to be herself. She had played a man's game and gotten incredibly far. But what a price she had to pay.

Mary left her alone then.

Maighread continued to watch. Young Sophia was holding hands with a nice-looking young man. That was no surprise; Sophie was particular, but didn't shy away from a boy she was interested in.

The whole spectacle looked more entertaining than concerning. Maighread had faith her girls would be just fine.

An image flashed, catching her attention. Maighread zoomed in. Lillian was leaning in close to a tall, broad-shouldered man. He was looking at her like a man did when he found himself enchanted with a woman. He also had an elemental sensuality to him. He would give her granddaughter a merry—and very satisfying—chase.

"Well done, girl. Well done."

This whole expedition to Canada was proving as interesting as she had anticipated. Good.

But all was not well, yet.

Fernando was going to be a problem. Maighread knew what she wanted to do—nothing that would pass the Geneva Convention.

An eerie thumping sound drummed against her office windows. The storm had not relented. Torrents of rain blasted the windows in chaotic bursts. It was a wild, powerful night. The wind, unpredictable.

Her phone rang, a staccato to the storm's milieu.

Maighread crossed to her desk. Agent Forest was on the line.

"She's requested an INCEPT check."

Maighread looked at the image on her laptop. Anyone her granddaughter cared for could potentially become a target.

"Have her security detail put surveillance and a tracker on him."

Chapter Twenty-Seven

Colt munched a large slice of red bell pepper. The tangy sweetness gave a satisfying crunch.

"Why is it when I cut vegetables they taste like vegetables, but when you do it, they're good?"

Tucker grinned and finished loading shrimp and vegetables onto the skewer in his hand. "Because you're a brute with no finesse?"

"Says the belligerent cop."

"That's Detective Belligerent Cop to you."

Colt snickered. It was good hanging out with his brother again. "Don't you still have your detective training wheels on?"

"Shut up, asshole. Want to hear something fucked?"

"Do I have a choice?" Colt took another bite of bell pepper.

"Remember the guy that got shot at dad's wedding?"

"No, I forgot."

Tucker looked up.

"Of course, I remember the dead guy at dad's wedding."

"Right." Tucker used the kabob he was loading to enunciate. "His prints were found on the gun that was recovered when Gabe was shot on his last CSIS assignment. He's a known international arms and drug dealer. Gabe was right."

Colt stilled. "What does that mean?"

"That's not the really fucked-up part. Dad routinely called this guy since before Gabe was shot."

Colt let that sink in.

"Dad's been hanging out with international arms and drug dealers?"

"Yeah, weird, right? I mean, Dad moves a lot of money for a lot of different clients, and he has to fill out paperwork to demonstrate everything is legal, but there's nothing to say he couldn't move money legitimately for a client who also happens to be a criminal."

"Does Gabe know?"

"Not yet. He took Savannah up to Jasper. They should be back tomorrow."

"What about Becca?"

Tucker looked out the kitchen window, no doubt assuring himself Becca was still outside in the garden, before he shook his head. "Not yet. You know she'll freak. And she's already stressed enough with getting this place ready for her opening."

"So, what, we just lie to her?"

"*No.* I just need to find a non-scary way to tell her, that's all."

Dad bought me the old Chasseur place.

Becca should have partnered on it with Officer Chasseur instead of Bruce Tanner.

Colt picked up his beer and took a swig.

Tucker loaded the last skewer. "Until we find out more, I say we stay as far away from dad as possible. It's not like that'll be hard. I'll find a way to tell Becca. But enough about that, what's with you and Lillian?"

"I just met her."

Tucker gave Colt his best annoyed-little-brother look. "You've never brought a woman here before."

Colt shrugged and took another sip of his beer.

Tucker pressed. "Dude, she's way out of your league."

"Thanks, asshole."

"Calling it like I see it, but seriously, how did you snag her? And you hate reporters—though, I get why you're making an exception with her. *Damn*."

Colt took another pull from his beer. "She's different. And completely immune to my charm."

"You don't have any charm."

"The ladies would beg to differ."

"Groupies don't count, dumb-ass."

"She defended me today, with the groupies, I mean. It was kinda hot. Until she insulted my integrity, intelligence, and career choice." Colt munched another pepper. "Does a man really need an ego? Mine is taking a beating with her."

"Sorry about that."

It was Lillian. She was standing in the doorway of the kitchen.

Chapter Twenty-Eight

The two men swung their gazes to Lillian. The phrase *deer in the headlights* came to mind.

Lillian held up her hands. "Don't stop on my account. I was enjoying your banter."

And the view. Colt had been leaning against a massive island counter, sipping a beer and munching from a pile of fresh vegetables. His brother, handsome in his own way, had been going between the chopping board, food processor and his own beer.

Lillian turned to Tucker. "Is he always like this?"

Tucker laughed. "Nope, must be you."

Colt moved then, stopping just in front of her. "Don't listen to him. Want a beer?"

"I'll have one later." She motioned at the preparations underway. "How can I help?"

Colt nodded behind Lillian. "Becca's out picking a salad, if you want to join her? You know, if ketchup won't cut it."

Lillian smiled. "Give me a bowl, cowboy."

Tucker snickered. Colt pulled out a hand-thrown ceramic dish and handed it to her. It was beautiful and surprisingly light. She was worried about breaking it until she cradled it in the crook of her arm. It nestled securely.

He would have followed her, but she shooed him back. "I got this. Drink beer with your brother. And Colt?"

"Yeah?"

"I'm not totally immune."

Those North Sea eyes flared.

She smiled and stepped out the back screen door, and her breath caught in her throat. She was in the midst of the largest residential garden she had seen on this continent. She felt pulled by a hundred shades of green. Lillian stepped off the wooden deck stairs into the main garden. The fragrances of various lush foliages tickled her nose. Keeping the ceramic bowl nestled securely in one arm, she let her other arm trail through the leaves of vibrant, plush plants crowding the garden-stone pathway.

The sun had just started to set. The slanting light accentuated the magic of the enchanting garden.

"I'm over here." Becca's voice called from deeper in the garden.

Lillian picked out Colt's sister's form, crouched low, and made her way over. An assortment of spinach, arugula, and red and green lettuces were already in Becca's bowl.

"I saw you come out." She held out her hand. "I'm Becca, by the way, nice to officially meet you."

Lillian shook the woman's hand. "I'm Lillian, and likewise." She waved at the garden. "This is incredible. What is this, zone three?"

"Zone two, actually. I can't cook worth a darn, but I can rock a garden, and a salad."

"How do you get your produce to thrive here? I haven't even tried to start a garden here, I assumed it would be pointless."

Becca laughed. "Patience, trial and error, and strong, high fences to keep out the wildlife. And Colt helped me build a greenhouse. Our elevation is high, and summer is short here. We try to soak up every minute."

"No kidding." A series of low rocks beyond caught her eye and Lillian gasped. "Is that a Chartres labyrinth?"

Becca straightened and smiled. "It is."

"It's beautiful." Lillian said in awe. The garden was built to nurture the body and soul.

"You can have a go at it whenever you like." Becca spread her hands wide. "And pick what you like. We have plenty."

The garden was an unexpected oasis. Soon, plump cherry tomatoes, bright radishes and crisp snap peas filled Lillian's bowl. She knew they were crisp; she had tried three. She popped a cherry tomato into her mouth and the fresh burst of flavor delighted. Her garden back home had been filled with her prized, but precise flowers. This one had raised beds with rows and clusters of vegetables and fragrant herbs, and wildflowers that even now, honeybees were buzzing among. It was a garden that nourished and nurtured.

Headlights flashed down the long drive and Becca swore.

"Who's that?" Lillian asked.

"I'm guessing either my mom or dad."

From her tone, neither was a welcome development.

As the vehicle got closer, Becca stood and swore again. "It's not my parents."

Lillian watched, curious, as Becca dusted off her hands and self-consciously patted down her hair.

The headlights swung around, and the car parked. Lillian followed Becca around and out a side garden gate. An RCMP cruiser was parked in the driveway. Officer Chasseur stepped out and Lillian heard Becca's intake of breath. Lillian noticed his uniform, and the cruiser, were now pristine.

Sophie and Craig climbed out. Sophie bolted for Lillian and wrapped her arms around her aunt.

Lillian hugged her back just as hard.

Sophie straightened. "We're okay, that just really sucked."

Craig took Sophie's hand in his. "I didn't mean for you to get caught up in this, I'm so sorry."

"It wasn't your fault. Your stepdad's an ass."

Lillian knew she would get the full account. For now, it was enough that Sophie was safe. And Craig—he really did seem like a good kid.

"You guys are good?" Becca asked.

Both Sophie and Craig nodded.

"Good." Becca took a cautious step toward Officer Chasseur. "Can I talk to you?"

He was standing in the open door of the RCMP cruiser, one hand on the roof of the car, one hand propped onto the top of the open door. He would not look at Becca. His face could have been carved in granite, and his mirrored sunglasses hid anything his eyes might give away.

The officer's jaw clenched. "No."

"Jason—"

"Please address me as Officer Chasseur."

"So that's how you want it?"

"That's how it is." He took off his mirrored sunglasses then. He addressed Craig and Sophie then, "Stay out of trouble. I mean it, the gun and ten thousand dollars behind the seat of the truck is a problem."

Lillian's head was swimming. That was enough money to get people bent out of shape, including judges or border control.

"Auntie, I swear it wasn't ours and we certainly didn't know it was there."

Officer Chasseur agreed. "Just keep your noses clean. And for the love of God, don't borrow any more vehicles. We'll get this is sorted." Officer Chasseur turned to go.

"Is my NOC 5251 status affected?"

"You're an athlete?"

Sophie nodded.

"Depends what the judge says."

Colt's sister stepped forward. "But you'll help her and Craig, right?"

Officer Chasseur looked annoyed. "Why would you think I didn't already?"

Becca took another step towards Officer Chasseur. "One of these days you'll realize I'm not the horrible person you think I am."

The officer put his sunglasses back on before finally looking at Becca. "Prove me wrong."

A silver Jaguar pulled up then.

"Who's that?" Sophie asked.

Lillian whispered back, "I haven't gotten the spreadsheet yet."

A tall, thin man got out. The pallor and slight sag of his skin suggested he had been recently ill, though his features were still classically handsome. Except his eyes. They looked cruelly calculating. Lillian was immediately wary of him.

The man turned to Becca. "I forgive you."

Becca crossed her arms. "What are you doing here, dad?"

"You didn't attend my wedding. I'm here to tell you all is forgiven."

Becca turned to Officer Chasseur. "Can you arrest him? Like for anything, anything at all?"

The front screen door slammed open, and Tucker raced down the steps.

"Are you fucking kidding me? Get out of here. You're not welcome."

Colt strode out the front door, taking in the scene. He put a hand on his brother's chest, but he looked at Officer Chasseur. "That wasn't directed at you so stop looking ready to jersey Tuck."

Lillian leaned in towards her niece. "In what context is *jersey* a verb?"

"I think it's a hockey thing," Sophie whispered back.

Another pair of headlights rounded the drive and a red beemer with the top down came to a stop. A beautiful older woman emerged. She wore designer jeans and a bit too much jewelry. She leaned back in and pulled out two large take-out bags. In a sing-song voice she crooned, *"Surprise! I brought dinner."*

Lillian watched the older woman in awe as her face crumpled, as good as any starlet, and she said in a dramatic pout, "I see you invited your father instead of me."

Chapter Twenty-Nine

It was like watching a tornado get closer with no escape. Everyone started talking at once.

Colt leaned against the rough-hewn fence lining the yard, ignoring the angry remarks directed at him from both of his parents, when they weren't taking verbal shots at each other and their other children. Bruce yelled some rather slanderous remarks about Officer Chasseur's parentage while Becca was pleading with her dad to stop. Tucker was using his pissed-off cop voice, but neither parent was leaving.

Lillian walked up, her hands in her pockets. "A diagram would work, too."

"What?" Colt was embarrassed for the second time that day. It wasn't like he and Lillian were anything to each other, but did his family have to be themselves, now?

A half smile played at her lips. "You weren't joking about your family. A spreadsheet or diagram would be fine."

Colt crossed his arms. "Two days ago, my dad wasn't even speaking to Becca and Tuck. Now he shows up uninvited and blasts them for not going to his wedding?" Colt shrugged. "I have no idea why he has a hate-on for Jason, and my mom has an eerie talent for showing up with take-out when she wasn't invited to something."

Lillian flinched as Colt's mom hurled a particularly nasty comment at her ex-husband, then at Becca and Tucker.

"I don't think I've ever heard those phrases."

"Translates just fine." Colt said without humor.

"Are you usually the referee?"

"My older brother, Gabe, is way better at it than me. Tucker gets too worked up."

She leaned in and nudged him with her shoulder. "I've got your back."

"Thanks, I appreciate that." Colt pushed off the fence *"Enough."*

A stunned silence followed his command.

"Officer Chasseur, thank you for giving Sophie and Craig a ride. I'll call you tomorrow."

"Since when are you buddy-buddy with the Chasseur kid?" his father snarled. "And lookie there, little Craig Cameron."

"Not fucking now, dad. Don't be a dick."

Colt rarely lost his temper. It was gratifying to see Bruce take several steps back. Maybe Colt was channeling his inner Gabe.

He turned then, bringing his hands up in a prayer position. "Lillian, Sophie, Craig—I'm sorry you had to witness that. Could you please go inside with Becca and Tucker?"

When the five had filed inside, Colt turned to his parents.

"This is a new low, even for you two."

"Don't you want to spend time with me?" Tears threatened to spill from his mom's heavily made-up eyes.

"Mom, we both know those are crocodile tears."

Bruce smirked and Colt turned on him. "That was really shitty, to Becca and Tucker, and Office Chasseur and Craig."

"Don't use that tone with me, I'm sick."

His mom asked, "What do you mean you're sick?"

"He's not sick, ignore him." Colt pointed down the drive. "Please, just go, both of you."

His mom stepped towards Colt, whimpering. "Why don't you love me?"

Colt pointed down the long country driveway.

Bruce's face contorted. "This isn't finished."

But both parents got into their respective vehicles. In moments they were heading out the drive.

Officer Chasseur remained.

Colt watched his parents' taillights. When both vehicles were gone, he blew out a long breath.

"Gabe always was better at handling our parents. Does CSIS have dealing-with-whack-job training?"

"I don't know, you handled yourself pretty good." Officer Chasseur was thoughtful. "That was...shocking."

"That was one of the lighter blow ups."

The officer looked at him closely. "With bulls it's nothing personal?"

"Amen, to that, brother."

The officer nodded, like he had figured something out. "Do you have time for a chat tomorrow?"

Something in the officer's voice gave Colt pause.

"I'll make time."

"I appreciate that. Can Craig stay with you for a couple days?"

Colt nodded, curious.

"Good. I'll give you a call. I have to check a few things, first. Keep your eyes open."

"Always."

Officer Chasseur slid into his cruiser and drove away.

Colt headed up the porch stairs. He crossed to the porch swing and slowly lowered himself.

He felt every creak the swing offered up like it was his own. He pushed with his boot and the swing rocked gently. He hadn't felt this crappy since the last time he was home.

If it felt better to stay away, why did he keep coming home?

Chapter Thirty

"Is this seat taken?" Lillian gave Colt a cautious smile. He was sitting on the porch swing, his arm casually draped across the wooden frame.

She had a beer in each hand and held one out to him. "I'm prepared to bribe with libations."

He took one of the bottles. "That's an offer I won't refuse."

Lillian sat down next to him.

Colt twisted the bottle top and held the open beer out to her.

She hesitated a moment before accepting it, passing him the unopened one in her hand. Colt opened the second beer and took a long pull from it.

"You opened my beer for me."

"Is that a problem?"

"I'm just not used to men doing that."

"You hang out with the wrong men."

"So I've been told." She took a sip.

Colt moved one arm to the back of the porch swing again.

She was *almost* tucked into him. "That was kind of intense."

The swing rocked gently. "Sorry you had to see that."

"Is your family always like that?"

"Bat shit crazy? More often than not. They're like a bad adrenaline high to come down from."

"Not everyone understands adrenaline."

Those North Sea eyes held her gaze. "You sound like you do."

The only sound was the rhythmic creaking of wood as Colt gently pushed the swing with his boot.

She picked at a corner of the bottle label. "I used to be a war correspondent, and a courier for MI6."

He blew out a breath before taking a sip of his beer. "Well, that explains a few things."

"Not everything." She wanted to confide in him. "I'm broken, broken."

"You mentioned that." Colt stood. "Bring your beer."

"Where are we going?" Lillian stood, too, and followed him off the front porch. He walked around to the far side yard. A woodshed was tucked into the tree belt and about half full. There was a large pile of sectioned trunks waiting to be split.

"You've got anger built up, right?" Colt asked her.

Lillian thought back to their interview. She had been awful. "I try to keep it squashed down, but it bubbles out. Sorry I was such an arse earlier."

An axe was embedded in a large stump that sat about two feet high. Colt gripped the handle and wiggled it free. "Here."

"You're chopping wood?"

"No, you are. It's a pressure valve. Try it." His eyes were serious.

"I usually run."

Colt put a piece of wood vertically on the stump. It was smaller in diameter than a stove piping.

"Try splitting this." He held the axe back out to her. "Have you ever split wood?"

"No."

"Move back a sec." She backed up. Colt gripped the axe with two hands. He stood near the stump. His feet were about shoulder width apart. In a single smooth motion, he rounded the axe up before swinging it down. Lillian noticed him wince.

The blade bit through the chunk of wood, slicing it in two pieces that fell off the stump. He grunted a bit when he tugged the axe out of the stump and grabbed one of the smaller pieces. This time he held the smaller piece by the side as he tapped the blade in. Once stuck, he lifted the axe and struck the piece of wood sticking off the end against the stump. The heavy axe head sunk halfway through.

He repeated the motion, effectively splitting it through. "Still a little big for kindling, but you get the idea."

"You winced."

"I pulled the muscles between my ribs."

Lillian looked at her hands. Only scars remained, reminding her she had trusted the wrong person. If he could swing an axe with pulled muscles, she could give it a go. She held out her hand. "I'll try."

She tried to mimic his motions. Her first try sunk the axe head into the wood, grossly off-center.

"Tap it down," he said.

Lillian did as he suggested. With each strike, the metal head sunk lower.

"Really give it hell."

Lillian bit her lower lip and swung. The blade cut smoothly through. The two smaller pieces of wood dropped the ground in a satisfying plunk.

"That felt good."

Colt smiled and set up another block of wood.

Lillian lined herself up and hefted the axe like she saw Colt do.

Split.

"I did it!"

Colt smiled. "Yeah, you did." He set up another log for her.

This time it took her three tries before the axe bit cleanly through wood.

Several minutes later she was sweating, panting, and thrilled to see the growing pile of split logs.

Lillian swiped her hair out of her eyes and set up another one. "I average about a hundred kilometers a week running, but this—this feels incredible."

Colt was staring at her. "You run a hundred kilometers a week? Why?"

She tossed the last two pieces of wood towards the growing pile by the woodshed, before notching the axe back in the stump. "It's the only thing I've found to keep me together. Well sort of."

"I'm listening."

He was. Colt's face was open and curious, not a trace of guile anywhere. He wasn't anything like Fernando.

Lillian took a deep breath. "Two years ago, the guy I thought was my boyfriend, turned out to be a double-agent selling State secrets."

"Oh."

"It gets worse. He seduced me to get access to British intel—which I didn't have, and even if I did, I wouldn't have given that wanker anything, even before I knew what he was about. I was tried for treason earlier this year. I was exonerated, but not before my twenty-year career imploded. For two years the tabloids skewered me and my family, and most of my so-called friends abandoned me."

"Holy shit."

Lillian shrugged and picked up her beer. "The guy was an idiot. In the world of international espionage, I'm seriously a nobody." Ultimately, that's what had saved Lillian during her trial. "Worst boyfriend ever."

She took a long pull from the longneck.

"And that's why you're doing local interest pieces here?"

Lillian nodded. "The kind of stink I have on me doesn't wash off. My grandmum thought I should come here, with Sophie. The kid's on the British Biathlon team and they're training here."

She heard the pride in her voice. Sophie knew what she wanted. Lillian was a puppet, at least as far as Fernando was concerned, and possibly her grandmum.

"And you?"

Lillian looked across the ranch yard. The sun had sunk lower but was still a brilliant fiery ball in the fading blue sky. A few wisps of clouds, brushed golden pink, stretched across the sky. All of the trees ringing Becca's yard stood tall and proud, though it was the aspen that caught her attention. Their bright green, spade-shaped leaves made a cascading rustling sound as they fluttered against each other in the breeze.

She breathed deep, letting her surroundings sink deep inside. "Canada wasn't my first choice, but it's growing on me."

Those North Sea eyes were looking at her with a banked fire that made her feel warm all over.

It made her feel brave. "I didn't expect to like anything about this place. I didn't expect you."

"And what am I?"

"I'm still figuring that out.

"Your ex-boyfriend is an idiot."

Lillian felt the tug of a smile.

"And you are *not* a nobody."

Her smile faltered. Colt's words, so sweet, dared her to face a very old, very raw, wound within her.

"Come on, you're smart, you're beautiful." He gave an exaggerated sniff. "And you most definitely don't stink."

His humor wrapped around her, and she let herself laugh. "Liar. I was just chopping wood." She tried to discreetly tuck her arms tighter around herself.

His dimples reappeared. "You're good with an axe."

"It was kind of perfect."

"Come over anytime." Colt tugged the axe out of the stump and put it in the woodshed. "I try to keep ahead of it for Becca. The wood pile I mean. She hates asking for help, so I just do it anyway."

"I like your sister." Lillian felt a kinship to Becca. Maybe given a chance, they could be friends. Lillian dearly missed real friends.

"Good." Colt was standing close to her again. He smelled like forest and man.

"We should go in."

He looked into her eyes. "Why's that, U.K.?"

She blinked. "When are your finals?"

"You want to watch me ride?"

"Maybe." Lillian's skin tingled, including her lips. "Don't read too much into this."

"Into what?"

She leaned forward and briefly pressed her lips against his.

He licked his lower lip. "What was that for?"

"Research."

"Into me?" He sounded a bit affronted.

"No. Into me." Her body was tingling, and her heart was galloping.

He dipped his head.

Restless, maybe a little desperate, Lillian grabbed the back of Colt's head and gave herself to the kiss. Of all people, this considerate, *younger* cowboy had blown past her carefully constructed defenses.

Then he did something delicious with his tongue, resuscitating long-dormant passion buried within her. She kissed him back, harder.

The sound of a vehicle coming up the drive interrupted them.

Reluctantly, Lillian broke the kiss. They stared at each other, both breathing hard. Colt still had his arms around her.

Finally, she whispered, "Who is that?"

"Looks like Clint."

Lillian pulled out of his embrace. "Clint, who?"

"Clint Steele. He's an old family friend."

Lillian took another step back.

She didn't like coincidences, and there were too many stacking up. She needed that INCEPT check.

Colt waved to the approaching vehicle and started walking towards the front porch. Lillian hesitated before following him.

The older cowboy climbed out of his truck. He held a white bakery box.

Colt smiled. "Clint, I'm glad you're here. I'd like you to meet Lillian Kensington."

Lillian hoped her smile wasn't brittle when she said, "We've met."

"Pleasure to see you again, ma'am," Clint said, touching the brim of his cowboy hat. "This is—"

The screen door banged open, and Becca popped out.

"Oh, hi Clint. Perfect timing, dinner's ready." She eyed the white bakery box. "Ooh, what'd you bring?"

"Brownies." Clint nodded towards Lillian. "I see you've met Lillian. You can give her pointers on how to handle Colt."

Becca's gaze darted between Lillian and Colt. "Why would I do that?"

"She's the journalist I was telling you about. She's a hell of a reporter, with as much spunk as you, Becca."

Becca looked at Lillian with renewed interest. "Really? That's awesome news. I'm hopeless when it comes to marketing, and I already like you."

Colt was staring at Lillian. "You're the journalist?"

"You're my field guide?" Lillian's voice was an undignified squeak.

Becca raised both arms in a victory salute, laughing. "And I'm getting kick-ass marketing material. Pick up your chins, they both seem to have dropped to the ground."

Lillian tried to tamp down her rising panic. What was she doing? She couldn't afford to be so careless. Lillian had only been a pawn to Fernando, but he was possessive and dangerous. She cared for Colt, and his family; they were good people.

What if that made them all a target?

Chapter Thirty-One

"Thanks for meeting me." Officer Jason Chasseur slid into the worn cafe booth across from Colt.

Several locals stared. A few bold souls even turned around in their seats to watch. It was a small town and the rift between Jason Chasseur and the Tanner family was well-known.

A waitress with a bad dye job and a lot of makeup stopped at their booth and poured coffee in their mugs.

They ordered the breakfast special. When she lingered, Jason smiled. "Thanks, we're good."

When she still didn't leave, he raised an eyebrow. "Can I help you?"

She huffed off.

Colt doctored his coffee with cream and sugar. "I hate being a spectacle."

"Isn't your Stanley Cup in Vegas?" Jason took a sip of his black coffee.

"Point taken."

Colt tried his coffee. It was awful. "You were way nicer than I wanted to be."

"I'm a nice guy."

"I'm starting to figure that out. Why aren't we supposed to hang out, again?"

"Your dad got my dad arrested when we were in high school," Jason retorted.

"Right. What about Becca?"

Jason's eyes turned icy. "What about Becca?"

Colt could hear people murmuring. They still had an audience. "Never mind. Why did you ask me here?"

Jason lowered his voice. "What do you know about Lillian Kensington?"

"Next to nothing, why?"

"You were seen at Stampede with her."

Colt didn't like Jason's tone.

"Yeah, she was interviewing me."

Jason pulled out his cell phone and held it out. The screen showed a photo of Colt and Lillian on horseback, the day he had been moving cattle.

"Where did you get that?"

"There's more." Jason handed him his phone. There were images of Lillian trail running, driving, walking into stores. Colt enlarged the next image. It was a photo of her in a bookstore with Clint.

Colt looked up. "Is this a joke?"

Jason's face was dead serious. "No."

Colt scrolled through the rest. There were more photos of Lillian. The last several were of Colt and Lillian at Stampede, sitting at the outdoor restaurant and the picnic table near the food trucks.

Several scenarios started pinging through Colt's head. He had to stop watching so many cop television shows.

He handed the phone back to Jason. "What's going on?"

"I was hoping you could tell me. Do you know Craig's stepdad?"

"Just by reputation."

Everyone in town knew Philip Kasser. The guy was a bruiser.

Jason pressed. "Do you know why he has photos of Lillian?"

"Beyond him being a creepy fucking asshole? No." Colt grabbed Jason's phone and flipped through the images again. "Seriously, this is creepy fucking shit."

"The truck the kids borrowed had a duffle bag with over half of those images. They were printed on regular photocopy paper with a web code on the bottom. I did a search for that code and found an unprotected share site. That's when I found the rest of the photos."

"That sounds unreasonably easy."

Jason took his phone back and pocketed it. "Not every criminal is a mastermind, or they wanted us to find it. And to be fair, the photos are technically not criminal. The unregistered handgun and ten thousand dollars in cash is another story."

Colt's head shot up. "A gun?"

"The kids' prints are not on the gun, cash, photos or even duffle bag. I believed them, but it helps to have evidence back up their story."

Colt ran his hands through his hair and blew out a breath. "What the fuck."

"The gun, photos and cash are worrisome."

"You sound like Gabe or Tucker. Why don't you guys ever call it what it is? Bad. Dangerous. Shit."

Jason leaned back. "Jumping to conclusions is sloppy police work."

Colt raised an eyebrow. "If one believes the media, there are a lot of sloppy cops out there."

Jason held up a hand. "Point taken."

Colt waited a beat. "Rough time to be a police officer."

"It's a hell of a lot rougher for some of the public."

"Do you get stuck in the middle?"

Jason asked, "Being both, you mean?"

Colt nodded.

"All the time." Jason rested his elbows on the table and steepled his hands in front of his face.

Both men were silent.

Jason cleared his throat. "About Craig. His stepdad always has had a heavy hand."

This wasn't news.

"Craig isn't talking. I assume he's trying to protect his mom." Jason flexed his hand.

The nosey waitress came with their specials. She held the plates, waiting.

"Those ours?" Colt asked.

The waitress slammed them on the table before leaving.

Colt asked, "What is up with her?"

"I arrested her kid for cooking meth last month."

"Um . . . are you sure we should be eating this, then?"

"Her son had drained her life savings and started using her as a punching bag. She's probably more mad at herself than at me."

"You guys are mental. I don't know how you do what you do."

Jason picked up his fork. "You're a bull rider."

Colt sniffed the food. "Smells fine."

Jason had already started eating his.

"Craig has no backup in that house. His mom keeps choosing his stepdad over him."

Colt added ketchup to his hash browns. "How can I help? I mean, he's more than welcome to stay with me for a while longer."

"With your sister starting that highfaluting eco-inn and dude ranch, does she need a hired man, one that can bunk up there? He's a whiz as a mechanic, but I doubt what he's making at that garage is enough for him to move out."

"I can ask. You're looking to find him a decent job?" Colt's own upbringing had been fucked, but he had never worried about where he was going to sleep, or if his person would be physically safe.

"Yes. Craig needs someone who will give him a chance, so he can find his bearings. Becca's found a way to plant roots, in spite of your family's, shall we say, *challenges?*"

"I call it fucked up drama, but sure, we can go with challenges. I'll talk to my sister." Colt started eating.

"I appreciate it." Jason hesitated. "I wasn't sure you'd even hear me out."

There were a lot of more obvious options Officer Chasseur could have reached out to for help with Craig.

Why had the police officer chosen Becca?

Chapter Thirty-Two

Early morning light filtered into the compact condo kitchen. Lillian sat at the table, her second tea long forgotten at her elbow, and stared at the open letters in front of her. The package had arrived first thing that morning, as Omran said it would, and contained letters Piety had received from Obedience over a span of several years.

They were rather ordinary looking, considering they were penned by a daring adventuress, and Lillian wondered how many correspondences between women held similar treasures and whose stories would never be told.

Sister, this land is as wild as I have always wanted to be. The forests go on forever, and the rivers are watery roads to the unknown. You would be shocked to know the skills I am learning. Just yesterday I shot and killed an elk. That sounds as alarming as it is, but practical. The land and flowing water are the only markets, and one's ability to procure food from such matters quite strongly here. I do not care a wit that men are supposed to be the ones to hunt. Our provisions were running low—pray tell, what was I supposed to do? The creature was right there. As it was, my propriety misstep caught the attention of one of the men in our small group. His family hales from much further east, but he criss-crosses the land, traveling extraordinary far distances in his trading. Since the elk, he pays more attention to me, much to Seamus' irritation. The rules of civility are different here. We travel often between posts and forts, and I meet devils, angels, and all manner between. Seamus protects me, though he loses patience. I know at times I am a hindrance. Other times, I know I remind him of a softer existence, which I think he appreciates. The tension between England and France has spilled into everyday life, just like at home. The French traders are amenable to Seamus, though our countrymen are not. This year we are to travel further afield. We left the western most great inland seas weeks ago. Tomorrow we will make our way to the mighty river that will take us west to mountains bigger than I can imagine. Our destination is a post called Roche Cachée. I am told the journey will be long, but beyond that I can not say, sister. I am awed daily. I do not wish to alarm you, but sometimes I am frightened, too. I have made friends with some of the local women, and when we reunite after long trips away, I am happy they welcome me back, though this trip perhaps a whole year will have passed before I see them again. There are none of our countrywomen here, and as we know, men's company can get tedious without the respite of women's sensibilities. I miss you and think of you often. Though there are perils here, I can't imagine a life under Lord Brantford's thumb. I am thankful everyday with my decision to alight from Geoffrey's persistent attentions. And you? Are you well and happy? What news from Cornwall? How is your husband? Does Moma visit like she promised she would? I wake up wishing you good morning and fall asleep wishing you good eve. Your dearest sister, BeeBee

Lillian picked up *BeeBee's* journal. She studied each map critically, focusing on the information they were meant to communicate, instead of their inherent beauty. Again and again, she flipped back to the one with the line of chevrons.

Sliding her laptop over, she pulled up contemporary watershed maps of North America. As Lillian stared at color-coded images of watersheds, in her mind's eye, she tried to transpose *BeeBee's* maps over the contemporary data. The distances those in the fur trade traveled was truly mind boggling. Non-Indigenous women simply did not venture into colonial hinterlands. The contemporary applause the few wealthy Euro Canadian women of generations past continued to receive for having ventured beyond their gilded front doors was a split victory—it raised awareness of the containment and limited opportunity for white women at the time, while completely dismissing the very existence of Indigenous women. It was that automatic dismissal that needed to be healed. Promptly. *BeeBee's* maps illustrated her travels were outside of what would have been considered the outer most frontier spheres. Any woman in her life would have been Indigenous.

Lillian gently refolded the letter and picked up another.

I am married in the ways of the country, dear sister. I wish you could have been here. The ceremony was brief but meaningful. Seamus is not pleased, though I do not know why. I am a constant irritation to him and I am sure he regrets daily bringing me with him. I would think he would have been delighted. Dajoji is well-respected, a capable provider. Truly, I do not know what has gotten into Seamus. He barely talks to me now, and finds reason to go off on his own often. I do not know what to make of his behaviour, it is most vexing, indeed. I do not have much time to ponder, though. There is always much work to be done and I am sorry indeed my letters have been so scarce. As a married woman, that which is expected of me has shifted. Before, being unmarried, white and female, I occupied an uncategorized social space. Life is different now. I am often mistaken for local, my dark colouring that Moma lamented so loudly growing up, has served me well here. People see what they expect to see, and no one expects an Englishwoman. Seamus has long expressed fear I would be kidnapped, though I think he exaggerated to keep me reasonable. He needn't have worried, I would never have left his side for anything less than marriage. Oh dear, I just realized that must sound dreadfully dangerous. Sister, I assure you I am fine. Exhausted, but fine. Hello to your dear family. I miss you, sister. I try not to think of never seeing you in person again. Perhaps one day we will share our secrets over a pot of tea, like when we were girls. Much love, BeeBee.

Lillian's stomach growled and she stood then, stretching. She cleared her tea dishes and made herself a simple sandwich. She had resumed running outside with her security detail without incident, or inner alarm bells, but had skipped this morning's run when the letters had arrived. She paced the condo now as she ate, eager to stretch her legs. She made another circuit of the small living room as she contemplated *BeeBee*. In her inattention, she stubbed her toe on the carton of documents she had left in the living room.

Awareness tingled through her body.

Popping the last bite into her mouth, she dusted her hands on her shorts and looked down. Next to the askew carton, and partially hidden under the sofa, lay a single volume. Lillian picked it up. Gently, she opened the front cover and read the first sentence.

BeeBee is going to be the death of me.

It was Seamus O'Malley's journal.

Chapter Thirty-Three

Tucker pulled a longneck out of the refrigerator and sat down on his leather couch. He propped his feet up on the rough-hewn coffee table and pulled out his phone.

Gabe answered on the first ring.

"We have a problem," Tucker said.

"What did Mom or Dad do now?"

"Nothing. Well, mom has a new boyfriend, but that's not why I'm calling."

"Who?"

"Clarence."

"The only Clarence I know is dad's cousin."

"Yup."

"Gross. And he's a putz."

"I know that. But you know how mom gets. Anyway, do you still have spook buddies?"

Tucker waited for the familiar retort from his brother. He wasn't disappointed.

Gabe sighed. "They're not spooks, they're just regular people who happen to have spooky abilities."

"Like I said, spooks. Anyway, Colt's got a new lady-friend. Some sort of war correspondent—slash—MI6 courier."

"Colt?" Gabe asked, incredulous. "How did he snag a woman like that?"

Tucker dropped his feet down on the floor, siting up. "I know, right? The guy's got groupies coming out of his ying-yang, but he brings home a fucking war journalist. Clint recognized her straight off. Her grandma is some securities minister coalition lead—whatever the hell that is."

"Are you talking about Lillian Kensington?"

"Yeah, that's her."

There was a low whistle. "That family is connected." Gabe paused a beat. "Seriously, *our* brother and *that* woman? He's a bull rider. She's cultured and worked for MI6."

"You forgot smokin' hot. I will never look at women in their forties the same way."

"Damn." Gabe asked. "How did they meet?"

"That's the weird part. She was interviewing him. She's covering local rodeos."

"Wow, how the mighty tumble. You know she was charged with treason, right?"

Tucker sat forward. "No. How did I miss that? Anyway, she's gotten cozy with Becca, too. Something just feels off. And like you say, your friends have spooky abilities."

"I'll find out what I can. In the meantime, call Andy if you need backup."

"Is he cleared for duty?"

"Not even close, but he will know who to send if you need help."

Tucker cleared his throat. "How are you holding up?"

Andy was Gabe's best friend and had recently barely survived a bridge collapse in Northern Alberta.

There was a heavy pause.

"Jackass nearly died on me. Thank God his head is even harder than mine."

"Andy's a tough S.O.B."

"He is."

Gabe's brevity spoke volumes.

"Tucker?"

Gabe's voice gave Tucker pause.

"Yeah?"

"Sorry I kept you guys away five years ago, you know, when I was recovering."

After Gabe had been shot in the head on a CSIS mission. He had chosen to recover alone. Tucker couldn't blame him for keeping their parents out. It had stung that Gabe had kept the siblings out, too.

"No prob."

Tucker picked up his unopened beer and popped the top.

"Did you just crack a beer?"

Gabe's voice sounded almost wistful. Tucker wondered if his aloof older brother was a little homesick.

Tucker took a swallow of beer before answering, "You could have one with me. Are you guys still at Becca's? Why don't you drive into town, we'll make it a boys' night?"

"Can't, we're still in Jasper."

"Colt made the finals on Sunday. Will you guys be back by then?"

There was a brief hesitation. "Yeah, we can make that happen."

Tucker was surprised. His older brother avoided most family functions.

"Gabe?"

"Yeah?"

"You know how Colt doesn't get weird over women?"

"Uh-huh."

"He's getting weird over this one."

Chapter Thirty-Four

L illian drove with the window down and the radio off along the lonely township road. She thought of Seamus O'Malley. He had been in love with *BeeBee*, that much was clear from his writing. *BeeBee*, bless her heart, hadn't a clue. It must have gutted Seamus to see her marry another. Lillian still had to finish reading the letters. She hoped his story was more than unrequited love.

An image flashed in Lillian's mind, of the three young women who had all vied for Colt's attention during the interview. Lillian's love life was not faring any better than Seamus'.

The vehicle's GPS chimed, saving Lillian from exploring her crush on a man a decade younger, and she turned into Becca's long driveway.

Colt's sister's inn was situated about half a kilometer from the highway, but it felt much more isolated. The roll of the land hid all trace of civilization except the gravel road and a single power line wire. The mountains could be seen beyond, and looked impossibly large as the early morning sunlight lit their stark faces in brilliant beauty.

A hawk hovered overhead, and she slowed the car to a stop. Its wings beat as it held its position. Suddenly, it dropped out of the sky, landing on the ground with impressive speed. A moment later the hawk was holding the unlucky prey in its powerful talons, while it ripped apart the small rodent with its beak. Lillian stared at the raw scene unfolding before her, unsure how to feel. There was no ego, no agenda beyond survival—living for the hawk and dying for the rodent.

In that moment, nature made her uncomfortable.

Lillian gave the scene one last look before she eased off the brake and the car rolled down the lane. Her doctors were telling her she had to be the damn hawk.

The gravel drive widened into a courtyard of sorts, flanked by outbuildings and corrals. Solar panels covered the surface of every roof. Two oversized residential wind turbines could be seen in the pasture beyond. Lillian parked her car between a pickup and an ATV, or *quad* as she had learned they were more commonly called here, and got out.

Clint Steele waved at her. He was outside a corral, his boot resting on the bottom rail, as he watched Colt.

Lillian walked up. "Good morning."

"It certainly is." A smile lit the older man's face, before he turned back to the horse and rider in the corral. "That kid's a natural."

She watched, curious. "Why do you say that?"

"See how little he uses the reigns?" Clint pointed. "And he's riding bit-less. He's using his body to communicate, using pressure and weight changes, just enough, to let that mare know what he needs. And she's answering. Hell, she's hanging on his every word." Clint nodded his approval. "Yes ma'am, it doesn't get much better than that."

"Why doesn't he train full time? I mean, could he?"

Clint tipped his hat back and scratched his forehead. He resettled it before answering. "He's got a waiting list. He could be in horses as long as he wanted."

Colt stopped the horse next to the fence then. The large animal blew out a breath and glanced at Lillian before nudging her head at Clint.

"What are you guys talking about?" Colt asked.

"You." Clint rubbed the bridge of the curious mare's nose.

Lillian felt herself blush at the older man's frankness, but Colt misunderstood. "I'm all yours until the finals on Sunday. Have you had a chance to coordinate with Becca?"

Lillian nodded. "We worked out what she wanted, and what I thought she needed, last night. I'm ready."

"Good. I just need a few more minutes."

Colt waited for Clint to give the mare a final rub before he clicked, turning the mount.

In moments horse and rider had resumed their paces. She hadn't done much riding back in England, only paying enough attention to not completely disgrace herself during equine-themed social events. She leaned her crossed arms across one of the corral rails, resting her chin on her wrist, and watched. Clint was right. What she was witnessing was pure magic.

She gave a half laugh. "Why hasn't some woman snatched him up?"

Clint slanted her an assessing-kind of look. He turned back to watch Colt. "That one, he's skittish."

Lillian misunderstood. "What do you do with a skittish horse?"

Clint smiled. "Give them a reason to join up."

"I don't know what that means."

Clint pushed off the rail. "You will."

Chapter Thirty-Five

"Y ou ride, right?" Colt finished adjusting the bridle on Jörð, one of his sister's quarter horses. They were in Becca's barn. The morning sunlight flooded through the high, wide windows.

Lillian eyed the massive saddle already on a second horse. "I ride English."

"You'll be fine," Colt assured her.

He walked under the horse's neck and adjusted the bridle on the other side. Jörð leaned into him for a nuzzle. He rubbed the mare's muzzle and wondered how to tell Lillian what Officer Chasseur had found. He didn't want to freak her out, but she should know she was being watched.

"You're sure comfortable around horses."

Lillian's words pulled Colt out of his thoughts. "I guess. Holda's ready to go. You can put your gear in her saddlebag. Just let me finish with Jörð, then you can hop up and I'll adjust your stirrups."

"Your sister has interesting naming practice for her horses." Lillian tucked her satchel in the saddlebag. It looked bulky and he wondered what she had packed. A compact camera and lens already hung across her torso.

"She moved back from Germany, but not before it made a very favorable impression." He walked over. "Do you need a leg up or a stool?"

"I think I can manage. But first tell me what's bothering you."

"What do you mean," he said slowly.

"Come off it. Tell me, whatever it is, I can take it."

"Jason—Officer Chasseur—asked me how well I knew you."

"Why?"

Colt blew out a breath. "Because he found a duffle bag in the truck your niece and Craig borrowed. It was hidden behind the back seat and had several printed images of you, ten thousand dollars cash, and a gun."

Lillian held his gaze, silent. He could tell the wheels of her mind were spinning, though.

"I thought you'd be more upset." He was. He was pissed.

"It's not the first time I will have been the subject of inquiry." She pressed her hand to her ear, and he wondered again about the small ear bud she always wore. He had never seen anything like it.

"Are you in some kind of trouble?"

She paused. "With my former line of work, I always have to consider the possibility."

That was a non-answer, if he'd ever heard one.

Lillian turned her attention back to her horse. She retrieved the reins before planting her left boot in the stirrup, but stopped.

She looked over her shoulder at him. "Thank you, though, for telling me."

"You're welcome."

"Can you do me a favor?"

Anything. "What do you need?"

"It's been a long couple of years. Let's just have a good day."

"Yes, ma'am."

If she wasn't worried, he would try his best not to be. He was fairly certain she wasn't telling him something, but a person had a right to their privacy. He would do his best to make her day a good one.

She leaned up, grabbed the saddle horn and hefted herself up. The camera slung around her torso barely shifted. Colt smiled as she wiggled around, finding her seat.

She caught him watching her. "English saddles feel different."

Colt started adjusting her left stirrup. "Yeah, I know what you mean. Don't tell the guys, but once in a while I ride English."

Lillian smiled. "Your secret is safe with me." She paused. "I thought Jörð and Holda were Norse?"

"Your guess is as good as mine. History was never my strong suit." Colt gently moved her leg into her stirrup. "How's that?"

He thought he caught her indrawn breath.

"Perfect," she breathed.

"Good." He circled the mare before he had the chance to do something stupid like squeeze her leg. He adjusted her right stirrup as fast as he could.

He packed what he needed in Jörð's saddlebags and mounted.

"Shall we?"

Lillian nodded, smiling, and Colt fell a little harder. He led the way out the barn. They walked their horses side-by-side. The summer sun sparkled on the water in the outdoor trough, and the bright green aspen leaves stood still in the calm morning. He kept an eye on Lillian. Holda was one of Becca's most docile mounts, but Colt wanted to be sure Lillian felt comfortable. "You doing okay?"

She closed her eyes a moment. "This was exactly what I needed. Thank you."

A rush of pleasure filled him, and he was glad he had thought to pack them a picnic lunch. He had no idea how long she wanted to stay out, but Colt could happily lose himself riding all day, especially if she kept looking at him like that.

"Good, there's no wind."

Colt raised an eyebrow.

"I picked up a UAV a couple months ago, and finally got the licenses I needed a couple weeks ago. Mind if we take aerial footage first?"

Colt blinked, finally understanding. "You have a drone?"

"Yes, and a fistful of permits."

She looked so animated.

"Sure, I know a place."

They headed north by north-west across the field and picked up an old logging double-track that circled a particularly photogenic ridge.

At the top, Lillian pulled her horse up short. "*Ohmygod.*"

Colt stopped, too. "Beautiful, isn't it?"

The trail had been flanked by poplar and spruce, but opened up to steeply rolling foothills. Beyond, the front range of the Rocky Mountains opened up. The rising sun lit the scene in a magnificent amber glow. The illuminated greys and browns of the rock faces were in stunning contrast to the different shades of green of the undulating grasses, and surrounding forests.

"Breathtaking," she whispered. She looked down before holding up her arm. "Look, I'm glowing, too. We're included."

Colt agreed. Lillian was beautiful awash in the golden light. She leaned back and pulled out her notebook from the saddle bag and started taking photos. Her horse obliged, dipping its head and standing idle. She took several photos and jotted down notes.

She snapped a photo of him.

"What are you doing?"

"Your sister wants marketing photos."

"Of the land."

Lillian gave him an indulging look. "I don't think you understand. You're what is called 'very marketable.'"

Colt shook his head before looking across the valley, taking in the view. He liked that she thought he was 'marketable'.

"Do you mind if I take some drone footage here?"

Colt pulled himself out of the fantasy he was building in his head. "Of course, how can I help?"

"Actually, after I get set up, can you ride down the trail, maybe two hundred meters, and then ride back?"

Damn.

"That I can do."

Lillian leaned back again. This time she pulled her satchel out from one of her saddlebags. She slung the strap around the saddle horn, and one-handed, pulled out the drone and handset. She fiddled with a few switches and within moments, a quadcopter floated above their heads.

"That looks pretty cool."

"Wait until you see the footage. It's amazing what these little guys can do." Lillian piloted the small aircraft, making sweeps and flying over the ridge. "Can you head down that trail?"

He did as she asked. They worked like that for the next few hours. It was a bit awe-inspiring to watch her work; she had a graceful intensity about her—a competent directness paired with a witty sense of humor. She directed him with ease and took his lead for riding the steeper trails and river crossings.

"Are you getting hungry?"

Lillian noticeably perked up. "You have food?"

Colt nodded. "Follow me."

They rode higher. He led them into a subalpine meadow. It was still early in the season, but shades of pink, orange and purple wildflowers bobbed in the gentle breeze. The rising front range of the Rocky Mountains towered beyond.

They dismounted and he pulled out a lightweight blanket and the picnic lunch he had packed.

Lillian steepled her hands, pressing the edge of her forefingers against her mouth and nose, and hooking her thumbs under her chin. "I didn't think this day could get any more perfect, but it did!"

Colt ducked his head, shy over her praise. He spread out the simple picnic he had packed: apples, grapes, crackers, cheese, a vegan tapenade, and bottles of carbonated water.

He wasn't sure what to do next, so he just said, "Help yourself."

Colt waited until Lillian had dropped onto the blanket before he sat, too.

"This looks perfect." She tucked in and he started to relax. He made himself a plate, too, and began munching.

"Do you know this land well?" Lillian asked, spreading tapenade on a cracker.

"Well enough to not get us lost if that's what you're asking."

"I trust you."

She paused, seeming to weigh her next words.

"Just ask. Whatever has you vibrating." He popped the cracker and cheese he had been holding into his mouth and waited.

"I'm looking specifically for *Fort Roche Cachée*. Do you, by chance, know where it is?"

Colt stared at the beaming woman sitting next to him. She had a dizzying number of layers.

"That's incredibly specific. Can you give me some context?"

"If I'm lucky, *Fort Roche Cachée* is on your sister's land. I'm also interested in *Fort La Jonquière*, but scholars don't agree on where it is. I've come across some references to it."

Lillian stopped talking and was suddenly incredibly fascinated with her apple.

Colt was still lost. He would so fail a history test right now. He waited, curious, for her to continue. Clouds scuttled above, and songbirds sang around them.

Finally, she spoke, "I've found a couple of references to those forts in old family letters."

"Sounds cool." He wasn't sure what else he was supposed to say.

"It is!" She stopped. "One of my several times great-aunts ran off to the New World in the mid-eighteenth century and worked in the fur trade."

"Didn't a lot of people do that?"

"Not women, not into the hinterland, and certainly not well-bred daughters. Ms. Obedience Beatrice Evans ran off to avoid an arranged marriage."

Colt cringed. "Her name was Obedience, and her parents arranged her marriage?"

Lillian nodded. "Her sister's name was Piety. She stayed in England."

It was super sexist, but his first thought was the women must have been rather plain, with names like that.

He wasn't particularly versed in history, but Lillian's words hit him—the women's lives sounded severely...contained. Obedience must have been quite the woman to so audaciously challenge such restrictive gender roles.

"It gets better. I think she made her way out here." Lillian's eyes were twinkling.

Colt spread his hand wide. "Out here, as in what is now Alberta?" He pointed at the ground. "Or out here, as in *here*."

"That's what I want to find out. White men were not considered to have traveled this far west in what is now Canada that early, and white women did not venture into hinterlands at all, let alone outside the known trade routes. To top it off, I think she married a local Indigenous man."

"In the mid-seventeen hundreds?" Colt rubbed his jaw. "Damn—good for them."

"I know, right? Her family back in England would have been quite put-out when she ran off with an Irishman. Imagine their reaction to her being be-friended by Indigenous women, and then marrying an Indigenous man?" She leaned forward. "A month ago, I didn't know any of this. Now, I'm chasing the most fascinating story of my career. Honestly, I didn't realize history could be anything beyond damning. *BeeBee*—that's what her sister called her—is inspiring me."

Colt watched the play of sunlight on Lillian's face. If Obedience Beatrice Evans was anything like her great-niece, the man who married her must have been the luckiest guy in the world.

He cleared his throat. "I've never heard of either of those forts, but I'll help any way I can."

"Really?"

She looked so surprised and hopeful, and her lack of presumption only endeared her more to him. Lillian Kensington was a mix of English order and worldly chaos; she had backstory in spades.

Aw hell, Colt had fallen for her.

Chapter Thirty-Six

"Fernando Martinez checked his Cayman accounts. Tech was able to drain seven of them. They're working on the last three." Agent Omran Forest stood in Dame Maighread Evans Coille Kensington's office.

Maighread sat behind her desk. Several files sat open, covering the wide space.

"Do we know if he suspects my granddaughter stole the blueprints?"

"We haven't picked up any intel to suggest one way or another. I was careful two years ago, but Martinez was picked up immediately after. There was a small window for him to realize."

Maighread tapped her desk with her middle finger. "That caliber of hydrogen technology should be powering airplanes and hospitals, not weaponized."

Agent Forest shrugged. "Weapons are more lucrative."

"Tell me about it." Maighread looked at one of the files open on her desk. "Are these balances right? That kind of money could bankroll a small army."

"They're correct."

Maighread swore. "We know he's without access to most of his assets—"

Agent Forest's hand moved to his ear a moment. "The last three have been drained, mum."

Maighread nodded. "Good. Now we just have to find the bastard. If he suspects Lillian, we need to find him before he kills my granddaughter."

Agent Forest looked at Maighread. "We did the right thing."

Maighread knew either choice was wrong. "Saving countless lives or saving my granddaughter's life, that's a bloody awful choice."

Agent Forest looked grim. "We'll find him first."

Chapter Thirty-Seven

"Colt, what are you doing here?" Lillian looked up at him. She was sitting at a table in the large downtown library's local history section. Her laptop was open in front of her, and around her was a fort of books. Some were open, some were in piles. Nearly all had sticky notes poking out of them. A stack of photocopies—the top one was a grainy photo, and a spiral notebook was also on the table. Her favorite pen was in her hand.

Colt held up the paper bag he was carrying. "I thought you might be hungry. Becca mentioned you were going to be here all day."

Lillian's eyes widen. "You drove all the way into town to feed me?"

Colt shrugged. "I was coming into town anyway."

"For what?"

Busted. He scratched the side of his jaw. "Hoping to run into you."

The smile Lillian gave him made him feel ten feet tall. "What is all of this?"

"Research. After our ride, Becca and I went over more of her international marketing plan. Meredith called—that's your dad's new wife, right?"

Colt nodded.

"She said something about a pipeline notification had arrived on the shared land, although she couldn't seem to find where Bruce had placed it."

"Probably framed it."

Lillian eyed him. "Another Alberta joke?"

More like a Bruce joke. Colt pulled out a chair and sat down next to her. "Kind of."

He put the paper bag he had been carrying on the table.

Lillian's eyes lit up. "That's seriously food?"

"Who's your favorite cowboy?" Colt teased.

"Trick question. You're my only cowboy."

The words hung in the air between them.

Lillian broke the charged silence first. "You're feeding me again."

"Is that a problem?"

"Heck no. Bring it."

"That's what I was hoping you'd say." Colt started pulling out food containers. "This is from Becca's favorite Lebanese deli. I remember you had a Mediterranean wrap at Stampede, so I went with that spice palette. Everything in this bag is vegetarian." He held up his hands. "And compostable, including the forks. Becca has trained me well."

Lillian looked startled.

"What? Did I forget something?" Colt wracked his brain, trying to figure out what he could have screwed up.

"You remembered what I ate?" She spoke slowly, like she was speaking unfamiliar words.

Colt stared at her. Didn't she know she was impossible to forget?

He placed an extra tzatziki sauce near her. "Seems I did."

Lillian closed her laptop and tucked it into her satchel on the floor at her feet. She stacked the open books in neat piles.

She held up her hands, fingers splayed. "I'm going to wash my hands, I've been handling old books all day." She disappeared into the washrooms on the outside wall.

Colt smiled and finished unpacking their food. Suddenly, an uneasy feeling interrupted his good mood. The back of his neck felt like goosebumps and a feeling of *wrongness* came over him. The last time he'd felt this way a grizzly had charged him. He had also gotten the same warning when a bull had busted out of his buddy's branding chute. Urban threats, however, were not in his wheelhouse. He wasn't like Gabe or Tucker.

Colt glanced around. A man stood several meters away, where the local history section abutted the regular stacks. He was next to one of the self-checkout stations, though he had no books with him.

Another man was standing closer, in the library-use-only section. He held a book in his hand, but Colt would bet he wasn't reading it.

Lillian reappeared and the man standing closer gave no notice of her, but zeroed in on the man at the checkout station and started walking towards him.

Immediately, the check-out station man moved.

Lillian smiled at Colt and sat down. "Thanks again for bringing dinner. I have a couple more hours I'd like to get in, but I was getting hungry."

He shot her a quick smile, before turning his attention back to the two men. If there was an altercation, he wanted to be between it and Lillian.

But the man that had been at the self-checkout station was gone. By the looks of it, the other man didn't know where he was, either. Colt looked around. How did a grown man just disappear?

"Are you okay?" Lillian asked.

"I thought I saw something. It's probably nothing."

Lillian frowned and glanced around. Did her gaze hesitate on the man Colt had noticed?

Before Colt could decide, she smiled brightly. "Shall we eat?" The smile didn't reach her eyes.

Colt ping-ponged his gaze between Lillian and the remaining man. "Sure."

Tucker's words rang through his head. *She's way out of your league.*

But the uneasy feeling was dissipating, and he convinced himself he must have imagined it. They opened their cartons and started to eat.

Lillian closed her eyes. "This is so good."

"Glad you like it." Colt motioned to the piles of books on the table. "So what is all this?"

"What?" Lillian blinked. "I did it again. I get distracted when you're around."

Colt liked hearing that. Still, he apologized.

"You must be used to it by now." Lillian leaned over and squeezed his cheeks between her thumb and forefinger. "You're the *Archambeau* guy."

"Stop that." Colt batted her hand away and took another bite.

Lillian sat back, smiling. "Your annoyance at your high-end modelling career is most endearing."

Colt glanced around them and pitched his voice lower. "No one here knows. I'd like to keep it that way."

"Like I said, endearing. And there's no one around, unless you count the man using the fake plant as a urinal."

"What?" Colt snapped his head around.

"I'm kidding. He left like ten minutes ago."

Colt turned back around. "I don't think I'll ever get used to big cities."

Did her face just fall a little?

She toyed with her fork when she asked, "Have you ever been to London?"

"Your London?" He shook his head. "I'd never had a reason to go before."

"Would you go now?"

"If you'll be my tour guide, I'll go today." He started to stand. "We can be there in ten hours."

Lillian laughed and tugged on his arm.

Colt smiled at her and sat back down.

She was still looking at him—kind of staring actually—her face radiant. Without thinking, he blurted, "You are so beautiful."

Damn, that was too fast. *Be cool, be cool.* He dipped his fork in his couscous.

She ducked her head. "Thanks. And to *finally* answer your question, Becca asked that since I was doing historical research on this area anyway, if I could keep my eyes open for anything on her parcels of land, or the crown land she leases."

His fork paused mid-air. "What historical research were you already doing? You mean your several-times great-aunt's letters?"

"Yes, those. And I've been trying to find more references to the early fur trade activity in the area, including anything on the forts or posts that are mentioned in the journals I brought. This food is amazing, by the way." She took another bite.

"You brought fur trade journals to Canada?"

Lillian nodded around another bite.

"From where? Do you work for a museum or something?"

"No."

Lillian started pushing the couscous and herbs around the take-out container with her fork. Colt waited.

Finally, she looked up. "They're from our family's estate library. Some of our ancestors worked in the North American fur trade. When they returned, they brought their journals home with them and they ended up in our library."

Not what he had been expecting. Colt wondered how many private family collections had historically significant artifacts.

"To us, they're family heirlooms; personal belongings that now have historical significance."

"I guess I never gave that sort of thing much thought."

Lillian put her fork down. "The ones I brought are from the North American fur trade, so they would be considered Canadiana and Americana now."

"So, you're doing a genealogical study?"

Lillian hesitated. "I guess I was just looking for an interesting project."

Colt had the feeling there was more to it, but who was he to pry?

"Need help with anything? I'm not a historian," he glanced at the piles of books, "or the world's best student." Colt had never been so acutely aware of his lack of formal education. Both Gabe and Becca had gotten master's degrees and Tucker an undergraduate. Lillian must have a fistful. Colt rode bulls.

Lillian was oblivious to his sudden rash of insecurity. She read from her notebook. "Do you know a Rose Chasseur, by chance?"

"Yeah. You've met her son."

Lillian's face was blank a moment. "Wait, the officer that kept yelling in the mud?"

Colt nodded.

She glanced at a man looking at one of the bookshelves nearby before saying, "That's a weird coincidence."

Colt followed her gaze. It was a different man than the one who had been there earlier.

He answered her, "Not really. What's the population of your London?"

Colt relaxed when the other man wandered off.

"Why do you call it *my London*?"

Colt ignored the new man at the stacks.

"For Canadians there are two: yours, and a town in Ontario with the same name. Great hardware store, by the way."

"'My London' is nine million, give or take."

"Combined, the prairie provinces—that's Alberta, Saskatchewan and Manitoba—are maybe seven million."

She looked startled. "Oh. That is a lot of low-density land."

"Welcome to western Canada. Playing six-degrees here is kind of not fair."

Lillian's shoulders visibly relaxed. "Then I guess it's not that weird. Her name came up in a few of the local histories I was reading. Her articles have a lot of great information, and photos, too. One of the forts she wrote about is called *Roche Cachée*. It's in two of the fur trade journals I have, too, but I haven't managed to find mention of it anywhere else. Some of the journals I have also discuss a *Fort La Jonquière*. Apparently, it is the earliest known western-most fort in what is now Canada, but historians don't agree on its location. Becca perked up when I mentioned *Fort Roche Cachée*. I'm guessing that pipeline notification has her a bit worried, and she's hoping for a re-route."

"I'm not an archaeologist like Gabe, but I think if an archaeological site is found and deemed significant enough by the provincial regulators, a pipeline could the-oretically be re-routed to avoid it. I have no idea how often that happens, though."

"Ms. Chasseur agreed to meet with me next week."

"She's a neat old woman."

"Colt!"

"What? She is interesting. And old."

Lillian picked up her fork again. "Can you still take me out sometime this week to work on the marketing content?"

In a heartbeat.

"Sure. I'm supposed to meet the guys tomorrow for lunch, but I can move it." Colt would rearrange his entire schedule if it meant he could spend more time with Lillian.

"How about we go the day after? Then you don't have to change your schedule and it'll give me extra time to make more of a plan and sketch out some content ideas."

"Sure, sounds great." Damn. Colt didn't want to wait an extra day before he got to see her again.

"Speaking of *Fort La Jonquière*, do you know where Fort Calgary is?" Lillian asked before taking another bite of food.

Colt hooked his left thumb and motioned behind his back. "Right there."

Lillian leaned over in her seat, looking beyond Colt's back. "You mean the white buildings with red trim?"

Colt turned in his chair. Being on the fourth floor, and the wall of windows, gave them an excellent view. "Yup. That's the one."

He turned back around. Genuinely interested, he asked, "What does *Fort La Jonquière* have to do with Fort Calgary?"

Lillian flipped back in her notebook. "According to an Inspector Brisebois of the North-West Mounted Police, the place he established as Fort Brisebois was built over what he thought was *Fort La Jonquière*, though that is still openly debated. It's one of four possible locations I've found so far. Anyway, Brisebois was apparently a bit of a wanker," she glanced up briefly, "I'm paraphrasing here, of course. From what I read, he was an abysmal leader, made irrational decisions and routinely abused his subordinates. During the Great March West—do you know what that is?"

Colt shook his head. He hadn't paid attention to local history beyond Stampede.

Lillian smiled. "I didn't either."

Colt snorted. "You're not from here."

"Don't ask me my take on English history: war, more war, marrying off our daughters to lecherous old men, still at war, noblemen—I'm using that word ironically—impregnating servants . . . did someone say war?"

Colt stared. More layers revealed.

She misunderstood his silence. "Sorry. I do value history, it's just so damn dark." She hesitated. "I try to find the bright spots of history, too, the flickers of hope."

"Tell me about the Great March West."

Lillian leaned forward. "Ottawa had been increasingly concerned about American wolfers and whiskey traders—hard men made harder by the U.S. Civil War—who were routinely coming north of the new border to sell booze and generally raise hell. The forty-ninth parallel was fairly porous at the time. In 1873, a group of them violently murdered approximately thirty Indigenous Assiniboine—many were women and children, allegedly over the perceived theft of horses. The massacre gobsmacked the Canadian public, which prompted government to finally create and deploy the North-West Mounted Police. It sounds like the Colonel who led the Great March West was a complete pillock, and the Great March West total omnishambles."

"Is that British for *shitshow*?"

"Yeah. It translates."

"What's a pillock?"

"An idiot. Colonel French led the march, and history has not painted him with a smart brush. Nor Brisebois. In 1875, he named a fort after himself and the men under his command were bloody unimpressed. Apparently, they thought him an elitist wanker. Instead of mutiny, they brought their grievances to Colonel Macleod. Macleod was well-respected and competent. He also outranked Brisebois. In 1876, Macleod renamed Fort Brisebois to Fort Calgary. Everyone was happy, except Brisebois, who resigned shortly thereafter in a huff."

"Your voice changed when you mentioned Colonel Macleod."

She sat back in her chair. "It did?"

"You respect him. Just like his men did."

Lillian paused. "I guess I do. There was a Superintendent Walsh, too. From what I've read, in a time of colonial ambitions, Macleod and Walsh appear to have been solid leaders. And unexpectedly sensitive to the Indigenous experience. Walsh gave Sitting Bull and his warriors ammunition to hunt and feed themselves. They had made it north of the border, but were starving after being aggressively hunted by the U.S. Calvary and out of ammo. Who does that? To act in trust and kindness during unstable, fractured times is rare, and beautiful." Lillian shrugged. "Of course, the books I'm pulling all of this from are history books, written with angles and agendas. Who knows, maybe everything I just said was white washed, too."

"Do you think it was?" Colt asked.

"I really hope not. We need those flickers of hope. We need stories of the kindness that occurs, not just pain."

Lillian suddenly sat up, her eyes shining. "*Ohmygod,* Sophie was right!"

"Sorry?"

"Just something my niece said." Lillian was glowing.

Her joyful outburst had lightened the mood. They talked and laughed as they ate their dinners. Lillian was smart, and nowhere near as stuffy as he had first suspected. Her obvious compassion and caring was paired with a wicked sense of humor.

Too soon, the food was gone. With dinner over, he should probably make a graceful exit. Instead, Colt motioned to the stacks of sticky-noted books. "Are you sure I can't help?"

"Really? Most people think this kind of research is boring."

Undoubtedly. But *she* wasn't boring, not by a long shot.

Colt shrugged. "Why not?"

"If you don't mind, then yeah, I'd love the help."

She handed him a neat, handwritten list of personal and place names.

"Can you check the indexes of those books," Lillian pointed at a stack, "with this list of keywords? And put a sticky note wherever you find them?"

"That sounds easy enough."

As Colt checked the indexes for the keywords and flagged them, Lillian went through the already-flagged books, making notes in her laptop. When he had finished his task, he picked up one of the books and started reading, paying special attention to all references of Macleod and Walsh.

When a librarian announced the library would be closing in fifteen minutes, Colt was surprised how much time had passed. He sat forward and rubbed his eyes. He had never spent this much time in a library before.

A young librarian wheeled a mobile book cart over to their table, asking Lillian, "How's the research going?"

"Great, thanks again for your help today."

"My pleasure." The librarian left the cart before heading off.

"You made friends with the librarians?" Colt would have been too shy to ask for help.

"Absolutely. Kindred spirits, and all that."

Colt felt on the fringe, though he had just gotten absorbed into reading a history book.

Lillian was shelving the library-use-only books onto the cart. She stopped when she noticed him looking at her. "What?"

He had never considered his world small, far from it. But hanging out with Lillian was expanding his. "Thanks."

"For what?" She looked up briefly. "You helped me."

"It was more interesting than I expected," Colt admitted, stacking books with her.

"Careful, you'll get sucked down researching rabbit holes. You can get lost for days."

Colt could think of worse things, like missing the chance to hang out with her.

"Thank you for your help. That went way quicker with two of us."

"Anytime." He meant it. "Are all of these books going on the cart or are you checking any out?"

"Most of these are library-use-only ones, but no, I don't have a library card."

That was a surprise.

"It should be easy enough to get one."

"I'm only in Canada two more months."

Her words dropped like a ton of bricks.

"Oh."

She gripped the handle of the cart. "I still have two whole months here, that is if you're not naffed-off with me?"

He wanted a hell of a lot longer than two months. For the first time since his imminent retirement, he felt a flicker of relief—he wouldn't be on the road the entire time she was here.

"I'd like that."

"I'll see you at Becca's the day after tomorrow, then?"

He nodded. "Can I give you a lift now?"

Lillian slung her satchel over her shoulder and ducked her head. "That's okay, I'm good. I travel light."

She wasn't blowing him off, but he had the sense she was keeping something from him, not that she owed him any explanations. Lillian glanced at him again but said nothing. It was then Colt noticed that the same man from before, was back.

"I'll walk you out."

She nodded. "I'd appreciate that."

He looked behind them. The man could have been discreetly following or ambling towards the exit. It was closing time.

"Mind if we take the stairs?" Colt asked. "That was a long time sitting."

"Sure."

The stairs were built as an architectural feature and not the most direct route anywhere. Colt slipped his hand around Lillian's. "Is this okay?"

She squeezed his hand in answer and Colt felt like he was walking on air.

Until they got to the main floor.

The first man, the one that had disappeared, was there watching them.

Chapter Thirty-Eight

"And I'm telling you we were being followed." Lillian was still in her running clothes, standing in the kitchen of the condo she and Sophie shared. Having a security detail at her disposal meant she could—in relative safety—run whatever time of day she wanted. Precious few women had that luxury. Fer-nando wasn't the only creep out there.

"The guy who followed you wasn't just one of the Jordemorden guys?" Omran asked over her secure phone.

"Positive." Lillian took a quick pull from her water bottle. "This guy was different. Not my first rodeo, you know."

"Again, with your vocabulary. I daresay you are as-similating."

She wasn't assimilating, she was falling for a damn cowboy.

"You're positive Fernando is in Europe?"

"You know I'd let you know if we thought he wasn't."

Lillian blew out a breath. She hated this not knowing.

"Bye auntie, I'm heading to practice."

Lillian scrambled around the kitchen corner to the living room. "Wait—"

But Sophie didn't hear her. The front door had already clicked shut.

She sighed.

"I heard that."

"You heard nothing. Remind me never to have kids. It's pure hell worrying about them constantly."

"She's a grown woman."

"She's nineteen," Lillian countered.

"Like I said."

"Agree to disagree. Anyway, I want to know who the man was at the library. My detail took a pic, but didn't get any hits back yet."

"I'm on it."

Lillian heard typing on the other end.

"His eyes were eerily icy." Though she wouldn't have classified them as mean, just cold. "And I'm pretty sure Colt noticed one of the Jordemorden guys."

"They're usually more covert than that."

"I know. I think they hovered tighter because of the other guy. I think he made them uneasy, too."

"Did you ask them?"

"No."

"Why not?"

"Because if I talk to them beyond the bare minimum, it hurts more when they die."

But she had slipped. She had looked the Jordemorden team in the eye, seen their intelligence and wit, felt their compassion and competence. If anything happened to them because of her, it would crush her that much more.

"Lillian—"

"Don't. It's how I've learned to cope." Or tried to. As a correspondent, she had witnessed the deaths of nine people protecting the different deployments she was in.

She thought of them often. Josh, Ethan, Martin, Frank, Eric, Sammy, Jesse, Paul and Sharon, bright lights blinked out way too soon.

Wiping her eyes, Lillian looked down at the encrypted email in front of her.

"Are you sure this INCEPT check is right? You did get it back rather fast."

Suspiciously fast, truth be told.

Omran cleared his throat. "I started it after your cattle drive escapade."

"How did you know it was him? I didn't even know who he was then."

"How do they say it there, *Gretzky is denied?*"

Lillian dropped her head back, staring at the ceiling. "I still hate your security clearance. It gives you more access into my life than I have."

Omran waited. It was an ongoing friction between them.

"I know who Gretzky is now."

"Congratulations." Omran said dryly.

"He's a big deal here."

Lillian always felt insecure when she moved somewhere new. It was hard to fly under the radar when she didn't understand the most basic of cultural nuances.

"Pretty sure he's on the citizenship test," Omran teased.

Lillian ignored the quip. "You guys had already done a standard check, why did you run the deeper check then?"

"You like him."

The words dropped between them.

"You could tell that from one encounter?"

Lillian felt exposed.

"Am I wrong?" Omran asked quietly.

"No."

"He's good for you."

"I'm a decade older than the guy," Lillian countered.

"I don't hear him complaining."

"He's a golden boy." Everybody loved Colt, his fans, his community.

Omran sighed. "And you lost your luster? That's really what this is."

"Maybe." Lillian bit her lip.

"You know that's not right." Omran paused. "Are you going to tell him?"

Lillian blinked, wiping at her eyes. "That he has a half-brother he doesn't know about, that his father lied about having cancer, or that his father was in business with the drug and arms dealer who tried to execute his older brother five years ago?"

Without missing a beat, Omran answered, "D—all of the above."

"Seriously? You would tell him everything?"

Omran blew out a breath. "From all accounts, the incident from five years ago is dormant."

"We both know how fast things can flare-up again."

"There is that. And if his father participated in Gabe's attempted murder, who's to say he won't try with another sibling, including Colt?"

Lillian's stomach twisted.

"The half-brother thing, I'd want to know. And the fake cancer thing? His dad is clearly unstable—families should know what they're dealing with."

"All of these things will crush him. Colt keeps his distance but his family matters to him, deeply."

Bloody hell.

Lillian asked, "What did you guys do with the intel about his dad?"

"We sent it to the RCMP. It's in their hands now."

In Lillian's experience, files passed to other jurisdictions sat unopened until it was too late. Colt might hate her for digging into his past, but she had to tell him. Gabe should also know his father was in business with those who tried to murder him five years ago.

How the hell did one drop those bombs on a family?

Chapter Thirty-Nine

Fernando Martinez woke up to his phone pinging. The woman in bed next to him was snoring softly. He frowned in disgust.

As he grabbed his phone she turned over. Her curvaceous backside made him hesitate.

His phone pinged again.

Fernando immediately picked up when he saw who it was, and let himself onto the balcony.

In the pre-dawn light, the sleepy medieval village below was still quiet.

"Good work planting the duffle bag with the photos of that bitch. The money and gun were a nice touch."

The man made a non-committal sound.

Fernando narrowed his eyes. If he didn't know better, he'd suspect the man was bored.

"I want to see true fear in her eyes before I kill her, do you understand? Toy with them, or whatever it is that you do. And grab that damn file. I want to know what they're working on. No doubt it has something to do with me. She always was obsessed."

"*Right.*"

Fernando bristled. He had never heard the word laced with so much loathing.

"What did you say?" Fernando snapped.

"The deal was the women would have British security details."

"So?"

"You gave us the British playbook. These guys are not British."

Fernando scoffed. "Then who the hell are they?"

"That's not my problem. You broke the deal."

"They can't be Canadian. Who are they?"

"You know the change fee. And Martinez?"

"What?"

"I know what you did to Chad."

The line went dead.

Fernando scoffed. He had made Chad. His former second in command was a nobody. The mercenary was bluffing to get more money. Or Fernando was a fool to think he could control him. His mind whirred.

Money. He needed money. His unprotected assets had been legally seized by several governments around the globe, and his offshore accounts were being methodically hacked and drained. He was dangerously low on cash, which was why he needed those blueprints.

His mobile pinged.

His officer wasted no time. "The blueprints are missing."

They were a license to print money.

Fernando set his phone down and wrapped his arms around one of the large potted plants. Grunting in effort, he hefted it over the balcony, screaming. It shattered far below.

He grabbed another pot. One after the other, he launched the pots over the rail, screaming.

If he didn't have the blueprints, he didn't have anything. Everything he'd built would be gone.

There was only one person who could have possibly stolen them.

Lillian.

Fernando grabbed his phone and stalked back into the room.

It was empty. The expensive piece of ass had fled.

Fernando made another call. That bitch, Lillian, would pay for stealing from him.

Chapter Forty

Lillian sat at the kitchen table as bright afternoon sun glittered through the condo. She would tell Colt what she found out tomorrow on their ride. She was meeting him at Becca's in the morning. That gave her the rest of the day to bolster her courage. He was going to be angry at her for doing the background check, and what she had found out.

He might never speak to her again.

Pain lanced through her.

On the table sat her ever-present tactical pen and notebook, her laptop, the grimoire, carton of fur trade documents and package of letters. After Omran's call, she had showered, changed, and ate a hasty lunch, eager to lose herself, and her churning emotions, in research.

She dipped her hand into the carefully wrapped parcel of letters and removed the next one. She gently unfolded it, honoring the moment. Likely no one had opened these treasures since Piety. It sounded fanciful, but to Lillian, the yellowed paper and faded ink was a tangible bridge to an intangible—but no less real—connection to her long dead kin. Lillian read.

This can't be all there is for me. I daresay I fear I never realized the effort our staff put forth. It feels like all I do is work, and doubt. Sister, I was a foolish girl, and now I am a woman with regrets. As is the custom here, my husband, Dajoji, has taken a second wife, one who is from the base of the mountains. She is beautiful and kind, and if we were not sharing the same husband, we would quite probably be friends. She is already with child. I think that is why he took another so soon; I have not provided him with a son, or daughter for that matter. I was right to wait. I really must write down those herbals from grandame, women need options. I am never without my slumber vial. Between Seamus and then my husband, I have had rare need to use it, as most men keep their distance. Besides having protectors, I am too strange, too different. I make men uneasy, though women don't find me odd. Do you not think there will come a time when a woman's value is assigned by her individual merit instead of her ability to be a broodmare? I could have stayed in England for that. Surely I am meant to be more than an obedient wife and dutiful mother, when I long for so much more? I can read and write, and do arithmetic, surely I could keep the ledgers at Fort Roche Cachée, it can not be harder than the ledgers back home when papa was ill. To be but given a chance. Do not fret dear sister, my husband is more amenable than Lord Brandtford. I just—this can't be all there is. Perhaps you found the last good man. I am happy for you. Love is rare. I rarely see Seamus, though I hear talk he is expected back to this area soon. Not that he speaks to me anymore the few times a year I see him. When we were girls growing up, I never dreamed this is where I would end up. There is discussion the French are building a new fort in view of the mountains. We shall see. Remember when we used to walk in the rain? Someday, I would like very much to do that with you again. I miss you, and hope this letter finds you well and truly happy. Your Loving Sister, BeeBee.

Lillian's hands were shaking. She reached for the grimoire, flipping to the pages of elixirs, and scanning for word of a slumber vial. It was a recipe for a fast-acting elixir, easily kept handy in a small vile worn around the neck. In the event a woman found herself needing to protect herself, she need only pass the uncorked vile under the would-be assailant's nose, rendering a grown man unconscious and giving her time to run away. No wonder some men were afraid of potions, they gave women a fighting chance to defend their person.

Lillian hugged the grimoire to her chest, wishing she could hug away millennia of violence. She was safe. Sophie was safe. They didn't need folklore recipes, they had the elite special ops of a sovereign nation protecting them. The women of her family who needed to use and pass on such protections, flimsy though they were, were long gone.

Lillian closed her eyes, hearing the voices, and screams, of millennia of women that had been silenced by disregard or violence.

She stood in a rush, nearly knocking over the kitchen chair. Anger and fear vibrated through her. She carefully placed the grimoire down before pacing the small kitchen. She felt like she needed to erupt, the pressure of long ignored emotions boiled within her. A little frantic, she looked around the kitchen. Her gaze stopped on the block of kitchen knives, but chopping anything right now, productive or not, was a recipe for disaster. One of her therapists had suggested beating pillows to release anger. She glanced at the sofa in the living room.

What she really wanted was a large pile of logs to split. Lillian paused.

She did have men in her life who valued and respected women. Colt did. He was filling in the sharp edges of Lillian's heart. And how he spoke of his sister, Becca, made Lillian love him all the more.

Bloody hell, she loved him.

She swiped at her eyes. Fernando had taken more than she thought. In her fear, she had isolated herself, particularly from men. She did have good men in her life; Colt, Omran and her security detail, Clint Steele, Tucker and Officer Chasseur. Even young Craig. Some men could be trusted. It wasn't just trust in herself she was rebuilding since the *unfortunate incident*, it was also her trust in men.

Tears streamed down her cheeks, and she gripped the kitchen counter.

Sophie's words pinged around her head. *ReWilding as in returning to the core of who you are, the real you.*

The real Lillian wanted to be able to trust men again. The real Lillian trusted Colt, completely. And in protecting herself, finding this space, she might lose him forever.

Could life really be this unfair when she was finally pulling herself back together?

The front door opened, and Sophie called out, *"Auntie, we're here."*

Lillian dropped behind the kitchen counter.

"Auntie, are you home?"

Lillian scrubbed at her eyes and blew out quick, soft breaths.

"Craig's here with his stuff. I told him you'd be cool with it."

Like a jackrabbit, Lillian popped up. "What?"

"Oh good, you're here." Sophie turned behind her. "Craig, come on, my aunt doesn't bite."

Lillian swiped at her eyes one last time and plastered a smile on her face. "Hi you two."

"Auntie, are you okay?"

Lillian pressed the heel of her palms against her eyes. "Onions."

Sophie smiled, relieved. "We were going to ask you if you want to go out to dinner with us to celebrate?"

Lillian felt her smile slip. "What are we celebrating, dear?"

Sophie looked alarmed. "Craig, moving in here for a bit. I didn't think you'd mind."

"*Sophie—*" Craig's voice was a mix between a plea and pride.

"What? You said it yourself, you barely know Colt Tanner and you don't want to impose on him. Stay here."

Lillian looked at the young man in front of her. From the stories, he hadn't had much experience being welcomed. She could relate. People needed a place to belong.

"Of course, you're welcome to stay. Sophie will show you to the spare bedroom." She looked pointedly at her niece. Sophie rolled her eyes.

"Don't look at me like that, people need their space. You'll thank me, later, I promise."

Craig's face was somewhere between disbelief and hope. "Are you serious? I can pay rent. Whatever you need."

"I wouldn't joke about this. I don't have a sense of humor, just ask Sophie. You are welcome here."

No kid was going to feel less-than worthy if Lillian could help it.

"I'll pay rent," he repeated.

"We can sort rent out."

The young man stood straighter, and his chest puffed out a bit. Lillian was pleased she hadn't, in-kindness, dismissed him and his ability to pay rent. She needed a reason to get up in the morning to feel worthy, and it seemed this kid needed to pay his own way, to feel the same.

"Craig doesn't have a lot of stuff, so it won't take long to unpack."

"While you guys do that, I'll get groceries and make a nice dinner. Don't get used to it, my cooking is sporadic at best. But tonight, we celebrate."

Sophie whispered to Craig. "Told you she's awesome."

Craig held out his hand. "Thank you, Ms. Kensington. I really appreciate it."

Lillian stepped forward and shook his outstretched hand. "You're welcome. And please call me Lillian. Any food concerns?"

Craig shook his head.

"Sounds good. I'll be back." Lillian grabbed her purse and tried not to look like she was running out the door.

"What about the onions?" Sophie called after her.

Lillian just waved before closing the door behind her.

As she walked to the grocery store, she replayed what had just happened. Had she made the right decision? She was in a position to help, and Colt said people help each other here.

Colt. She smiled at the thought of him.

Her phone pinged and her smile vanished.

It was her doctor; her time was up.

Chapter Forty-One

"Lillian?" Colt had just parked on the far side of the small grocery store parking lot when he noticed Lillian. She was sitting on the grassy median under a tree.

He walked up. "What are you doing? Need a ride?"

Lillian briefly looked up, shielding her eyes with her hand from the bright sun. "Oh. Hi."

Gone was the fire and spark from their time at the library. She was downcast, sullen even.

He had never had such a start-stop relationship with a woman, if one could even call this a relationship. With Lillian, he couldn't seem to find a gear, any gear.

"I can give you a lift if you're waiting for a ride?"

"It's not that."

Her voice gave him concern. He squatted low, bracing his arms on his thighs. "What's going on?"

Lillian plastered her fake smile on her face. "How have you been?"

She was clamming up.

"I'm fine. What's going on?"

"How are Becca and Tucker?"

"*Lillian—*" In a softer voice, he said, "I'm here. Tell me what's going on."

"Oh, bugger it." This time when she looked up, he could see her eyes were red. "According to my doctors, my body is shutting down and digesting itself."

Colt sat down before he fell down.

"How exactly does that work?"

"I need to eat meat." Lillian covered her face with her hands, mumbling, "What the bloody hell is wrong with me?"

Relief flooded Colt. He even smiled. "So you'll be okay if you eat meat?"

Lillian looked up at him, her eyes filled with fresh tears. "You don't understand. Millions of people around the world live healthy, normal lives eating plant-based diets. This is another way I'm broken."

She buried her head in her hands and her shoulders shook.

He sat, crossed legged, and laced his fingers together in his lap. "Lillian—"

She turned her head to look at him. "What?"

"I know my choice of career path has made you strongly question my intelligence."

She cracked a smile at that.

"But aren't humans technically omnivores, like from a science view, or whatever?"

Her smiled widened at his clumsy question. "Yes, humans evolved to be omnivores."

"Then why are you so sad you are one?"

She pushed strands of hair back from her face. "You don't understand. I can't be a part of brutalizing animals. I just can't. There are a lot of really crappy things I can't control in my life. Not eating flesh; that I can control, or at least thought I could."

"And current industrial agricultural practices are a freight train to crazy town?"

"I've never heard that particular way of phrasing it, but yes."

Colt shrugged. "Becca's rubbed off on me. She was a regenerative agriculture specialist in Germany before she gave it up to come home and run an eco-inn."

"Why did she do that?"

"No idea. She's tight-lipped about it and I won't pry."

Lillian admitted, "I've ignored my doctors about this for years."

Panic flared again. "Will you be okay?"

Lillian put her hand on his arm. "Sorry, yes. No permanent damage. Yet. I don't get it, though. Eating too many animal proteins can cause so many issues in the body. Even spiritual texts point to eating a plant-based diet."

"This might be oversimplifying things, but cut yourself some slack. So, your body needs animal proteins. It's not like your doctors are asking you to shoot heroin. They're asking you to what, eat a burger occasionally?"

"Something like that." She pressed the side of her curled hand against the bridge of her nose. "This just feels like another thing broken with me."

Colt looked across the parking lot. "The finals on Sunday will be my last ride."

Lillian's head shot up. "What? Why? You love rodeo."

Colt lifted his right arm. "My body doesn't."

Compassion lit her eyes, and she placed her hand on his arm. "Oh, Colt, I'm so sorry. I know how much rodeo means to you."

He placed his hand over hers. "My body needs me more."

She held his gaze.

He continued, "I can't ignore the damage I've been doing. And I'm not telling you this to be unkind, I'm telling you this because in my own way I understand."

He didn't add she had been part of his decision to retire. She was the only woman he could see himself settling down with.

"My family doesn't know, please don't tell them. Becca would worry more about me riding on Sunday than she normally does."

"I won't." Lillian promised.

Colt hesitated. "You're not broken."

Lillian pulled her hand away. She seemed to shrink in front of him.

"My sister does that, too. Why do you guys assume there is something wrong with you, if something doesn't go perfect?"

Lillian's shoulders hunched over more.

Colt berated himself. Why had he said anything? He should have kept quiet.

But she was laughing, hard.

"What's so funny?"

She kissed him on the mouth, making his lips tingle and his cock wake up.

"What was that for?"

Her eyes dimmed a bit.

"More than I can tell you right now. But I can say, you just helped me unpack one more kernel of my suppressed feminine."

"I don't know what that means, but I will help you unpack anything you want me to."

She stared at him a long moment. "I know you would. You're a good man, Colt Tanner."

Now his whole body felt tingly.

She reached for his hand again. "I am sorry you are retiring from bull riding."

"How hard was that for you to say?" Colt smiled, wanting to lighten the mood.

Lillian grinned. "Excruciating! But I am. I didn't understand it before. I think I might, now. It's part of who you are." She paused. "When I first saw you riding, horses mind you, during the cattle drive . . ." She shook her head. "I've never seen anything like it."

"I was just working."

"Colt, you have a real gift. Your ability is pure poetry."

Her praise was almost painful. No one understood his reverence for animals, particularly livestock, with the possible exception of Clint. It was unsettling to be seen so clearly.

"Anyway," she continued, "it's part of you, and I like you."

"I like you, too."

The space between them crackled.

Lillian inclined her head in the direction of the chain grocery store. "Will you go in with me?"

"I will go with you to buy meat, but we're not going in there. I'm taking you to Bill's."

"Who is Bill?"

"He's a local, non-judgmental carnivore type, and the best butcher I know."

She raised her eyebrows.

"You're not the first plant kiddo who had to go omnivore."

"I am not up for a lecture right now—"

Colt held up his hands. "I'm certainly not going to give you one. Neither will Bill. He's cool. Live and let live, and all that."

"Okay." She paused. "Thanks for telling me about Sunday."

He nodded, still unsettled by her insight, and what he had shared.

They both stood. Colt tried not to notice as Lillian brushed the loose grass off her shorts.

"I'm making dinner for Sophie and Craig tonight. Want to come?"

Hard yes.

He coughed. "Sounds great. What can I bring?"

"How about dessert?"

He gave her an intimate kind of smile, and she turned a lovely shade of pink.

Lillian clarified, "I meant something like cake or cookies."

"Anything you want, U.K."

They walked several steps in silence before Lillian took his hand in hers.

Colt had to ask, "Why didn't you call me? This is pretty big; you don't have to do it alone."

She looked at the ground. "I felt stupid. I should have. I'm glad you're here."

He was, too. They walked, holding hands.

She whispered, "I tried so hard to get my body to work."

Colt looked down. She looked so sad. It fired up every protective instinct Colt had.

"There is nothing wrong with you."

Didn't she know she was perfect in every way?

He gently squeezed her hand. "Come on, U.K. Let's go buy some meat."

Buying steak, he could handle. The incredible woman walking beside him not knowing she was enough as-is, that was knocking him to his knees.

Chapter Forty-Two

Lillian's condo was typical mountain chalet meets conservative urban, but somehow it worked. Tall, log beamed ceilings, wood plank trim and flourishes, a fireplace, and windows capitalizing on peak views, combined with muted colors and tight lines. A couple of shelves of books were the only thing that could be considered clutter. Colt liked it. Lillian was like a world-weary, sexy librarian that had every masculine part of him on high alert.

They had just finished dinner. Lillian folded her hands together. "If you two are going to make the movie, you need to hurry."

Sophie stood from the table. "We'll cook and clean up tomorrow, promise."

Craig placed his napkin on the table and stood, though he looked undecided.

Colt felt for the young man; Sophie and Lillian were quite a force. "Go on. I'll help Lillian with clean up."

Craig looked relieved. "Thank you again for dinner, and for letting me stay."

Lillian darted Colt a cryptic look before answering, "It's no trouble, really."

Her smile reached her eyes, though, and Colt knew she meant what she said.

Within minutes, the door closed behind the kids, leaving Colt and Lillian alone.

Lillian jumped to her feet and started clearing the table with lightning speed. Colt felt compelled to match her pace.

"You okay? I didn't realize this was a race."

"I just want to get these started."

She seemed jittery. Was she upset about dinner?

"Was the roast okay?"

"It was fine. Oddly delicious, actually."

Silently, they worked in tandem. All too soon the dishwasher was running, the pots and pans washed and put away. All that was left was for her to boot him out the door.

Colt hung up the dish towel. "I think we set a land speed record."

He hoped he had kept the disappointment out of his voice. It wasn't her fault she didn't dig him.

She spun around from wiping off the stove. "What?"

It was worse than he thought, she was breathless. Lillian had been rushing so damn fast to get him out of there, she was short of breath.

"Never mind."

She crossed to the sink and rinsed the cloth. In her haste, water squirted across her shirt.

It was unbelievable how badly he had misread the dinner invite. Resigned, he shoved his hand into his jeans pocket and pulled out his truck keys.

"I should get going. Thanks for dinner."

"What? No. Where are you going?"

She scrambled to wipe her hands dry on a tea towel.

"It's okay. I can take a hint. I've never seen anyone sprint through dishes that fast in my life."

"That's not why I was going so fast."

"Seriously, it's all good." It wasn't, but he couldn't make her be into him. He respected her choice.

He turned to go.

"I want you to stay. Like *stay-stay*. Please."

It took Colt a half second to switch gears.

He tossed his keys onto the table, before planting his hands on her hips. In a fluid motion he had her picked up and settled on the now-clean kitchen counter.

"Oh. Right here on the counter—"

He kept his hands on her hips. "Is this okay?"

She laced her hands behind his neck and whispered, "this is why I was racing," before claiming his mouth with her lips. It was the hottest kiss of his life. He squeezed her hips. She bit his lip before wrapping her legs around him. He lifted her off the counter, ignoring his protesting shoulder, and carried her to the living room.

"Bedroom," she said breathlessly, pointing.

"Yes, ma'am." He changed course, feasting on her neck as he carried her into her bedroom.

He stopped at the bed, and she released her legs from around his waist and stood, her arms still locked around his neck.

"Colt?" She started kissing his neck.

"Yeah?" He couldn't think.

"I've wanted you since the cattle drive," she whispered.

This woman was burning him alive. He covered her mouth with his.

She slid her hands to the hem of his t-shirt and tugged it over his head. She let her hand trail down his bare torso to the front of his jeans. She stopped at the bulge she found and palmed him.

He sucked in a breath. When she gently bit his nipple, he leapt in her hand.

"Check my pocket." He nuzzled her neck.

She dragged her hand across him, then slipped her fingers into denim. She pulled out a strip of small foil packets. Her smile was as old as Eve's. "Only five?"

Colt's jaw dropped a bit. Um, what was she thinking?

"Check my pocket," she whispered.

He did, pulling out two. "Only two."

She squeezed him gently again. "I have more in my nightstand, satchel, the glove box in my car," she smiled, "the glove box of your truck."

He groaned.

"I wanted to be ready when you were."

Holy fuck.

"I'm ready, swear to god, I'm ready."

Colt had never been this hard in his life. He let Lillian pull him to her bed. When his shoulder protested, he winced before he could stop it.

"Your shoulder—"

"Will be fine," he interrupted in a haze.

She gently sat him down and stood between his legs. He wrapped his arms around her, kneading her bum as he planted kisses on her stomach. She held up her arms and he slipped her t-shirt off. Her bra was a black lacy number that had his mind short circuiting.

She led his hands to the waistband of her shorts. He slowly slipped them off her. A scrap of black lace remained.

She gently pushed him back, following him onto the bed. He scrambled out of his jeans and boxer briefs. She retrieved one of the foil packets and sheathed him.

When Lillian straddled him, pressing herself against his straining erection, he thought he would come right then.

He breathed out her name.

She started to lower herself onto him and he grabbed her hips, stopping her. "Wait, are you ready? I mean—"

Then she stroked against him and whispered, *"I'm ready."*

He could feel that she was.

"God, yes, Lillian."

She slid over him then.

She did things to him—he felt things—he had never experienced before. She took him on a tour of the galaxy, and then did it again.

They lay on her bed, staring at the ceiling, Colt clutched the light blanket to his chest, still breathing hard.

"I didn't know sex could feel like that."

Lillian turned her head and kissed him on his shoulder. She whispered, "Only with you."

Colt wrapped his arm around her, holding her close. "Only with you."

She snuggled into him. Colt felt completely at peace.

Suddenly Lillian sat bolt upright, swearing. "The kids are home!"

Chapter Forty-Three

"Go! Go! Go!" Lillian dove out of bed, scrambling into her clothes. Colt was hopping on one leg, trying to pull his jeans on when she fired his t-shirt at him.

It was tight. "What is this?"

"Does it matter?" She hurdled over the bed, grabbing his hand as she passed and pulled him out of her room.

They dropped onto the couch, exhaling. Lillian lunged for the remote and snapped on the television.

The sound of the key in the front door lock made them both freeze.

"Nice save, U.K.," Colt whispered.

The front door opened. Sophie and Craig walked in holding hands and both looking a bit dreamy. Sophie's makeup was smudged, and Craig's hair was tousled.

"How was the movie?" Lillian asked, fiddling with a pillow.

"Fine." Sophie looked at Lillian, then Colt.

"Why's Colt in your British Aerospace t-shirt?"

"His got wet doing dishes and he borrowed one of mine."

Sophie raised an eyebrow. Craig looked anywhere but at Lillian or Colt.

Colt tugged at the small t-shirt, but the soft fabric clung as tight as before.

An awkward silence hung.

Craig noticed the television. "Your aunt likes MotorTrend? Cool. This is a good one."

Sophie grabbed his arm, tugging him towards the hall to the bedrooms. "It's late. I have training tomorrow. Good night, guys."

"But MotorTrend—" Craig started.

"Watch it online." She pulled Craig towards the short back hall.

"What about Becca—"

"Tomorrow." Quieter Sophie hushed, *"Let's give them some privacy."*

"Goodnight." Craig called before dutifully following Sophie down the hall.

Colt waited until the kids were down the hall and he heard doors close.

"My shirt got wet?"

Lillian smiled. "Close enough. I got wet, does that count?"

Heat flared in Colt's eyes.

Lillian held out her hand. "Not with the kids here."

He puckered his lips in a fake pout. "Fine. Nice parenting."

Colt looked down at the tight shirt. "Did you work for British Aerospace?"

"No, I dated a physicist." Lillian shrugged. "He was petit."

Colt's eyes flashed in alarm.

"Totally kidding. You should see your face."

Colt closed his eyes. "You're a grown woman, your body, your business. I just don't want to hear about the guys before me. Call me old fashioned. Is that okay?"

Lillian didn't want to hear about the women Colt had been with, either. "Fair. Same."

He nodded.

The shirt hugged every muscled contour of him. Lillian wanted to run her hands over the soft cotton, every seam, contour and hollow.

"I know it doesn't matter, but the t-shirt's mine. I did a story back in my early days." She tilted her head and made an appreciative sound. "Darling, how your muscles are straining those seams makes me want to use my mouth to remove it."

Colt snaked his left arm out and pulled her close. He gave her a sizzling hot kiss. She kissed him back.

He pulled away first. "See you tomorrow?"

She nodded.

They stood. She walked him to the door. "I want you to stay over, but I feel weird with Sophie and Craig here."

"I understand, and it's sweet." Colt cupped her cheek with his hand and kissed her. "See you at Becca's tomorrow."

Lillian nodded, closing the door behind him, and setting the locks.

"Please don't break my heart," she whispered.

Tomorrow he might hate her.

Chapter Forty-Four

Lillian walked into Becca's barn, her heart hammering. She had never taken sex for granted, but last night with Colt had been on a level she never even knew existed. She was feeling things—like settling down kind of things—that scared the shit out of her.

It was a bittersweet realization. There was a very good chance he wouldn't be speaking to her after she told him about the INCEPT check.

She saw him, then. He had just finished saddling Jörð and was whistling to a quick tempo country western song on the radio. She memorized the image.

Feeling like a coward, she called out, "Good morning."

He turned, dimples appearing. "Morning."

"Nice song."

"A two-stepping classic."

She stared blankly.

"Oh, no way." Colt walked towards her. He took her right hand in his left and wrapped his right arm around her waist. He was so close, his arm around her felt so good, so strong, even his scent fueled her growing fantasy.

"What are you doing?"

"You've never two-stepped, right?"

She shook her head, holding that smoldering North Sea gaze.

"Hang on." With that cryptic remark, he led her into a spirited dance through the barn.

He had meant literally.

She clung to him. Once she found her steps, she let herself follow his capable lead. It was fast-paced and deliciously fun. When the song ended, she was breathing hard and laughing. He gave a final twirl and she ended pressed flush against him. He dipped his head and Lillian kissed him back with everything she had.

"Sorry, sorry."

Lillian broke the kiss, pulling back at the interruption. Craig stood at the opposite end of the barn, eyes awkwardly closed.

Colt whispered in her ear, "To be continued." He called out to Sophie's beau, "Craig, man, what are you doing here?"

Craig opened his eyes, standing straighter. "Becca hired me, for barn chores and stuff."

"That's great news." Lillian was thrilled for him, he looked so proud.

"You're not mad?"

"Of course not, why would I be?" Lillian asked.

Craig squirmed. "Sophie kind of put you on the spot with me moving in. Becca called when we were on our way to the movie. The job offer includes room and board."

"Congrats, man," Colt said. He led Holda, saddled and ready to go, out of her stall and handed Lillian the reins.

"How did you get here?" Colt asked.

Craig smiled. "Clint sold me his old work truck. Said it would just rust out back, if no one was driving it. He said I could pay him a couple hundred dollars each month until it was paid off. Can you believe it?"

"That's Clint," Colt said.

Craig hesitated. "Becca asked if I was going to school, if I had to work around a school schedule."

"And?" Lillian gently prodded.

Craig kicked at the concrete floor. "I've never thought about it before. I always kind of thought school was for other people. But with a job and a truck, maybe I could go to school."

Colt looked thoughtful. "You're handy with a wrench. Have you looked at SAIT?"

"Isn't that for like helicopters and airplanes?"

"They've got engines, don't they? I think they have an auto program, too, though I'm not sure if you'd learn new stuff. I hear you're pretty damn good."

Craig ducked his head at the praise.

Colt untied Jörð.

A spark of an idea flickered as Lillian stashed her satchel into one of Holda's saddle bags. "Are you into racing?"

"Formula One is cool. Nascar's okay. I've worked a few pit crews, just for local stuff. It's pretty fun."

Lillian needed to check into a few things.

"We should be going, but maybe we can talk more later. And Sophie should be done training by four."

"She's here," Craig said, confused.

Lillian had left quite early to make the dawn meeting and figured Sophie had still been sleeping.

"Oh, I didn't realize."

She had thought Craig had been sleeping, and he turned out to be here, too.

"Did I say something wrong?" Craig asked.

"No. No biggie." Why was Sophie skipping practice?

"Do you want me to get her?" The poor kid was looking terrified.

"No, no." Lillian plastered a smile on her face. "I'm sure I'll see her when we get back."

"Shall we?"

Lillian nodded.

To Craig she waved. "Have a good first day."

He was so desperate to please that she wanted to put his mind at ease before they left.

Craig waved back, looking relieved and already moving on to his next barn task.

Colt led the way out of the barn. The wind was firm, tossing the branches of the trees that lined the inn's yard. Lillian eyed the sky. Heavy storm clouds were gathering in the west even as the bright summer sun rose higher in the east. If they were lucky, the contrast would make for excellent photos for Becca.

Her stomach turned over. She had to tell Colt. Lillian would savor these few precious hours she had before the truth exploded whatever was building between them.

"You seemed surprised about Sophie."

They had ridden halfway across the field, and Lillian measured her response. "It's not like her to blow off practice, and I thought she would tell me if she wouldn't be home, as a courtesy. I did. I worry about her. And Craig. I left so early, I just assumed they both were still asleep."

"I imagine it's pretty tough raising kids. How do you find that sweet spot of giving them enough space to grow and spread their wings, while also keeping them safe?"

"Let me know if you find out. Sophie is nineteen, old enough to make her own choices. When I think of what I did when I was nineteen . . ."

When Lillian didn't finish, Colt laughed. "She's a good kid. I'm sure everything will be okay."

"I haven't seen much of her since we moved here. I always just assumed she was training."

Colt was quiet. "Maybe her priorities have changed." He looked at her. "Mine have, since meeting you."

Lillian knew just how hard losing your career was. "I am sorry about Sunday being your last ride."

"I wasn't talking about bull riding," he said quietly.

Lillian's whole body tightened and Holda shied, sidestepping. Lillian thought the horse was going to bolt, but Colt had immediately moved Jörð in. He reached for Holda's reins and drew out a long, low *woah*. The normally docile horse responded to Colt's instructions.

"You good?" Colt asked.

Lillian nodded, resettling the reins. "Thanks."

"Anytime."

She leaned forward, speaking to Holda, "Sorry, honey, I just got so excited." She added, *"And I think he was talking about me."*

Holda turned her head, bobbed once, before facing forward and walking again.

Lillian sagely added, "Holda gets it."

Colt grinned, his dimples making an appearance. "You ladies talk as much as you like."

Lillian tried to shift to a work gear. "Where are we going first?"

"Becca drew a map of places she thinks will make good material. I thought we'd head to the furthest ones and work our way back. She loved your drone footage, by the way. And your write-ups so far."

Lillian smiled, pleased. She waved a hand. "The land did the heavy lifting. I mean, just look at it."

They were on a winding trail wide enough to ride side-by-side. Poplar trees dominated the lower slope, while spruce and fir trees were more prevalent on the upward slope.

"What kind of tree is that?" It was coniferous, or cone-bearing, and shaped like an oversized arrow—strong and incredibly straight.

Colt looked where she was pointing. "Lodgepole pine."

Lillian took in the undulating foothills, big sky, and ever-present mountain peaks. "I get it now. Why people live here. You must have missed this terribly when you were on the road."

"You saw it, home's complicated."

Lillian's heart tightened. He didn't know half of how complicated his family was.

"Can you un-complicate any of it?"

"You sound like Clint."

Lillian looked sideways at him. "What's his deal?"

"Clint's? I don't know." Colt shrugged. "Old rancher?"

"No, I mean, does he have any family?"

Colt shook his head. "No one really knows Clint. He'll give you the shirt off his back, and is always quick to lend a hand, or ear, for that matter. But no one really *knows* *him*. He's a private man."

Lillian understood.

"Any more leads on *BeeBee*?"

"Seamus was in love with her. I found his journal."

Colt was quiet before saying, "And she married another."

"I don't think she had a clue about Seamus' feelings for her, and her husband took a second wife. It didn't sit well with her."

"What happened? What did she do?"

"I don't know. Their story is likely lost to history. I thought I might have tracked down another journal of Seamus' at one of the archives in town, but my appointment to view it was cancelled. Apparently the journal was misplaced. The archive moved buildings a few years ago and it's not uncommon when items are moved that something gets misplaced in the shuffle. Or it could have been lost decades ago and no one noticed."

"I'm sorry, Lillian. I know how important their story is to you."

"It was a long shot anyway. From what I can tell, the maps of *BeeBee* and Seamus' I do have look to be between the upper Missouri's tributaries and the south fork of the Saskatchewan River. There is a lot of information for this part of Alberta starting in the second half of the nineteenth century, but *BeeBee* and Seamus lived a century earlier. Seamus didn't have a license from the French, nor did he work for the HBC. Any trading activity he would have done would have been considered illegal by the French or British. Meaning the forts Seamus was trading in wouldn't have a commercial paper trail to find as they would have wanted to stay under the radar. And any forts that were here at that time predate colonial government-sanctioned ones." Lillian paused. "It's incredible we found what we did."

"I had no idea." Colt looked around them. "Dang. We passed the first spot Becca wanted."

They backtracked and Lillian went to work, snapping pictures and taking field notes that she would write up for various marketing content. She tried to capture the landscape in its most unexpected, not simply the typical awe-inspired mountains scenery. Each spot Colt took her to made her breath catch and her heart yearn.

The landscape was as remarkable as her guide. Colt was rugged and beautiful, and with a calm strength and grace. He only gave a half-hearted protest when she asked him to be in some of the shots. Lillian finished snapping photos and taking notes of their final location before looping the camera strap around her neck. They were on another ridge, their trail playing peek-a-boo with the surrounding forest.

Lillian gasped. Below them was a cobbled floodplain with a braided river.

"Can we go there?"

Colt eyed the cloud cover. "We'll probably get wet."

"I don't mind if you don't."

The smile he gave her was like a little kid given permission to explore. "Let's go!"

Colt led his mount off the trail, his movements fluid and confident.

Lillian, on the other hand, had her doubts.

After several minutes, she asked, "Is this safe?"

The vegetation had thickened, and Colt ducked under a tree branch. "Off trail, or here in general?"

"Off trail."

"We're following landforms now. They're another kind of trail. Keep talking, though. There has been some bear activity where we're headed."

Lillian had read a brief bear awareness brochure before running on the mountain trails, and had always carried bear spray, but maybe she should have taken them a bit more seriously.

"Bears don't like talking?"

"Most bears don't give a fig about people, but they are curious. Talking lets them know we're here. Once they know you're a person, they pretty much leave you alone. They don't like being surprised, though, and really don't like being cornered. It's possible to encounter a predatory bear, but it's rare. Most negative bear-human interactions were from habituated bears."

"What does that mean?"

"Human behavior—like leaving out food, either on purpose or in ignorance—habituates local bear populations to seek out human contact as an easy food source. You get a hungry bear who actively ambles into campsites, towns or ranch yards expecting lunch, and usually ends up with the bear being put down, or relocated. Relocated bears still know people equal food, so there is still the threat they'll be put down next time."

"You should be a guide for Becca's eco-inn."

"I'm supposed to be a silent partner." He looked over at her. "Humans and bears can coexist; we just have to be smart about it."

Her security detail were used to two-legged threats. Leading them into an area with bear activity was something else.

Bugger it, it was time.

Lillian tried to memorize Colt's smile, those North Sea eyes. She wanted to remember the way he was looking at her right now, before her stupid reality got in the way.

She pressed a button on her earpiece. "Confirming you guys caught that. The bear thing?"

"Copy that."

Colt asked, "Who are you talking to?"

Lillian took a deep breath before giving him a high-level briefing about Fernando, being tried for treason, and her security detail.

"That's what that thing constantly in your ear is?"

She nodded.

"They're following us right now?"

She nodded.

"They were at Stampede?"

"They were the ones who told us to take cover in the funhouse."

"And at Becca's?"

"They were surrounding the house," Lillian confirmed.

"They were at the library?"

"They've been following us the whole time."

"The whole time?"

She nodded. "They knew you were at the condo last night."

Colt kept riding.

"Please, say something."

"Give me a sec, that's a lot to take in."

Lillian swallowed hard. The biggest news was yet to come.

They wound their way down to the floodplain. The dappled light of the forest made the setting magical. If only she had magic to somehow make this all better.

But she didn't. There wasn't a grimoire on the planet that could fix the mess she had made of her life.

They dismounted on the floodplain. Left alone, Lillian could spend hours exploring the braided river and shoreline. Instead, she sat on river cobbles and waited. When Colt hobbled their horses and walked downstream, away from her, her heart broke.

Wiping at her eyes, she pulled out her notebook. At least she could help Becca. When Lillian finally looked up from her work, the sun was gone, the clouds ominous, and she had pages of notes. Becca might not want anything to do with her after today, but Lillian wanted to turn something in to her.

Lillian re-read what she had written. She had always thought writing notes in the field was like doing a field sketch, but with words, except now she was writing marketing content instead of gripping first person narrative.

How quickly her life kept changing. Like the sand in front of her. The floodplain held braided, shallow, fast-flowing channels of water that flowed over the land. River cobbles and boulders, for the most part, stayed put. As did the areas that grasses and a few scrubby trees had taken root, or the downed tree trunks from floods past, wedged to a stop, had landed.

The sand, though, was at the mercy of the water and the ever-changing conditions.

"It's weird, but I do get it."

Colt stood over her. He had come back.

"May I?" He asked.

She nodded, quickly moving her satchel out of the way.

He sat down next to her.

"I'm sorry I didn't tell you sooner about the detail."

He was looking out across the floodplain. "I can't imagine what you've been through. My superfans are creepy, but not dangerous."

"Well, you don't think so, anyway." It was a macabre way to try to lighten the mood. Lillian took a deep breath. "There's more."

Colt sat straighter. "I don't think I like the sound of that."

"I trusted Fernando. He destroyed my life and killed people. I've been scared of trusting the wrong person again, of my mistake hurting people, myself included."

"I remember when we first met. You weren't comfortable with me."

"It wasn't you, I didn't trust anyone, especially men. But I started liking you and it scared the shit out of me. So, I had a background check done on you. A deep one."

Those North Sea eyes gave the slightest flash. "Okay. Seems reasonable, given the circumstances."

"You're not freaking out?" Lillian ran her hands over her jeans. "This was the point I thought you'd be yelling."

Colt dipped his head, trying to catch her gaze. "You liked me enough to get a deep background check done?"

She nodded. "You have to understand, I was almost killed for falling for the wrong guy. I didn't trust my radar—"

"I get it."

Lillian still felt like she had to explain. "Anyone near me gets vetted. My grandmother is a high-ranking securities minister. I didn't disclose my relationship with Fernando to her because I was afraid he would be upset at the implied breach of trust." She eyed Colt. "How are you being so calm about this?"

Colt actually laughed. "I don't have anything to hide. And rodeo superfans can be seriously scary. I would love having access to background checks."

"Hold that thought." Lillian swallowed. "The background check was thorough."

"It can't be that bad. I've always considered myself kind of boring."

Her heart was pounding so bloody hard. *Just tell him.*

"How many siblings do you have?"

"Three. You know Becca and Tucker, and you'll meet Gabe this weekend. Him and Savannah have been in Jasper since my dad and Meredith's wedding."

"Shortly after Gabe was born, I think your dad fathered another son with a woman named Doris Stone."

Colt stilled.

"Your dad paid child support for eighteen years for a kid named Tanner Stone." Lillian pressed on. "When Gabe was with CSIS, he routinely ran checks on Tanner Stone, your half-brother."

Colt shook his head. "No way, Gabe would never keep a secret like that from us. My dad having an affair and a secret child? That's messed up, but feasible. But Gabe not telling us? No way."

"Maybe the intel made a mistake." She knew it didn't. Not for something this routine.

Colt ran a hand through his hair. "Holy shit."

Lillian steepled her hands in front of her face, her heart still pounding.

Colt looked at her.

"Aw hell. There's more, isn't there?"

She blurted, "Your father does not have, nor has he ever had, cancer."

Colt's shoulders visibly relaxed. "I already guessed that. Whew, you really had me worried there."

Lillian waited.

"There's more?"

Lillian was watching him, and he turned to her, picking up her hand. "Hit me with whatever's left."

"Five years ago, your father was in business with the drug and arms dealer who shot Gabe during his last CSIS mission. This year, that communication resumed. The international law enforcement agencies connected to the case have long suspected an internal leak, however there is no intel."

Colt scrambled to his feet. He walked several steps away before he stopped, hands on hips, staring downstream.

He spun around. "You're saying my dad tried to have Gabe murdered? Why would he do that?"

Lillian stood, too; her voice unsteady when she spoke, "I'm sharing the intel I received. I don't know what your father's connection is, just that there is evidence of a business connection. I thought you had a right to know."

"Who the fuck are you?"

"I'm a nobody," Lillian whispered. Tears brimmed. She swiped the back of her hand across her eyes, now was not the time to cry. She knelt and started collecting her things.

A hand touched her shoulder and she flinched.

"Please look at me."

Lillian swallowed, but looked up.

Colt's eyes were still stormy. "I meant who is courageous enough to share something like this with someone they just met?"

Unable to stop them, a torrent of tears streamed down her face. "It's not like I had a choice, this shit's bad. I didn't want to hurt you, but I couldn't not tell you."

She swiped at her face, before slamming her notebook and water bottle into her satchel. She pocketed her tactical pen and stood. Her life couldn't get more broken.

"Lillian."

She stopped. Colt was holding out his hand to her.

She stared at it.

"Lillian, I'm not going anywhere. We'll figure this out together."

She loved to hear her name on his lips.

Lillian closed her eyes. "I really want to take your hand—"

"So why aren't you?" He sounded hurt.

She held up her hands, hiccupping. "Mine are wet and gross."

The dimples appeared and he wrapped his arms around her.

She held him tight.

"Lillian?"

"Yeah?"

"You know I've had bull snot on me, right?"

She smiled and burrowed deeper against him. They stood like that for a long moment. When she tilted her head up, his mouth dipped lower, and their lips meet.

When he did that delicious thing with his tongue, she sighed.

Remembering, Lillian pulled back. "*Shit.* They can hear everything I do."

The look on Colt's face could best be described as masculine pride. "You mean they just heard you moan?"

"I sighed. It was a very dignified sigh."

"Yes, you did." He pointed his index finger up and made a small circle. "Are they watching, too?"

"They'll be close enough in case we need them. I'm not certain if they have a visual on us, want me to ask?"

He held up both hands. "Nope. I'm good."

"*Affirmative.*"

Lillian looked at Colt.

"They just said something, didn't they?"

She nodded.

He dropped a kiss to her forehead. "I'm going to need a minute before I can get on my horse."

This time it was her feminine pride that surged.

He cleared his throat and walked a few steps away, shaking out a leg.

Lillian pressed her hand to her chest, taking a deep breath. That had gone better than she would have dared hope.

Suddenly she spun around. She had been so focused on telling him about the INCEPT check, she forgot the biggest threat.

Lillian called his name and Colt turned.

She blurted, "At my treason trial, the double-agent swore he would kill me." She held up her hands, palms facing out. "But that's it. No more surprises, I swear."

Chapter Forty-Five

Dame Maighread Evans Coille Kensington heard her office door click shut behind her assistant, Mary. She had just walked around the front of her large desk when a disturbing image flashed through her mind and her knees buckled. She scrambled to the settee and sat down. With shaking fingers, Maighread reached for the phone.

Agent Omran Forest picked up on the first ring. "Mum?"

"Fernando's in Canada. You need to go, now!"

Chapter Forty-Six

A tractor turned circles as it grated the outdoor arena's dirt. Lillian sat in the stands of the in-field, behind the bucking chutes. Sophie and Craig were there, along with Becca, Tucker, Gabe and Savannah. Lillian would have pegged Gabe's background even if her detail hadn't mentioned it. He moved like an agent. Lillian was fairly certain Gabe didn't like her. Savannah was warmer to her, but not much.

Lillian sat on the edge of the group. Sophie and Craig had folded naturally into the lively banter. Her niece always had an effortless comfort with people, and working for Becca was doing Craig a world of good. Sophie said he liked living in the bunkhouse, though it was quiet. Her staff would start in a few months.

Lillian smiled, but did not join in. From their in-field seats, the bright afternoon summer sun was at their backs, and she watched as the stadium filled.

She saw Colt then. He had looked up into the stands and she smiled, giving him a small wave. She could tell the moment he saw her, his face lit up. Her heart thudded in her chest. She didn't think she'd ever tire of the jolt of awareness she got whenever she saw him. She had made more progress in a few days with Colt than months of therapy. With him, she felt like she was living again, maybe more than she ever had before.

Gabe leaned forward. "Why are you wearing an earpiece?"

Everyone stopped talking.

She folded her hands. "Work."

"Reporters wear government grade earpieces now?"

Lillian met his stare. "No. I wear them. And your intel is incorrect. This piece blew past government grade five versions ago."

Her earpiece hummed to life, chastising her. *"Easy there."*

Lillian glanced at Sophie. Her niece looked guilty. She must have taken hers out. Lillian would have to have a talk with her.

Gabe pressed. "You didn't answer my question."

Becca's voice held censure. "Leave her alone, Gabe. Not everyone is a security threat."

Pop, pop.

Lillian instinctively went to duck, but it was only a pyrotechnics display exploding on the in-field. The rodeo had started.

Gabe shook his head and turned away from her.

The next two and a half hours were brutal. Lillian tried to watch with an open mind, but it was difficult. When barrel racing was announced, Gabe's girlfriend, Savannah, turned to Becca. "Do you ever miss it?"

"Not really . . . maybe. I guess, sometimes."

Tucker piped in, "Is that your final answer?"

Becca elbowed him. "I'm a complex woman."

"We know." Tucker rubbed his ribs. "Ow. Save it for Officer Chasseur."

A flush crept up Becca's neck.

Lillian asked, "Becca, can you explain barrel racing? I've never seen it."

Becca threw her a grateful smile and started explaining the sport. Starting with what the field crew was doing, setting up the barrels.

As the event started, she continued. "See the turn?" Her voice was filled with a hushed respect, "Her horse— so beautiful. She nailed that," Becca pointed, "that's what you're going for."

Lillian could pick out the difference in IEDs, but each horse and rider running around the barrels looked the same to her.

Tucker rubbed his hands together. "Bull riding's next."

They had a front row seat with the bucking chutes right in front of them. Lillian watched. As cowboy after cowboy took his turn, she felt more sick to her stomach. The bulls were stomping, snot-flinging, bucking fury.

Lillian wrung her hands. "What's with the clowns?"

"They're not clowns." Tucker pointed. "Those two are bullfighters, and the one over there is the barrel man. Don't let them hear you call them clowns."

"Than why are their faces painted like clowns? And why does the barrel fellow have clown trousers on?" She heard the petulance in her voice and knew fear was shredding any diplomacy she had.

The next cowboy was bucked off unceremoniously. Lillian breathed a sigh of relief as he hobbled out of the way and the stocky bull trotted out of the arena.

The announcer said Colt's name and Lillian's stomach rolled. She covered her mouth with her fingers.

"You okay?" Tucker asked.

She swallowed. "This is barbaric and dangerous and—"

Tucker raised an eyebrow.

"*Ohmygod*, this is terrifying."

"Was that so hard to admit?" Tucker actually smiled. "He knows what he's doing. Colt's been riding bulls for years."

Tucker didn't know how injured Colt was riding. She shook her head. "He's putting himself in harm's way."

"Didn't your career put you in harm's way?"

Lillian snapped her head around. "That was different."

Tucker shrugged. "If you say so."

He turned his attention back to the chutes.

Colt was next, but the bull was slamming itself against the bars of the chute. He hovered above, his boots on the upper rungs of the shoot, waiting for the animal to settle.

Their seats were a little too good. She looked up at one of the large screens at the end of the field instead. Several hands and shoulders were in the shot, helping Colt.

The bull stopped slamming and Colt lowered himself onto its large back. With precise, quick motions, he intricately wound a braided rope around his gloved hand, the bull giving nary a snort that he noticed.

The next pause Lillian would never forget.

On the screen, there was a look of fierce focus in Colt's eyes. Then he nodded. The gate swung open, and the bull exploded out. A fraction of a second later, it launched backwards, back into the chute. Men in cowboy hats scrambled out of the way.

Colt's body had nowhere to go.

Lillian winced each time he was slammed between the metal chute bars and solid animal.

The bullfighters darted forward, luring the heaving animal out of the chute.

Slam. Slam.

Lillian watched in horror as Colt's body took a beating.

The bull gave a final push, crushing Colt's body against the metal bars one last time before charging out.

Colt held on and the buzzer sounded. He vaulted off the bull and stumbled, before regaining his footing and trotted off to the fencing of his own accord, and well out of the bull's way.

Lillian couldn't breathe. "Excuse me."

She fled, getting as far as the garbage can behind the bleachers before she was sick.

Tucker approached her slowly. He held out a bottle of water out. Lillian accepted it.

"Are you pregnant, or something?"

"A woman is sick and the only thing that crosses your mind is she must be pregnant? No, Detective Cracker Jack, I am not pregnant." She took a drink of water. "I'm literally worried sick."

"Oh."

She took another sip of water. "Sorry. I get snappy when I'm upset."

"You and Becca both." Tucker paused. "You get used to it, Colt riding, I mean. Becca says it gets easier."

Lillian pressed the back of her hand against her mouth. Watching Colt get battered like that had been one of the hardest things she had ever watched in her life.

Tucker angled his head at the announcer's words.

"Colt's got a re-ride."

"Beg your pardon?" She couldn't have heard him right.

"A re-ride, the bull didn't give him a chance to score, so the judges gave him a re-ride."

"He's going back on a bull, today?"

"Yes, and soon. He was the last rider."

Chapter Forty-Seven

"Remember, Flame Thrower tosses his head like a damn slingshot." Shayne fist-bumped his left shoulder. "Have a good ride, buddy."

Colt nodded in his helmet, before he climbed up onto the chute. The bull he would be riding was Flame Thrower. The bull's half-brother, Fury, had gored him pretty bad four years ago.

Jake grinned, holding his end of the rope. "You got this buddy."

Colt lowered himself onto the large animal's back and went through his routine. Distantly, he heard the sound of the crowd erupt at whatever the entertainer was saying. When he was tied in and the tail of the rope draped over the bull's shoulders, Colt slid up on his rope and into position. He bit down on his mouthguard and nodded.

The gateman pulled hard, swinging the heavy metal gate open, unleashing bull and rider. Colt turned his heels in as the bull leapt out and spun left. After bucking hard twice, Flame Thrower torqued right and started spinning. Back and forth, Flame Thrower spun, bucked and torqued under him. Colt rode and spurred, keeping his center just enough to hang on.

The buzzer sounded.

Colt went to release his riding glove, but the bull planted his front feet and bucked hard before tossing its head back. Colt had bounced off the bull's back and was already airborne when Flame Thrower tossed his head. Colt shoulder made a sick popping noise before he was tossed, still tied.

Colt scrambled to get his legs under him. The popping sound had been his right shoulder dislocating. He was hung up, his right arm flopping useless, on the side of the heaving, bucking bull. In a moment he would be dragged under.

One of the bullfighters appeared beside him. Another on the opposite side of the bull. Two mounted units were coming in.

Seconds passed as the first bullfighter worked to free Colt's rope. Colt managed to keep his footing enough to stay partially upright, only half-dragged by the bull.

Finally, the rope gave.

The bull stopped suddenly and shouldered Colt hard. It would have knocked him to the ground if the bullfighter hadn't grabbed his safety vest, holding him up. The second bull fighter dashed in. The bull charged left, giving Colt and the first bullfighter a safe opening. Stumbling and in near-paralyzing pain, Colt let the bullfighter help him off the dirt to where Jake and Shayne were waiting.

The bullfighter called, "Good ride, bro. Pop that shoulder back in," before trotting away.

Shayne whistled. "Shit, that looks bad."

Colt's stomach rolled. He breathed through his teeth and tried not to pass out. The pain in his shoulder had blown past excruciating about seventy seconds ago, and Colt could see white sparkles dancing at the corner of his vision. He looked up, nodding to Lillian and his family, wanting to reassure them, but their stark faces only made his pain more acute.

"Ninety-One!" The announcer's voice boomed. *"Colt Tanner rode for a ninety-one folks, we have our Stampede Bull Riding Champion!"*

Colt turned away and willed the nausea down. A medic waited. He was wobbly on his feet, but Colt made himself follow the medic. He focused on the sound his boots made—click-thump, click-thump—as he cradled his right arm in his left. When they made it to the treatment room, he crawled onto the medic's table, still gripping his useless arm.

As stars continued to dance at the edge of his vision, he remembered.

His career was over.

Chapter Forty-Eight

"I'm fine." Colt hung up his cowboy hat on one of the numerous hooks lining Becca's foyer, before using the boot jack, only wincing a little. He toed his boots to rest neatly on the mat.

Lillian closed her eyes and all she saw was Colt hung up, dangling from the side of the huge, stomping bull. She didn't know if she'd ever get over that kind of fear. Besides the sling his arm was in, protecting his shoulder, he didn't look any worse for wear. But Lillian had seen his eyes. She knew that look because she'd seen it in her own reflection. His career really was over.

She quickly toed out of her own shoes and placed them next to his boots, before following him through Becca's living room and down the hall towards the kitchen in the back. The thought of him in pain made her feel nauseated all over again. "I can go fill your prescription. Honestly, I don't mind."

"I'm good." Softer, he added, "Thanks, though."

"This whole cowboy-up thing sounds like masochism."

He gave a bleak half-smile. "It's not that."

The tone of his voice had warning bells firing. Lillian instinctively placed her hand on his arm.

He stopped.

She asked, "You dislocated your shoulder, why won't you let yourself take any painkillers?"

Those North Sea eyes flashed briefly. "Because I used to abuse the shit out of them."

He covered her hand still on his arm.

"I can live with pain. I couldn't live with doing that to myself again. Darkest damn year of my life."

Lillian swallowed hard. "That's why I run so much. I'm scared to death of the abyss."

Colt looked at where his hand covered hers.

"I found the right doctor. He believed I could change, and I didn't want to let him down. It worked. Now I don't want to let myself down."

Lillian fell even harder. She pressed a kiss against his hand. Colt had his demons, but his was a texture of depth and integrity. He was real, like the North Sea his eyes reminded her so much of.

He's a golden boy.

And you lost your luster, is that it?

She had scoffed at a bull rider being news worthy.

Now, Lillian wondered if she was worthy of him.

Loud laughter drifted down the hall.

Colt lifted his left fist up, notching it over his lips. "I can't—"

Lillian waited, afraid what he was going to say.

His voice was barely a whisper. "My family doesn't know."

She blew out the breath she had been holding. "You have my word."

He gave her an inscrutable look. His voice was hoarse when he said, "I mean it."

"So do I."

He blew out a breath. "Thanks."

She nodded and squeezed his good arm. "Always."

Colt turned and walked the rest of the way down the hall.

When they entered the kitchen, Becca looked up. "Hey guys! Hope you're hungry, Tucker has outdone himself again."

Tucker was doing food prep at the large island counter; Becca was standing next to him. Gabe and Savannah were sitting on stools on the opposite side of the island.

Colt looked at his sister. "I thought you'd be swarming me."

Her smile faltered. "It's taking everything I have not to launch myself at you."

He held his left arm out and she gave him a hug, before wiping her eyes. "You scared the shit out of us today."

Lillian stood off to the side, silent.

Colt cleared his throat. "It wasn't my favorite ride, either."

Tucker looked at him. "So that's it?"

Colt nodded.

Gabe said, "Sorry, man. That sucks."

Savannah looked asked Gabe. "What sucks?"

"Colt's wreck—"

"—was a career ender." Colt shifted his arm, resetting it in the sling, but he hadn't looked at Gabe yet.

The room fell silent.

Becca hugged Colt again in a gently fierce hug. He hugged her back. "We all knew this was coming."

She nodded and stepped away from him. She wiped at her eyes, again.

Colt cleared his throat. "What's Tucker got cooking? It smells incredible!"

Lillian stepped forward. "It certainly does. How can I help?"

Tucker nodded towards a slip of paper. "If you can follow a recipe better than Becca, want to give that glaze a go? Her try was a disaster."

Becca's smile was watery, but real. "Duh. I can barely boil water."

Lillian, relieved to have something to do, started reading the recipe. The disapproving looks Gabe was shooting her was making her nervous, and Savannah appeared only marginally less hostile.

Tucker wiped his hands on a tea towel. "Good. I'm going to start the grill. Don't let Becca touch anything."

"It's my kitchen."

"Yeah, I know. It's like giving a Maserati to a child, you have no appreciation for it."

"Someday, you're going to come crawling here, begging me for your dream job."

"I keep telling you, cooking is my hobby."

"Only because you're too stupid to make it more. You have a gift."

"Yeah, catching bad guys." Tucker picked up the tray holding a full salmon. "This is ready to go."

He looked at Gabe, who straightened.

"The men are going outside now."

Tucker's tone had definitely changed.

Lillian glanced at Gabe. Colt's oldest brother's eyes were frosty, and Savannah wouldn't meet anyone's gaze.

Colt still hadn't looked at Gabe. He squeezed Lillian's hand. "I'll just be on the back deck."

She nodded.

Lillian's heart was pounding as she watched Colt walk out the back kitchen door with his brothers.

She had told him everything. There was nothing left to hide.

So why did it feel like her life was about to explode again?

Chapter Forty-Nine

Colt followed his brothers outside. Tucker went straight to the grill on Becca's back deck, igniting it, before giving Gabe a hooded look.

Colt eyed the two men. It was hard to look at Gabe, though, he had been lying to them for years.

"What do you know about Lillian?" Gabe was leaning against the railing, his arms crossed, and frowning.

"Why?" Colt adjusted the sling. His shoulder was throbbing.

"I mean it. What do you know about her?"

Colt met his stare head on. "Apparently more than I know about you."

"What's that supposed to mean?"

"Told you. He's mooney over her," Tucker interjected.

Colt felt his anger slipping the leash he had put it on. "What's this all about?"

"Lillian is not who she says she is."

"Really?" Colt's voice dropped low. "And what, exactly, is that?"

Tucker shot Gabe a look. "What Gabe means, but is sucking-ass at communicating, is that we're all worried about you."

"Because of her past?"

"How do you know she has a past?" Gabe demanded.

"Because she told me."

Gabe scoffed. "Right. I'm sure she was completely honest with you. Do you know she was an MI6 courier? Did she tell you that?"

"Yes, she did. How long is this going to take?" His shoulder was throbbing.

"Colt, use your head. She was tried for treason. She was in bed with a double-agent."

Colt saw red. He launched himself at Gabe. He landed a left-handed punch before Tucker managed to wedge himself between them.

Tucker shoved them apart. "That's enough."

Colt's shoulder and ribs were on fire. Gabe was breathing just as hard as he was.

Colt shrugged Tucker off. "You're right. It took her almost a whole week to mention the shit storm that blew up her life and the security detail following her."

"She told you all that?"

"She also told me about the INCEPT check she had done on me."

Gabe stilled.

Colt's laugh was bitter. "That's got your attention. But you already know what she found, don't you?"

The color drained from Gabe's face. "I was going to tell you guys, I swear. I just didn't know when was the right time."

"Nice try. You had decades and still couldn't figure it out."

"Will someone tell me what the fuck you guys are talking about?" Tucker demanded.

"Gabe has the balls to say Lillian can't be trusted. Which I find hilarious, because Gabe has known for years that we have a half-brother. Tanner Stone."

Tucker stared in shocked silence.

"That's different," Gabe said.

"How, big brother? How do you justify lying to us for years? Enlighten me, I'd love to hear this."

Gabe's face had turned ashen. "It's more complicated than that."

"Dad banging some woman and knocking her up is not complicated. It's par for the course. Finding out you knew and didn't tell us—that we have another brother for chrissakes? That's the part I'm having a hard time dealing with. You lied to us, for years."

"We have another brother?"

Becca stood at the back door, Lillian and Savannah next to her.

Colt didn't think it could have gotten worse until Savannah dipped her head.

"She knows?" Colt felt his temper explode. "Your fucking girlfriend knows, but you couldn't be bothered to tell your family?"

"Savanna is my family. It's not like—"

"Fuck you." Colt was shaking he was so pissed.

Becca repeated, her voice was dazed, "We have another brother?"

Colt crossed the deck. "The math works, because as far as I'm concerned, we just lost one."

Lillian gasped, her face white.

"By the way, her intel also said dad never had cancer, and was in business with the guy that tried to murder you five years ago."

Silence.

Becca shook her head. "This is too much."

Gabe lashed out at Lillian. "Are you happy?"

Lillian stood proud and straight. "You knew about Tanner and chose not to tell them. That's on you, not me. Do not for a second try to pin your shit on me."

For tense moments, no one spoke.

Tucker broke the silence. "Let's just pause the whole half-brother thing a moment. I know dad's a dick, but in business with the guy that tried to kill his own son?"

Lillian sighed. "I'll forward the intel."

Gabe's face was like stone. "Why would you do that?"

"Let's be clear, I don't like you, either. But you should know what you're up against."

Becca stepped forward. "What exactly do you mean? Is anyone in danger?"

Lillian sighed. "Your father keeps very bad company. Better to know what you can, so you guys have a better chance of staying out of any splash zone. Hell, Gabe might have already been burned by it."

Gabe shook his head. "You go too far."

"No, I know what betrayal feels like." Lillian looked at each one of the faces staring back at her. "It's devastating. In my case, and possibly Gabe's, it was also very nearly deadly. I would save every single one of you from that." She gave Gabe a hard look. "All of you."

Dead silence.

Colt took Lillian's hand. "Time to go. You don't need to explain anything to them, and I need to be anywhere but here."

She nodded, squeezing his hand, back. It killed him to see tears in her eyes.

He turned to his brothers. "You guys are assholes. Don't call. Don't stop by. As far as I'm concerned, you both can go fuck yourselves. Never ambush me again."

Chapter Fifty

"I've never seen Gabe like that." Becca poured three glasses of wine. Lillian, Becca, and a quiet Savannah were in Becca's large kitchen. Lillian had leapt at Becca's invitation to come over for a glass of wine; she hadn't been nearly as thrilled to see Gabe's girlfriend, Savannah, was also in attendance. They sat at the island counter, an obvious distance between them, while Becca stood next to it. Lillian noticed the woman rarely sat down.

Becca pulled a small pouch out of a kitchen drawer. She opened the drawstring and slid the contents out. Small glass beads and silver charms caught the afternoon light as they tumbled out onto the counter. "I always forget to use these."

Lillian picked up one of the wine charms. It was handmade and lovely. She glanced at Becca. Her eco-inn was filled with mindful expressions of strength, beauty and grace. A lot like the woman herself.

"And I think it's good for him. For Gabe, I mean," Becca added.

Savannah straightened in her seat and Lillian thought she looked ready to do battle. Gabe was lucky to have someone so protective in his corner.

Becca selected a charm and put it around the stem of her glass. When she looked up and saw Savannah, she asked, "What did I say?"

Savannah slid off her stool. "Maybe I should go."

"No really, what's wrong?"

Savannah glanced at Lillian before turning back to Becca. "I don't want to get in the middle of this, whatever this is. Gabe is crushed Colt isn't speaking to him. This is what he was afraid of, why he didn't say something sooner about Tanner."

Becca slid a glass of wine closer to Savannah. "Easy there, princess warrior. Gabe's still recovering from all of us growing up."

"What do you mean?"

"He's the oldest. He's always been a super serious overachiever, and his sense of responsibility is off the charts. For over twenty years he's carried the burden of our dad's indiscretions. To be honest, it would have broken me, knowing that family secret and terrified I would slip and fracture the family unit, dysfunctional though it was. I know why he didn't tell us about Tanner. Our asshole father terrorized the poor kid, putting the blame on his young shoulders. That's classic Bruce. And don't get me started on him being in business with the fucking mercenary who nearly killed Gabe." Becca squared her shoulders. "But I don't want to talk about that piece of shit. Colt's upset. When he calms down, he'll understand why Gabe made the decisions he did." Becca paused. "And sorry for all the cussing, I'm angry and trying to sort this all out."

Savannah hesitantly sat back on the stool.

Lillian accepted the glass Becca handed her. "I never meant to make such a cock-up or hurt any of you. I certainly didn't intend my actions to put a wedge between you guys."

Becca waved her words away. "When our parents split, we all broke in our own way. To be clear, we weren't the poster family for functional families, either, far from it. Still, we were a family. It's been five years since our parents divorced and none of us have found our footing yet."

She clinked her wine glass with Lillian's. Savannah grudgingly joined in.

Becca took a sip of hers, looking thoughtful. "Honestly, I have high hopes this upset will blow out the pipes. Give us a chance to start fresh. If anything, you unstuck a wedge that had been festering for years."

Lillian sipped her wine and hoped Becca was right.

Becca nodded, as if answering an inner question. She took another sip. "I think I would get a background check done. I mean if I was into a guy, and I had the means to."

Savannah's eyes widened. "You don't think that's invasive?"

Becca snorted. "I know you and Gabe are tight now, but if I'm not mistaken your last serious boyfriend is currently in custody."

Lillian raised her eyebrows. "Do tell."

Savannah toyed with the charm on the stem of her glass. "It's embarrassing."

"Exactly! Don't we all have at least one boyfriend we'd rather forget existed?" Becca asked.

"Don't remind me." Savannah took a cautious sip of her wine. "I guess I could have used one of those INCEPT checks for Blaire."

Lillian set her wine glass down. "The last time I fell for a guy treason against the Crown was involved. My career imploded and I was nearly murdered."

Savannah sprayed red wine across the island counter. She clapped her hand over her mouth and nose, her eyes wide.

Becca busted out laughing. She laughed so hard, she snorted. She grabbed two tea towels and wet their corners at the sink. She handed one to Savannah, and started wiping up the sprayed wine with the other.

"*I am so sorry.*" Savannah's voice was shaking as she mopped up her face and hands.

"Don't be. That was funny. I needed that." Becca topped up her glass of wine. "This is all very weird—I have another brother." She picked up her own glass and took a huge swallow. "And you two are the closest I have to having sisters. I've decided I'm keeping you both."

Lillian and Savannah glanced at each other.

Becca took another long drink. "Basically, you're stuck with me. Do try to get along. Sisters that fight piss me off. Don't they realize how lucky they are?"

Savannah cleared her throat. "Gabe didn't mention those details about your—"

"My grandmum calls it the *unfortunate incident.*"

"It certainly sounds like it." Savannah said diplomatically. "What happened?"

Memories flooded Lillian. Instead of pushing them back down like she always did, she let them surface. "I had just finished a rough field shift. It's always harder, reporting on what's done to women and children."

Lillian closed her eyes. She could still hear the sobs of mothers and grandmothers long dead, but not before they buried their children and grandchildren. She inhaled, the memory of burning buildings and charred flesh stung her nostrils.

Her stomach rolled and her eyelids flew opened. "The men were just trying to protect their family—no man should have to face that. And no one outside cares. We're too busy drinking five-dollar coffees in single-use containers and complaining about a carbon tax or how slow the WiFi is. So I'm a mess and this guy, this *really* handsome guy, chooses me. *Me.* And I'm starved for something good, because there is just so much bad out there. Not to mention, I was breathing down forty. If there were any warning bells my heart or mind may have thrown at me, I ignored them, because he was paying attention to me. And listening. And he doesn't seem to notice or mind I'm broken." Lillian looked down. "I didn't realize at the time that it was because he didn't care."

Becca and Savannah looked at each other.

Lillian rushed out, "Colt will come around. It'll be okay. Gabe and Tucker's protection of Colt is a beautiful thing. They just don't want him to get hurt."

Savannah picked up the bottle of wine and topped Lillian's glass up. "Honey, we're talking about you now. Go on. We're listening."

Then Becca reached out and rubbed Lillian's shoulder. "I've got a whole case of that. We're not going anywhere."

A sob hit the back of Lillian's throat, and she swallowed hard, blinking. "Thank you."

Both women gave her watery smiles, moved by her experience.

Lillian blew out a breath. "As a war correspondent, I had contacts and access MI6 found useful. I was useful. They recruited me to be a courier, though I think my grandmum had something to do with it. I jumped at the chance to be able to help more. And make her proud. I did what I was told, and kept my mouth shut."

Lillian pressed her palms against her eyes a moment and took a breath. "When I met Fernando, I thought I had snagged this incredible catch. He played the woke boyfriend; how important my work was to me, my friends and independence, how I had no intentions of getting married or starting a family. Meanwhile, he was installing spyware on everything, including on any of my contacts he could get close enough to. I was a nobody, but my friends and family weren't. When he would ask to read my notes and articles, I thought he was being supportive, that he valued what I did. But he was just looking for encrypted codes and messages." Lillian shook her head, disgusted. "Do you know how hard it is to write persuasive pieces on hell, in the hopes that an apathetic world will give a damn? I mean, women are being brutalized and he's looking for fucking codes to sell."

Savannah scooted her stool closer to Lillian. "I had no idea that was your job."

"How could you? I'm covering bloody rodeos."

Becca wrapped her arm around Lillian.

Lillian squeezed her hand over Becca's. "At my trial, Fernando was there. He broke free of the guards and grabbed one of their guns to kill me. He was tackled, but not before his shot was thrown high and killed a reporter in the gallery. He murdered a hideous, weasel of a man from one of the meaner tabloids, but the guy didn't deserve to be murdered. When will the killing stop?"

Lillian pulled back and wiped her eyes. "In the world of espionage, I was a nobody. I have no idea why Fernando thought different. Seriously, I'm a nobody."

"Stop saying that. Every woman is a somebody, and that's why you do the work you do, right?

Lillian blinked at Savannah. "Damn, you're right. How did I miss that?"

Savannah took another sip of her wine.

It was the first time Lillian had opened up like that to other women. It was oddly comforting.

Becca leaned back against the island counter, elbow bent and holding her wine glass near her nose.

"What are you doing?" Savannah asked.

Becca closed her eyes and inhaled. "This smells so good, and Lillian's story was so sad."

"Wine and tea do make most things better." Lillian smiled, inhaling the bouquet in her glass. "Who is your sommelier?"

Becca pulled the wine glass away from her nose. "I don't have one. I was hoping my chef could handle it—crap, by the look on your faces that was really naive, wasn't it?"

Savannah shrugged. "Maybe your clientele won't mind."

Lillian knew the crowd she typically ran with would expect one. "Get a sommelier. The best one you can afford. They'll be worth it."

"Okay." Becca nodded, before her face crumpled. "What was I thinking? Opening an eco-inn by myself? I am in way over my head—"

Lillian rolled her eyes. "Said no man ever. Did you know that statistically men apply for jobs if they meet at least sixty percent of the requirements? Apparently, women only apply if they have them all. You got this. What you don't, you'll figure out."

Savannah raised her glass. "Amen, sister."

Becca blew out a breath. "I second-guess myself a hundred times a day."

"Means you're growing," Lillian wanted to assure the woman.

Becca stood straighter. "I know my brothers are stubborn, we'll get to them in a sec." She looked at Lillian. "How do I reach out to Tanner Stone?"

"Like, right now?"

Becca nodded.

Lillian had a contact number listed for him from the INCEPT check. She pulled up the file on her secure mobile. "Here you go."

Becca stared at it. "I'm scared."

"So's he." Lillian reasoned.

Savannah grabbed a sticky pad and pen and wrote the number down. She handed it to Becca. "For when you're ready."

Becca looked up. "Let's do this."

Savannah glanced at Lillian.

Becca picked up her mobile, but stopped. "I don't even know how to dial this. Where is this number from?"

Lillian looked at the number. "It's an Australian mobile number. The international access and country code is included."

Becca dialed. She held her mobile up to her ear and looked a bit queasy. Her gaze darted between Lillian and Savannah. After a few moments, her shoulders slumped. Suddenly she tensed. "Um, this message is for Tanner Stone, it's Becca Tanner. I'll call back." She hung up abruptly, nearly dropping it.

"I think I'm going to puke."

"You did great." Savannah encouraged.

Lillian handed her her wine glass. "Yes, you did."

Becca's eyes were round. "Okay. Now, about my other brothers."

Chapter Fifty-One

"You can't ignore your brother forever." Lillian whispered to Colt. They were back in the local history section of the downtown library. It had been a week since the disastrous blow out between Colt and his brothers.

"It won't be forever." Colt resumed reading the history book in front of him.

She placed her hand on his arm. "Honey, please. You're obviously hurting."

"So? I'll get over it. I'm just not there, yet." She called him Honey.

"This is my fault." Lillian started tapping what he now knew was her tactical pen against the table. "If I hadn't gotten that INCEPT check done, none of this—"

"No, my brother's a selfish ass who didn't find time in two decades to mention we had a half-brother."

"Would you typically describe Gabe as selfish?"

"No."

"Exactly. Hear him out. I've met bad people. Your brother is not one of them."

"He doesn't need to be an international arms dealer to be an asshole."

"So, he was an asshole. We all can be from time to time. Hear him out."

Colt made a frustrated groan, deep in his throat.

"I know, this whole thing is not on. Please, just talk to him. To both of them."

"Fine, I'll talk to Gabe and Tucker."

Lillian dropped her head down to the library table. "Thank the lord."

He smiled. "You're cute when you're frustrated."

She popped her head up, sweeping her hair back from her forehead. "Thank you for noticing."

Lillian glanced at the book in his hand. "What are you reading?"

He shrugged. "Just a collection of letters and stuff. Your research got me interested in history."

She smiled. "Told you it's addictive. Now," she looked at her laptop, "I think I have Becca's report ready. I just have to print it—and send."

Colt had no idea what she was talking about.

Lillian pointed to a printer a few meters away. "I just sent the report to that printer."

Colt started to stand, and she snaked her hand out. "Nope, I got it. Stay down."

He bristled. "I'm not feeble."

"Never said you were." Lillian stood and headed to the printer.

"My legs still work," he called after her.

She tossed him a very feminine smile as she picked up the copies.

Lillian came back from the printer, report in hand. "Any chance I could see what else works?"

Heat flooded Colt, and more than his shoulder was throbbing. "Now. I am so ready right now. Let's go."

Lillian grinned. "You're going to a rodeo with Shayne and Jake tonight, and I'm meeting with Rose Chasseur." She tidied the stack of papers and slid them into a large envelope. "But . . . I could come over, after."

"I'll skip the rodeo; you reschedule with Rose." He leaned in, nuzzling her neck with soft kisses.

Lillian turned her head and he slanted his mouth over hers. Without breaking the kiss, she dropped the envelope on the table and twinned her hands around his neck.

Long moments later she pulled back with a sigh. "I *love* when you do that with your tongue."

"Say the word, and I will do anything you want me to with my tongue."

She made a frustrated sound. "To be continued, tonight. Go see your friends. I'll meet with Rose. And I'll meet you at your place after."

"Promise?"

Lillian pressed her lips to his quickly. "Yes."

She handed him the envelope with the report. "Here. Can you give this to Becca tomorrow? While you're there, you can talk to Gabe. He and Savannah are still staying with her."

Colt accepted the report, frowning.

Lillian snatched the report back. "Tonight is not conditional upon that. That's not how I roll."

It was Colt's turn to hesitate. "I didn't think so—"

"Tonight is only about you and me, right?" Her voice shook with emotion.

"Of course."

He had forgotten about her ex. He hadn't meant to be insensitive; he didn't like it when people used sex as leverage, either.

She blew out a breath. "I'll understand if you want to change your mind. I told you, I'm broken."

He tucked a strand of hair behind her ear. "You're wild, not broken."

Lillian's eyes glassed with unshed tears. "That's the sweetest thing anyone has ever said to me."

"It's true." He gently took the report from her other hand. "I will give this to Becca tomorrow. No promises on talking to Gabe. Be patient with me."

"Absolutely."

He tucked the envelope under his arm sling and held out his left hand to her. "Come on. I'll walk you to your security detail's car." He stopped. "They heard all of that?"

"More or less."

"They know where I live, don't they?"

She nodded.

Colt was still wrapping his head around Lillian's world.

He just hoped when the two months was over, there would be a place left in it for him.

Chapter Fifty-Two

"And this remote will activate it?" The mercenary confirmed.

His brother nodded. "Yup. Let me just get it into place."

Christopher Fischer could blow things up like any brute, but Austin made sophisticated incendiary devices. He also was currently using his latest UAV—a drone that was able to scramble current surveillance methods—to rest the small, unmarked package against Colt Tanner's door.

Lillian Kensington's security detail was proving to be rather tenacious. Since Lillian and the bull rider started spending time together, they periodically swept the bull rider's house. Since they started sleeping together, they did daily sweeps with surveillance.

Christopher frowned, scanning the perimeter. Kensington's security detail were good. One misstep could get Austin and Christopher killed.

"It's in place." Austin piloted the drone back and quickly packed it up. "I still think it's possible she won't come straight here."

Both men got back into the truck. Christopher had parked them on a nearby road allowance. To a casual onlooker, they simply looked like ranchers. Christopher started the truck, before activating the bomb.

"People like her are predictable. She'll come."

He pulled out onto the rural highway.

Austin tapped his knee with his thumb, and he stared out the window.

"Fernando Martinez is a jackass."

"So?"

"So, don't you ever get sick of dealing with jackasses? I mean, the money's good."

Christopher slanted his brother a look. "Only if they pay. We just activated a motion-sensitive bomb to murder a woman because her old boyfriend doesn't pay his bills on time. One could argue that's a fairly asshole move."

"What do you think she has that Martinez wants so bad?" Austin asked.

"Don't know, don't care."

"It's probably worth a lot of money."

"Chasing shiny objects is a good way to get dead."

"*Stay focused,* I know," Austin grumbled. "You have a lot of rules."

"Keeps us alive." There was only Austin and Christopher left. The rest of their family was dead.

Unlike the living, there were no regrets when you were dead. And Lillian Kensington wouldn't be alive to regret getting tangled up with Fernando Martinez for much longer.

Christopher's phone vibrated.

Martinez had paid them what he owed and sent new instructions.

"What about the bomb?" Austin asked.

Christopher kept driving. "That's our insurance. It's time to go to work."

Chapter Fifty-Three

Colt stared through the windshield of his truck. He was parked in the cut hay field that made up the parking lot of the small-town fair. The sun had set but it wasn't full dark. He could see the lights of the midway blinking in the summer night. The halo of lights ringing the rodeo arena illuminated a swirling mass of bugs at each light.

Classic rock was playing from several midway rides, punctuated by the calls of the rodeo announcer. This had been his world for so long, it was weird not being a part of it anymore. Colt hooked his thumb on the bottom of the steering wheel. Maybe he'd go in in a few more minutes, though he'd already missed half of it. He hadn't been able to make himself get out of the truck. Since the wreck, people treated him different. He couldn't deal with the looks, the earnest words of regret. Bull-riding had a shelf life. He had always known that. That wasn't what had him turned inside-out.

Lillian.

He didn't know if he was coming or going because of a woman. If she were here, she would turn that beautiful smile on him. He'd tell her he changed his mind, that he didn't want to go in. She would nod, place her hand on his arm and calmly say in that adorable accent, *So, come on then, in you go.*

And he would. With Lillian he could do anything. She was the strongest person he knew. Fearless.

"Oh my god." Colt covered his mouth with his left hand.

He loved her.

That smart, beautiful, uptight Brit had blown past his carefully constructed fortress of solitude.

What was he doing here? He didn't want to be out of town, he wanted to see her, to tell her. He wanted her. More than just sex, though that was incredible with her, he wanted her. Forever. He had to tell her.

But first, nature called. There was no way he would make the drive home without stopping first. He could see a row of porta-potties lining the edge of the field parking lot and got out of the truck.

As he was making his way back between the rows of ranch trucks and SUVs, his shoulder ached something fierce. Colt adjusted the arm brace he was wearing and smiled. Like he told Lillian, there were worse things in life than physical pain.

He couldn't wait to see her.

A blunt thump sounded as pain exploded in his head.

Then everything went black.

Chapter Fifty-Four

"Thank you so much for meeting with me." Lillian sat at Rose Chasseur's kitchen table. A fresh pot of tea sat between them, as were fresh-baked muffins.

"Oh, my pleasure, dear. I'm just happy someone is interested."

Lillian could see the sun setting beyond Rose's kitchen window. The sun had painted the sky in brilliant shades of orange and gold.

She stared, enchanted. "I've never seen a sunset like that."

"They are pretty, aren't they?" She motioned to the tin of muffins. "Please help yourself. I baked these fresh this afternoon."

Lillian felt her chest squeeze briefly. She smiled at Ms. Chasseur and dutifully placed one on the small plate Rose had put in front of her. She took a nibble.

"These are amazing." They were better than anything from her favorite cafés in London. She took a bigger bite.

Rose beamed. "Glad you like them. I've seen you with that nice young man, Colt Tanner. I hear his brother, Tucker, is quite the chef."

Lillian fidgeted. Since the blow-up, Colt and Becca were the only Tanner siblings speaking to her. In a conspiratorial whisper, though, she said, "I hear the real treat is his brownies."

Rose clapped her hands together. "I do love a man who can cook. Now, how can I help you?"

Lillian was more than happy to change the subject. "I was hoping you could tell me what you know about *Fort Roche Cachée* and *Fort La Jonquière*." Lillian pulled out her notebook.

She rubbed her chest again. Her stomach wasn't feeling well, either.

Lillian cleared her throat. "I'm still learning North American fur trade history, but my research has led me to *Fort Roche Cachée* and *Fort La Jonquière*. They both are quite mysterious. Academics don't agree where *Fort La Jonquière* was, and your article for the historical society is the only one I found that mentions *Fort Roche Cachée* at all."

Though Rose Chasseur seemed like a kind woman, Lillian erred on the side of caution, and did not divulge her family connection to the fort.

Rose leaned forward. "I've always wondered about both of those, too. I have old family documents that mention *Fort Roche Cachée*." She raised her forefinger like a school marm. "However, it is important to keep in mind fur trade posts and forts could be seasonal, and their names and locations could be quite fluid."

"Are you serious?"

Rose nodded. "The names of forts or posts could, but not necessarily, change when the chief factor changed, too. A location one year might be moved the following year or even years, for various reasons. Sometimes the fort or post retained the same name, other times it changed. Sometimes if it moved again, it took a former name."

"Ms. Chasseur, you don't know how relieved I am to hear you say that. I was having a heck of a time, trying to keep everything straight."

Rose threw her hands up. "I hear you, dear. It is a logistic researching nightmare. Fur trade houses, like Edmonton House, once they were established, tended to stay put and with the same name."

Lillian nodded. Her chest was still feeling *weird*. She surreptitiously rubbed where her sternum met her rib cage.

"Please, call me Rose. And I remember when I first started researching, the rabbit holes I would go down trying to make heads or tails of the information. It is quite a merry chase." Rose paused. "It can also be incredibly frustrating. Are you following a family history?"

Lillian couldn't see a problem with sharing part of the truth. "I'm helping Colt's sister, Becca. She's interested in protecting the history of the area."

Rose brightened considerably at that. "I haven't seen Becca in ages. How's she doing? I hear she's opening an eco-inn. How exciting. I can't imagine doing something like that when I was her age. You young women, you have so much spunk. Come to think off it, that sounds like a lot of work. I'm guessing she has a partner to help her?"

"I don't think so, and she's run pretty ragged. Her launch is in a few months."

Lillian really wasn't feeling well.

"That's so much work to do by herself." Rose stood then. "Hold on a second. I would love to help Becca any way I can. I'll just get those documents we talked about."

When Rose left the kitchen, Lillian undid the top two buttons of her blouse. Her breath was coming in too fast and her heartbeat felt erratic. She closed her eyes and a vision exploded in her mind.

Colt.

Rose walked back into the room. "Is everything all right, dear?"

Lillian could barely breath, the vision had been so visceral. "I do apologize, an emergency has come up."

"Is there anything I can do to help?"

"No, thank you." Lillian scooped up her notebook and satchel. "I'm so sorry. I'll call again."

She dashed out the door without a backwards glance.

Chapter Fifty-Five

Colt woke up in a rush. His shoulder was screaming at him, and he was laying on his side, his hands bound behind his back. He blinked, trying to focus in the dim light. He was alone in the back of a large vehicle, like a cube van. Empty racks lined the spacious cargo area.

He could very well die here. He thought about his brothers wouldn't know that he was sorry. That it had been his angry pride that stopped him from calling them back.

And he thought about Lillian.

He had to get out of here.

Colt wiggled his wrists, trying to find purchase. Gabe or Tucker would know what to do. Colt worked his wrists again. They gave the slightest fraction of an inch, but his shoulder was screaming.

A dark idea surfaced.

He didn't know how much time he had. It might be his best shot.

Colt maneuvered himself over to one of the vertical metal rack posts framing the back of the van. Positioning himself, Colt gritted his teeth and slammed his right shoulder into the frame.

Searing pain lit through his whole body. Stars dances through his vision, and he nearly passed out, but he hadn't heard what he was going for.

Sucking in air through his teeth, he positioned himself again, this time slamming his shoulder harder against the metal posts.

Pop.

He slumped over. Counting his breaths, still alive, he wiggled again, this time his defunct shoulder allowed him to slide his bound hands to his front. He bit, jiggled, and finessed the ropes until he got one loose enough to slip.

He pulled off the other one. Then he shoved the rope between his teeth and lined himself up against the metal frame. He closed his eyes.

This was going to hurt.

Slam.

Colt swayed as stars danced in his vision again.

He lined himself up again.

Slam.

He heard a click. And swayed in pain.

Tentatively, he moved the fingers on his right hand before testing his shoulder.

His shoulder was back in its socket.

Colt looked around the empty cargo space. The only weapon he had was the rope and surprise.

He hoped it would be enough.

Chapter Fifty-Six

"Do you think they saw us?" Sophie was scared. They had just left the lights of the small-town rodeo behind.

"I don't think so." Craig squeezed her hand before returning both hands to the wheel. "That was Colt Tanner, right?"

"It was hard to tell in the dim light, but I think so. If it wasn't Colt, it's somebody else who needs our help." The man had been jumped from behind and stuffed into the back of a cargo van before it sped away. They were following at a discreet distance.

Earlier, Sophie had snuck past her security detail. She had just wanted to hang out with Craig, and she hadn't told him the whole truth about her 'bodyguards' as she called them.

For weeks, Sophie had chatted up her security detail, playing the pliable nineteen year old who would never dream of sneaking out. Now she wished she hadn't culti-vated such a believable persona. Her security detail was so vigilant for external threats, they hadn't seen her deceit coming, and now she needed them.

Craig said, "We should call Officer Chasseur. You still have his number, right? He's the one officer I trust. My stepdad has buddies in the RCMP."

"Remember I told you that half my family are overachievers?"

"Yeah."

Sophie rushed out, "My aunt was a war correspondent and courier for MI6 before she was duped by a double-agent who swore he would kill her."

Craig turned his head quick. "Jesus, Sophie, you're just telling me this, now?"

"Focus Craig." Sophie motioned with her hand in the dark. "This shit, has that wanker written all over it."

She pulled out her phone.

"You're calling Officer Chasseur. Good."

"No, darling, I'm calling my security detail. I slipped them earlier tonight."

Sophie started texting her security detail.

"Who are you? What is happening?"

She kept typing as she spoke, "Stop being so dramatic. I wanted to hang out with you, you know, *without* an audience."

Craig's mouth dropped open. "Are you serious?"

Sophie looked up from her mobile. "I wanted our first time to be special. And private."

Craig audibly exhaled.

The moment was ruined when the cargo van in front of them slowed.

"Shit, what do we do?" Craig asked.

Sophie hit send. "Pull into the next side thingy."

"Do you mean Range Road or road allowance?"

"Dude, you're speaking Greek. I don't care. Just take your first right after the driveway. I'll figure it out. I've been trained for this since I was a kid. My grandmum made sure of it."

Chapter Fifty-Seven

The sun had nearly set by the time Lillian pulled into the narrow lane of Colt's rural ranch yard. No lights were on inside the house. A lone yard light cast long shadows in the dim light. Colt hadn't answered his phone in the ten minutes from Rose Chasseur's house, nor had Becca. She didn't have Gabe or Tucker's numbers. Fear like she had never known pressed in. Lillian launched herself out of the car, calling Colt's name.

Her detail intercepted her several steps from Colt's front stairs.

"Get back in the car."

Her detail's voice wasn't frosty, just dead serious. Lillian automatically started backing up.

Then she noticed there was a package resting against his door.

"What's that?" She pointed.

"Stop, don't move."

Lillian froze.

Gabe stepped out of the shadows.

Three more of her detail emerged, pulling their sidearms, all aiming at Gabe.

Gabe held up his hands.

Calmly, in full control he said, "Call them off."

"What are you doing here?" Lillian dared a glance around the yard. Something felt off.

"Shayne called. Colt never showed up." Gabe's voice was bleak. "It's my brother."

One of her detail stepped forward. Gabe allowed himself to be patted down.

Still holding his arms up, he said, "I'm not carrying. But I'd bet that package has a bomb in it."

A second of her security detail had already cautiously moved to the stairs. He pulled out a handheld device and briefly waved it over the envelope.

He slowly stood and started backing up. "Motion-sensitive, remote activated. Blast ranking three with a range of six, plus or minus two degrees."

The detail that had patted down Gabe said, "Both you guys, get in the car, now. It's reinforced."

A dark SUV pulled into the narrow drive, swerving around them.

Omran was driving.

Lillian swore. Her lack of security clearance was doin' her head in.

Omran rolled down his window. "I put a tracker on Colt. I'm sending the coordinates link. I'll take care of the bomb. Go get your boy."

Gabe and Lillian piled into the backseat and the SUV sped off.

Gabe eyed the two men in the front seat. "They're not here officially, are they?"

Lillian rubbed her temples. "If they get Colt out safe, does it matter?"

"No. Colt's the only thing that matters right now."

Her detail in the front passenger seat said, "We have his location. ETA twenty minutes."

Seventeen minutes later her mobile rang.

It was Fernando.

Chapter Fifty-Eight

It hadn't been enough. Colt strained against the new ropes that bound him. A man he had never met was beating him. Colt tried to blink. Two men stood off to the side. One was younger. Both looked unimpressed at the guy beating him.

The guy was screaming, taunting Colt.

Spit flew from his mouth. "She thought she could go slumming?"

Thump. Thump.

Colt grunted with each vicious kick to his ribs.

"She thought she was smarter than me?"

This time the guy kicked Colt in the head. Pain exploded between his ears.

"Lillian is nothing!" he screamed. "She's a nobody! Do you hear me? A nobody!"

The guy's shrieks were maniacal.

Colt focused on Lillian; she had an elite security detail. She would be safe.

His deranged attacker rained more blows down on him. Colt took it. If they were beating him, they weren't attacking Lillian.

She would be safe.

Lillian had to be safe.

Colt had no idea how long he had been here, or how much longer his body would hold up.

Then everything went black again.

Chapter Fifty-Nine

A cruel laugh sounded. *"Your boy is still alive. For now."*

Lillian's stomach dropped. She put the phone on speaker.

Fernando was still talking. *"Your boy can take a hit, I'll give him that."*

Lillian's gaze flew to Gabe's. "Fernando, what did you do?"

"You have something of mine, so I took something of yours."

"What are you talking about? I don't have anything of yours."

"What do you think I am, stupid? Who else could it be?" It came through as a shriek.

Lillian closed her eyes. Fernando in control was dangerous. Fernando out of control was terrifying.

Gabe made a circling motion with his hands. *Keep him talking.*

"What do you want? I'll get whatever you want."

"You know what I'm talking about. I want the blueprints back."

"What blueprints? I'll get them, just tell me where they are, or what they are. I'll find whatever you're looking for."

The line went dead.

Lillian's gaze flew to Gabe's. "I have no idea what he's talking about. How can I deliver something I don't have?"

Chapter Sixty

"They just turned into that small ranch yard." Sophie squinted. Moonlight glinted off rows of twisted metal. "Make that a weird junkyard. We can't leave Colt in there. What if they're torturing or murdering him?"

"That escalated fast." But Craig slowed the matte black three-quarter ton he had bought from Clint Steele only yesterday, to the side of the road. He backed into the unused road allowance a few hundred meters from the junk yard drive. Tall prairie grasses swayed around the truck. The full moon shone bright overhead. The matte black of the truck blended well with the inky darkness of the horizon.

She pulled out her phone.

"What are you doing?"

"Sending my auntie a pin of where we are."

She added a brief text message. *I think Colt's been kidnapped.*

"Now, I'm calling Officer Chasseur." He answered on the first ring. She put him on speaker.

"Chasseur here."

"Officer Chasseur, it's Sophie Kensington. Craig and I saw two men jump who we think is Colt Tanner at the Black Gold Rodeo grounds and put him in their truck. He wasn't moving after they hit him on the back of the head. We followed them."

"Do not engage—"

She interrupted him, "Duh."

"Stay on the line," Officer Chasseur said.

Sophie heard muted voices over a radio.

"They turned into a small ranch yard, it looks like a weird junkyard." Sophie pulled up the map app on her phone and rattled off the nearest intersection to where they parked.

"I know the place. I'm on another call and can't leave. I'm calling it in. You kids get the hell out of there, now!"

Sophie looked at Craig when she answered, "Of course, Officer Chasseur."

"Why didn't you call nine-one-one?"

"You mean because our last run-in with law enforcement went *so* well?"

"I know the system isn't per—"

Sophie hung up.

"Did you just hang up on him?"

"We're fine. He'll thank me, later."

Sophie set her mobile on silent. She clicked the tactical pen her aunt had given her on her thirteenth birthday. And turned to Craig. "Darling, I love you, but you've had zero training for this sort of thing, I am not letting that tosser kill Colt. I'll go in from here."

Craig was staring at her. "You love me?"

Sophie stopped. "Yeah, babe, I thought you knew that?"

Craig gripped the steering wheel. "Um, no. You've never said that."

She pressed a hard, quick kiss to his lips. "I gotta go. I'll show you later how much I'm into you."

Sophie went to open her truck door.

"I'm not letting you go in alone."

"Letting me—"

Craig reached behind the seat and pulled out an oversized wrench. "I love you, too. I can't let anything happened to you. We'll go in, together."

Sophie pressed her index finger against his lips. "I have combat training."

"Seriously?"

"It's more like defensive training until my security detail steps in. They will be here in," she checked her phone, "one hundred and twenty seconds."

"I'm going with you." Craig flipped the switch so the interior lights would not come on when they opened their door.

Sophie looked up at the lights that didn't go on. "Can you sabotage the vehicle they just drove in?"

"Of course."

"Swear to god, if you get dead, I'll never forgive you."

"I know."

"Fine. Decommission any vehicle that looks drivable. Let's go."

Chapter Sixty-One

"*Shoot him.*" Fernando shrieked.

Austin looked at Christopher, eyebrows raised.

Christopher sighed. He could be enjoying a new Pinot noir at home instead of catering to this freak show—the double-agent was unstable and a huge pain in the ass.

The cowboy on the crowd groaned, and Fernando Martinez started kicking him, again. He had broken both of his hands beating the bull rider and couldn't hold a gun. Fucking moron.

"Control yourself, man." Christopher chastised.

"*Shoot him.*" Fernando shrieked, again.

Christopher gave him a cold smile. "That's not in our current contract. She was the target, not him."

"Aren't you waiting for blueprints of some sort?" Austin reasoned.

Martinez turned on him. "What do you know of those? They're mine. Do you hear me? Mine!"

The battered cowboy on the ground's eyes rounded and he held up his bound hands in warning.

But Christopher had already seen the Spaniard lunging for Austin.

He fired.

The Spaniard dropped to the ground, dead.

Christopher looked at Austin. "Never work on credit."

Chapter Sixty-Two

"*Clear.*"

As soon as Lillian heard the word, she blew past her security detail. She ran into the garage where a body lay unmoving on the floor. She dropped to her knees next to Colt. He was bound and badly beaten—alive, but just barely.

Tears streamed down Lillian's face, she wanted to clutch Colt to her, but without knowing what was broken, she didn't know what to hold. She said his name, over and over. Sirens sounded in the distance. Then Gabe was there, pulling her away. The paramedics were taking Colt away.

She screamed, trying to grab for him, her cowboy. Gabe held her up, half carrying her to their waiting vehicles.

Lillian saw him then—Fernando—dead on the ground.

It was over.

Except it wasn't. Colt was fighting for his life. As they followed the ambulance, Lillian rocked in her seat. *"He has to be okay,"* she repeated over and over.

The security detail in the front passenger seat handed Gabe a blanket. He gently wrapped it around Lillian.

"Colt's tough as nails," Gabe said quietly.

He didn't look at Lillian the rest of the ride.

Chapter Sixty-Three

It was taking longer than it should. Sweat gathered on the back of Agent Omran Forest's neck as he worked to defuse the bomb. He'd never seen the design before.

Neither had the agent on the other end of his earpiece.

Omran ran another set of diagnostics. He swore when it came up with nothing. Bombs going off tended to alert the highest levels of governments. No one wanted an international incident.

A dark SUV pulled into the small ranch yard. It was one of the Jordemorden crews. Omran stood and started walking over. Maybe they had seen the likes of it before.

Omran heard the blast before he felt the heat. He was flung forward like a rag doll.

The bomb had detonated.

Chapter Sixty-Four

"It's been four days. How long is she going to stay there?" Craig whispered.

Sophie stood next to him, in the small foyer of the hospital room. Colt lay in the hospital bed. He was heavily bandaged up, and had only regained consciousness twice, but his vitals were strong.

"As long as it takes." Sophie paused. "My auntie is loyal, sometimes to a fault."

Becca agreed. She looked at the woman, finally asleep in the chair. Lillian had pulled the chair next to Colt's hospital bed and had barely moved from her post, since. Sometime yesterday, she had allowed her niece to wash her hair, and run a comb through it. Lillian had also changed into one of the extra sets of clothes Sophie had brought.

Craig's voice cracked with emotion. "We got there too late, we should have done more."

Sophie shook her head. "Don't. That's basic head survival one-oh-one. You can't play that what-if game. We can't possibly know how it would have played out. They could have shot Colt if they saw us. And we still don't know who killed Fernando. I'd like to, I'd send them a fucking Christmas card, before—"

Becca cleared her throat.

A police officer walking past had stopped just outside the door at the word *shot*, and looked in the room when Sophie mentioned *killed*.

The audacious young Brit pointedly stared at the officer and waved. He shook his head before he resumed walking down the hall.

Becca wrapped her arms around herself. "Craig, I hear congratulations are in order. You were offered a Formula One crew position? That's amazing!"

Sophie snapped her head around. "What?"

Craig looked embarrassed. "An apprentice position. Before this all happened, your aunt contacted a couple crew guys. She mentioned me and asked if there was anything available. They called me for an interview two days ago. I had to do a few tests, too, but I was offered an apprentice position." He hesitated. "I have to tell them by tomorrow."

"This is like a dream job, you have to go for it!"

He looked panicked. "What about us?"

Sophie grabbed his face and kissed him, hard. "Babe, we got this. You do your pit crew thing, I'm going to drop skiing, get a political science masters and give my great-grandmum a run for her money. We'll figure the rest out as we go."

Craig was kissing Sophie back, Colt's machines were still beeping as they should, and Lillian was still asleep. Becca ducked into the hall, before she lost her nerve. She dialed the long number.

Voicemail picked up, again.

She swallowed the lump down in her throat. "Um, hi. This message is for Tanner Stone. It's Becca . . . again. I know this is all super weird, and I don't want to be a total pain bothering you, but Colt's been hurt, bad." She paused. "He's your half-brother, I just thought you should know."

Hands shaking, she hung up quickly.

She turned, staring at Colt through the window glass.

Chapter Sixty-Five

Lillian woke up with a start, and remembered. *Colt.* She stared at the hospital room ceiling and tried to prepare, in case—in case he was gone.

"Good morning, sleepy head."

Lillian's gaze flew down.

Not only was Colt alive, he was awake, and smiling at her.

"*Colt.*" Lillian launched herself at him, in slow motion. "Where can I hug? Where can I kiss that it won't hurt?"

His swelling had gone down considerably, and she could see his dimples again. She finally settled on gently holding his hand.

"*Well,* since you asked." He grinned, letting the words dangle between them.

Her heart felt like it would expand through her ribcage. "If you're thinking *that,* you must be doing better."

Colt was alive.

She swallowed a sob. Still clutching his hand, Lillian whispered, "I thought I lost you."

Colt cradled her cheek with his other hand. "Honey, don't cry. I'm here, we're safe. While you were still sleeping, an Agent Omran came in. He said it was over and that Fernando was dead. He also said something about a bomb, and that the front of my house blew up—"

Lillian's eyes rounded.

"It's okay, it's okay, no one was hurt. I'll care later about the details." Colt's face crumpled and he pressed his forehead to hers. "Right now, I just need you, safe and here."

Lillian gently snuggled next to him in the hospital bed. They held each other for long minutes.

Colt kissed Lillian. "I didn't get a chance to type it up fancy—not like you would have, but I found *BeeBee* and Seamus. They did get their happily ever after."

"What do you mean?"

"You were so sad with where the letter you had of *BeeBee's* ended that I wanted to see if I could find anything else. With the help of several patient librarians, and an archivist, we found Piety's letters. *BeeBee* and Seamus reunited, actually told each other they were in love with the other, got married, and moved back to Ireland. I have copies of their marriage certificate, and the baptism certificates for their four children—evenly spaced two years apart."

"You did all that research for me?"

Colt's voice was serious. "I wanted to give you a happy ending."

Lillian's heart surged. She knew he wasn't talking about *BeeBee* and Seamus anymore.

"For real?" she asked.

"For always. I love you. I know you're independent, I just hope there's room in your life for me. And I mean forever, if you'll have me. I want to marry you, but if that's too traditional—"

"Ohmygod, *yes!*" She blurted, "Wait, I'm late."

Colt stared and she rushed out, "I don't know if that changes things for you. I know we thought we were being careful." She stopped. "The only thing I know is, I love you, too. So much. Being with you feels like breathing. Completely, hopelessly, necessary."

"You love me." Colt hugged her tighter, before blowing out a breath. "I never considered having kids before, have you?"

Lillian shook her head.

"Want to?" Colt asked.

Lillian looked into those North Sea eyes. "With you, yes. Yes, I do. And it scares the shit out of me."

"Promise me we'll take turns freaking out?"

"Good call. We both can't freak out at the same time, that would be Barney Rubble."

He dropped a kiss against her forehead. "You are so adorable. I love you so much—ohmygod, a kiddo." He looked stunned.

"Maybe, I didn't take a test yet." She gently traced her fingers across his chest. "I love you, too. Whatever happens, we'll figure it out together. You saved my life, Colt."

"Pretty sure we saved each other. I talked to Gabe and Tucker."

"How long was I asleep?" Was she pregnant? "Are you guys good?"

"We're good." He waited a beat. "With you eating red meat again, does this mean we can serve steak at our wedding?"

"Only if we also have those little ketchup sachets."

Epilogue

Tanner Stone replayed the voicemail again. His sister seemed nice.

He ran a hand through his hair and blew out a breath he had been holding. He hoped Colt made it. His brother. That was still weird to say. He didn't know the guy, wasn't even sure he wanted to.

But they mattered to him.

His laptop beeped, a welcome distraction. He pulled up the encrypted email from his boss. His kill at Bruce Tanner's wedding had been verified. Tanner had been given a shoot-to-kill order by his bosses. The man he had taken out was wanted in seven countries. Gabe wasn't the only agent in the family.

Tanner was still putting the pieces together on who had tried to murder Gabe. From what he knew, there was no way Gabe would have knowingly corroborated with his father and compromised a mission. Bruce Tanner setting up his son to be ambushed and murdered? That was completely feasible.

His biological father was as dirty as they come. Tanner knew it. He just had to prove it.

DON'T MISS: NOT AN EASY TRUCE

Book 3 in the *Hearthstone* series

What if the one person you are trying to forget was your heart's deepest desire?

Becca Tanner is determined to make her dude ranch inn nestled in the foothills of the Canadian Rocky Mountains open on time and be a success. Nowhere in her business plan did she pencil in time for arms dealers and drug runners, manipulating fathers, or sparring matches with her one-sided, decade-long crush, Officer Jason Chasseur. She invested everything she had and more that she didn't into her dream and she'll go down swinging before giving up on herself or those counting on her.

RCMP Officer Jason Chasseur doesn't believe for a second Becca Tanner didn't know her father pushed him out of the chance to buy back his family's ancestral land. That sparks fly whenever she's near is irrelevant. When the land in question turns out to be an active criminal basecamp and Becca is forcefully recruited, he knows she is in way over her head.

As the time ticks down to opening weekend, Becca is running out of time. As danger mounts, she digs in deeper, determined to keep her livelihood and wits about her. Small consolation if she's dead, a fact Jason is quick to remind her as he hustles with everything he has to keep her safe. Family secrets keep pace with them as they run headlong into each new threat. Can they trust each other long enough to help a broken criminal family heal and finally accept the love that has always been between them?

Author's Note

Each author has their own creative process, and the characters who entrust me to tell their stories (because that's what it feels like) tend to take my hand and show me what their story is.

Years ago, Lillian and Colt came into my awareness. They gave me the start of their story and then quietly waited in the background as I paused my fiction writing to craft a non-fiction book with an active-duty homicide detective. After that project, they remained shy, silent even, while Becca and Jason from *Not an Easy Truce* started chatting like crazy.

Turns out my process isn't linear.

After I finished *Not an Easy Truce*, Becca and Jason's story and book three of this series, I came back to Lillian and Colt's story, book two. Although shy, these two characters have kept pace in my heart the whole time and I realized why they were quiet—I am a different person than the one who started their first scenes all those years ago. So is this planet. From climate instability to social justice movements, we are in times of great change. Some change I welcome with open arms, like a wise friend I didn't realize how badly I needed them until they came into my life. Now I can't imagine my life without them. Other change I can only hope spurs positive action, because the alternative can t be all there is.

When I was writing this book, there were three instances of lethal, brutal violence against women that made wide headlines. Let me repeat that—three made wide headlines. My mind short-circuits when I consider how many actual murders and violence against women occurred during that time. So does the number of catastrophic weather events, water instability, ongoing pollution crisis...the lists go on and on.

As I was writing *Wild Not Broken*, Lillian and Colt took me by the hand as I struggled with what is a reality for so many — violence, fear, instability and fighting for basic survival. The experience was not unlike writing the nonfiction police memoir with the active-duty homicide detective. There is a lot of darkness out there. When I would stumble writing *Wild Not Broken*, Lillian and Colt would remind me there is also great light. From woman reclaiming their inherent power to men reclaiming their inherent kindness; from regenerative agriculture to the energy transition, I feel we are on a path of deep positive change.

This is not an easy time, but we are making collective progress — why do you think the old systems are resisting so hard? We heal our beautiful planet, and our relationship with each other, by healing our relationship with ourselves. This is why I write the books I do; I want to open dialogues, expand awarenesses gently, and help readers connect to Momma Earth and themselves.

This is ReWilding.

Welcome Home.

Sarah

Jan 2022

Calgary, Alberta

Author's Notes & Acknowledgements

I can't imagine skipping down this crazy, beautiful path without the incredible people in my life. Writing this book has reminded me, in no uncertain terms, that I am surrounded by extraordinary individuals— kind, smart, generous souls who share their talents and wisdom, and make this world a brighter, happier place. Mark Leslie Lefebvre, your belief in me inspires me to keep expanding what I thought possible. Adrienne Kerr, you understand the very core of my work. Dawn van de Schoot, you are my artist touchstone. Scott Hamilton, for the twenty-plus year (and counting) fur trade conversation. Guy Slater, for introducing me to the concept of Post Traumatic Stress Injury. James Graham, you stepped in at the eleventh hour—mo carraig. To Harold and Joan Johnson, Tammy Lynn Carbol, Liz Anderson, Allison Gorner, Jessica L. Jackson, Susan Forest, Shelley Kassian, Tania Therien, Deb Draper, Dave Sweet, Lorraine Paton, June Baxter, Diana Mary, Randy McCharles, Val King, the Alberta Romance Writers' Association and When Words Collide communities, my friends and extended family, you all have helped me get here, my profound *thank you.*

I had generous support from Calgary Arts Development and The City of Calgary to write *Not an Easy Truce,* the next book in the Hearthstone Series. My process is not linear, and I needed to write *Not an Easy Truce* before I could write *Wild Not Broken*. That support changed my life. The magic from that experience continues to sparkle and shine through every facet of my life. I am deeply appreciative to Calgary Arts Development and The City of Calgary for giving me the resources and that opportunity to focus exclusively on creating my art.

James and Rubes—for always and everything. You make life beautiful, radiant, and positively lovely.

About the Author

Sarah Kades writes eco-thrillers, and narrative non-fiction as Sarah Graham. Her writing is largely inspired by her previous careers as an archaeologist and Indigenous Knowledge study facilitator, where she routinely lived in tents, caught rides in helicopters and gaped at the awesomeness of the landscapes around her.

Sarah is a two-time Energy Futures Lab Banff Summit storyteller, a recipient of the Calgary Arts Development individual artist grant, and has presented at the British Society of Criminology conference on the application of using arts-based approaches.

When she's not writing you can find her running, bumping into her next adventure, or trying to figure out where in the garden to put the makeshift wood fired pizza oven.

Learn more about Sarah online at:
sarahkadesgraham.com

Book Club Availability & Questions

Sarah is available for virtual book club meetings and is happy to connect with readers. If you are interested in having her as a guest for your book club, or if you are curious about purchasing bulk copies of **Wild not Broken** in print or eBook edition, please contact mark@starkpublishing.ca.

Below are potential book club questions.

1. Lillian did not want to relocate to Canada, though the move turned out to be a positive, life-changing adventure. Has there ever been something in your life you really didn't want to do and it turned out better than expected? Would you have done anything differently?

2. Colt's concept of home has been significantly impacted by his parent's divorce and their subsequent actions. What does home mean to you? What builds home? What breaks it?

3. Lillian resonated with her several times great-aunt BeeBee's life. Has there been a time in your life you connected strongly with a family member's experiences, whether living or deceased?

What was it about them that captured your attention?

4. While flying over Greenland, Sophie is awe-struck at the sight of the fjords. Have you ever been awe-struck by nature? How did it make you feel? What natural spaces to you gravitate towards?

5. Lillian's career did not survive being accused of treason. Has there been a time in your life where you were accused of something you didn't do? Has there ever been a time you realized you had falsely accused another? What happened?

6. For much of the book, Colt preferred living life on the road. What do you consider are the positive aspects of that? What are the negative? What do you feel the road gave him? Do you feel he missed out on anything? Which do you prefer? Why?

7. During the cattle drive, Lillian connected to a new landscape, nature, and allowed herself to contemplate other's perspectives. Discuss when you have connected to a landscape and nature? Has there been a time you have been surprised to resonate with a particular perspective? What happened?

8. Both Colt and Lillian have made choices that had a negative impact on their physical body. Has

there been a time you dismissed the signals your body was communicating? What happened?

9. Lillian has a complicated relationship with her grandmum. Do you have complicated relationships? What makes them complicated?

10. Gabe withheld his knowledge of a half-brother. His actions hurt Colt deeply. Do you think Gabe's actions were justified? Is there ever a time or circumstance you consider withholding information is the right decision?

11. Sophie is reluctant to tell her auntie she no longer wishes to compete. Has there ever been a time in your life you were ready to make a major change, but were reluctant at the reaction of your loved ones? What happened?

12. Lillian feels invisible in Canada, inspiring mixed feelings. Has there been a time in your life you felt invisible, or wish you were invisible? What happened?

13. Colt did not wish to disclose to his family his previous abuse of pain killers, and instead found a doctor he trusted who helped him. Under what circumstances do you think it may be easier to get help from a professional, instead of family members? Are there any circumstances this privacy would help relationships, or not?

14. Lillian is hesitant to connect on a personal level with her security detail in fear of their eventual demise. Has there been a time you withheld of yourself out of self-preservation? What happened?

15. In the beginning of the novel, both Colt and Lillian have chosen to not have children. This is a significant life decision, and many who make this choice feel social judgements. Have you or anyone in your life made the same choice? Were you or they criticized? Where do you think this comes from?

16. Lillian is a decade older than Colt. Do you feel their relationship challenges gender roles? Would it be different if he was the older one? If yes, how so? Have you been in a romantic relationship with someone older/younger? What happened?

17. Sophie is vocal in her irritation of historic and religious gender roles. When in your life have you encountered bias. Was it in your favor, or in opposition? What did you do?